Dreaming in Indigo

Indigo Kids

by Billie Angel ^i^

PUBLISH AMERICA

PublishAmerica
Baltimore

First printing

ISBN: 1-59286-404-X
PUBLISHED BY PUBLISHAMERICA, LLLP
www.publishamerica.com
Baltimore

Printed in the United States of America

Dedication

This book is dedicated to the memory of my mother and father.
To my mom
who introduced me to a world of higher awareness,
and to the idea of keeping an open mind.
To my dad
whose humor and laughter
matched his courage and devotion to his family.

Acknowledgements

Thank you doesn't seem like a strong enough statement,
but I would like to express my appreciation
to those who have encouraged me in this endeavor
and particularly my husband Bill
who not only gave me encouragement,
but also shared in the adventure.
And finally to my publisher,
who took the chance....

Prologue

The silence was ominous, like walking through a dark alley after nightfall; my senses were straining to hear any sound that might be an indication that we were not alone. The only sound I heard was the soft lapping of water against wood, and occasionally the sad call of a loon somewhere in the distance. I waited.

The baby was sleeping quietly and I prayed that she would remain asleep and silent. The heat radiating in waves from the tall metal walls was almost audible as it rushed across the open space, crashing against the opposite wall, and launching itself back across the warehouse to start all over again. The temperature was well over 100 degrees and sweat ran off of my body as if I were standing under a hot, steamy shower.

Suddenly, cool water splashed against my hot skin, cooling me as it ran the length of my body following every curve and ending by trickling off the end of my fingers and down my legs and into my shoes. I jerked myself back to reality. *My mind must be going to get caught up in an illusion like that*, I thought as I refocused on my hiding place behind the ropes that were hanging floor to ceiling on large hooks in the back corner of the metal building. I didn't have room to turn around or even move, each time I took a deep breath the rough rope fibers pressed angrily against my body filing through my skin. My tank top and shorts didn't provide much protection, so the skin on my arms and legs was already covered with bloody abrasions.

The spacious warehouse floor was littered with sailboats in various colors and stages of repair. Some were up on sawhorses and some were stacked against each other, while others leaned upright against the adjoining wall like silent sentinels watching and waiting. I peered towards the huge warehouse door, across the vast space, and it seemed to grow taller even as I studied it through the opaque waves of heat. That door was the only way out of the warehouse and beyond it could be safety. It also could be capture; in any case it would certainly be cooler.

Water lapped the dock just feet away from the door. I couldn't see it, but I could hear its soft voice calling to me. I could also smell its clean scent, and even feel its cool refreshing dampness, just out of reach. What I couldn't do was taste it. My mouth was so dry that my lips stuck together when I closed them. I was becoming weak and desperate for a drink.

I wondered when it would be safe to leave this dark cramped hiding place. I knew that I couldn't stay much longer, time was running out. I felt my instincts on full alert just like any trapped animal and although it was quiet and seemed peaceful enough, it didn't feel right to me. I decided to wait.

The cough came from outside, it was soft and muffled, but so close that it sent a shot of panic through me. They were there. Thank God I didn't try to creep out earlier. It was definitely a male voice. Then two male silhouettes moved into view in front of the open door, their forms seemed larger than life, as they moved in the rapidly gathering dusk. I heard their voices whispering as they moved out of sight their cautious footsteps receding along the dock's wooden surface. Realizing that this could be a ruse to flush me out of hiding, I once again decided to wait.

Slowly and carefully I wiped the sweat out of my eyes and shifted my cramped position, causing the rope to gash in new places. As I moved, the baby made a soft mewing noise, the kind of sound that only a very young baby makes. Change in plans. I'd have to make my break now, ready or not, before the baby became fully awake and started to cry. Standing up with the baby in my arms, I pushed my way past the collection of rope all in one motion, curling my body forward to protect the infant from the harsh ropes.

I gritted my teeth against the pain on my bare arms and shoulders, small red abrasions beaded up on my elbows and forearms.

Standing silent for a moment I wondered if I could do this. I was so tired, so lethargic in this heat, and my muscles were stiff and cramped from being in one position for so long. I felt more like a hunted animal than a young woman in her last year of college.

Slowly, I moved toward the door, just one step at a time, my lightweight canvas sneakers making no sound on the hot wooden floor. As I moved across the open space I could feel the heat waves as they vibrated around me, making it difficult to even breathe. Approaching the opening I could feel a cool breeze edging toward me, touching my hot damp skin and creating a coolness that acted as a stimulant which gave me that extra shot of energy that I needed to keep moving. Reaching the door I hesitated, looking longingly at the water. *What I wouldn't give for a drink of water, I can almost feel it trickling coolly down my throat.* I mentally dreamed for a second.

Shifting back into focus, I remembered that the men went to the left, so I edged my way along the building to the right, finding nothing but water. No land and no boats. I noticed a few lights along the bank to the right and felt a ray of hope. I was a good swimmer, and could swim the distance easily. Quickly I scanned the dock for something to use for the baby. A reed basket would be nice. It worked for Miriam who saved Moses from men who wanted to kill him, by putting him into a basket, and sending him off into the water. However, this was a very clean dock, and I could see nothing that could be used to float the baby.

The sound of men's voices at the other end of the dock jerked me out of my speculations. *Damn! They are coming back already.* Quickly, and very carefully, trying not to disturb the baby I put my arms through the straps of the papoose carrier, attaching the strap around my back so that the baby was on my chest facing me. It had been too hot to have her this close before, but now I would need to leave my arms free. The ladder leading down to the water was old and rusty, but it only complained softly as I lowered myself down the steps and into the water.

The water was tepid; not really cold, but more like a cool bath. Very slowly, an inch at a time, the water crept up our bodies cooling as it touched. Glancing at the baby's face I was startled to see that the small blue eyes were open and appeared to be studying me, but the wee baby didn't utter a sound. Smiling at the infant I prayed that she'd remain silent, because I could hear footsteps on the dock as the men returned.

We were up to our necks in the water and actually enjoying the refreshing coolness as it flowed over our bodies, rejuvenating our very cells. Letting the water run over my lips and into my mouth and throat was almost a sensual experience, I had never realized how good something could feel. Slowly I brought my hand out of the water and dripped the cool liquid on to the baby's lips. The response was automatic as the small lips formed into a sucking shape. I touched my wet finger to the pursed lips and watched as the baby drained my finger dry.

The men were close now and there were at least two more of them. They spoke quietly as beams from their flashlights darted around the dock, but their voices were quite clear. One in particular seemed to be very agitated.

"How could you let her get away? That child must be eliminated!" The words were spit out in a violent hissing whisper creating a visual picture of a pointed reptilian face to match the angry serpentine voice.

Cautiously I leaned my head back in the water and released my grip on the ladder. I was very careful; fear kept me moving slowly. I didn't dare make a splash or even a ripple. I floated for a second, and then started to carefully move my legs directing us away from the dock. This would have seemed easy, especially with the cooperation of the baby who seemed to be actually enjoying the cool water and the ride, if I hadn't been so terrified.

On the dock, lights were flitting around like fireflies and then they started searching the water around the dock shining out further and further into the darkness.

I started the frog kick in earnest now, fear giving me the strength to put as much distance as possible between us and those penetrating lights. I didn't plan a destination; I just headed straight out from the ladder as fast as possible which put me out into the middle of the small lake. The water was warmer than flowing water and had no current to tug at me.

The men must have assumed that I would head for shore near the dock, because their lights were now bobbing in that direction. I wasn't tired, the swimming was easy work and the baby was content, so I just continued out into the lake with no plan in mind other than putting as much distance between us, the dock and especially those men.

Night in the forest is very dark; there are no streetlights or lights shining down from windows or even lighted signs on buildings. The moon had not yet risen and only a few stars studded the blue-black sky. However, that was enough to guide me in a straight line, keeping me from swimming in circles.

I'd been in the water for a long time now and was starting to notice the strain, and was stopping more often to float and rest. Suddenly the roar of an outboard motor shattered the peaceful night. "Oh God no, they have a motorboat." Fear once again was clutching at me. The baby must have felt my surge of fear because she made a soft whimpering sound. Using both arms and legs I sent us shooting through the water. I had to make land, I just had to.

Just when it seemed I'd have to swim forever, my hand touched something that felt smooth and cool. I jerked my hand back thinking of some reptile, but discovered a tree limb, leaning out over the lake with its leaves lightly skimming the water, had touched my hand just before my shoulder bumped into a sand bank. The solid sand brought relief and fantasies of salvation to my exhausted mind.

I rested for a minute, just sitting in the water nearly in a stupor. Looking out across the dark water I could see that the boat appeared to be checking the shoreline closest to the warehouse, working its way around the lake on the right side of the dock. I had no way of knowing how much shoreline was between where they were looking and where we now sat, but I did know that

I must move now, we had to get away.

Without standing up, I turned and looked at the shore behind me. I assumed that they would check to see if there were footprints or splashes of water leading out of the lake. So I consider how I could get to dry land without making a wet trail. Finally I decided to use the tree. I worked my way through the water to the base of the tree where it leaned out, over the edge of the bank, with its branches arched downward delicately fingering the water below. I decided to just come up out of the water on to the tree roots, where the water wouldn't be so noticeable and there wouldn't be any footprints. It was for sure that these guys weren't Indian trackers. They probably wouldn't even notice.

However, it only took one attempt at grabbing the trunk of the tree for me to realize that this couldn't be done. I was an athletic person; working out in the school gym, jogging around the campus, and swimming regularly, but I just didn't have the strength to climb a tree trunk straight out of the water, with a baby strapped to my chest and half of the lake dripping off of my clothes. Plan B meant finding some low bushes growing close to the water and climbing over them, hoping that they'd hide the water trail from the probing lights.

I made my way over the bushes, my wet shoes making a squishing sound with each step. The sound seemed to vibrate in the quiet setting. I headed into the cover of the woods, and then turned to look back at the lake I saw that the lights were within shouting distance of the shoreline. Quickly I turned back to the woods, fear once again pumped through my veins pushing the blood along at a very fast flow. My muscles were screaming and threatening to quit altogether, but I coaxed them into just one more step... left foot, right foot... just one more step.

The darkness in the woods was complete, there was not even a star or a reflection. I literally had to reach out and feel for the next tree or bush to make my way. I knew that I was moving slowly, and that they would have no problem catching up to me with the aid of their lights once they found where I'd climbed out of the water, but I couldn't quit now. I struggled from tree to bush, bush to tree, while the leaves and branches grabbed and dragging roughly across my face and arms. The only sense of direction was my still activated survival instinct. I could actually 'feel' the difference in the damp air behind me from the lake, and the closer warmer air of the forest in front of me. From time to time I would hear some little critter scurry away in the undergrowth, and once an owl hooted off to my right. The baby was silent throughout this entire ordeal as if she understood the seriousness of the situation.

As the trees and brush closed out the dampness from the lake behind me the air became close and warm. Finally the trees and bushes thinned out and the pine needles and leaves underfoot became firmer more like walking across dirt. The blackness gave way to a dark gray rather than the absolute black.

Then the crunch of gravel stopped me in my tracks. Hoping I'd found a path or a road I stepped back and forth testing the sound between pine needles and gravel. I moved by listening to my feet, whenever the crunch of gravel didn't follow my step I'd angle the next step sideways trying to stay on the path.

Then without warning I saw what looked like the outline of a car looming ahead of me. It must be a gravel road after all. The car looked like it was parked on the other side of the road. There were no lights it just appeared to be parked there, it could be abandoned, or it could belong to them, set up here to block my escape.

I stood perfectly still, studying what I thought was the rear of the car, but suddenly the headlights flashed on proving me wrong and freezing me in the blinding beam. I felt just like a doe with her fawn, caught and blinded on the road by an on coming car before being run down. The silence was heavy. Even the night animals were quiet. No motor was running in the car, but someone was definitely inside. Then, in the stillness I heard the sharp metallic sound of the latch, as the car door opened.

Instinctively, I started backing up. It could be just some local kids making out in the car, but I didn't like the feeling I was getting. A man loomed in front of the headlights. He looked huge, with the lights framing his body. Then he started walking slowly across the road, his feet crunching loudly on the gravel, sending sharp staccato sounds crashing through the quiet forest. He had a slim yet sturdy looking body and appeared to be fair skinned, but the light was bright and I couldn't be sure. I couldn't see his features or the color of his hair, but his actions definitely didn't feel right. He hadn't called out and he had just been sitting in his car. He must be one of 'them' sent to guard the road.

I was now convinced that this was not the help I was seeking, and as I turned to run I came face to face with a large blur of white. Yellow eyes and long teeth formed the face of a huge white wolf. His lips were drawn back displaying long vicious looking teeth. I could feel his breath whiffing towards me from between those glistening fangs. Before I could even make a sound, let alone get away, the wolf leaped around me closing the gap between the man and us. He stood in a half crouched position facing the other figure. Intense energy filled the air as two male animals faced each other on this lonely road. The low deep snarl from the wolf left no doubt that he meant business and fully intended to fight.

As I watched the face off, the thought of a wolf challenging a man for the supper he'd found flashed through my head. As a young girl, I'd been very quiet, finding my adventures in books. I read a lot of stories about the adventures of people living in the wild and a lot of those stories dealt with wolves attacking livestock and also people and now I feared that I was about to experience that trauma first hand.

The man stopped dead in his tracks. The two held their ground for a minute longer, and then the man started backing up. When he reached his car he climbed in and fired up the engine, a deafening sound in this lonely forest, he started backing the car away from us. He obviously wasn't going to stick around to save us from the wolf. When he was down the road he whipped the small car around, spewing gravel in every direction, and drove quickly away.

As the taillights of the car disappeared around a curve, the darkness closed in once more. I thought that I was too tired to feel any more fear, but to be eaten alive by a wolf pushed me into sheer panic. I decided right then that I'd rather be shot by the men than be eaten by a wolf. As I saw the white body move in the dark I bent down and scooped up a handful of gravel. It wasn't much, but maybe if he were really peppered he'd decide to find a new meal. Raising my arm with the rocks, I waited until he got closer.

Without warning, the baby started cooing, gurgling, and waving her arms. She had hardly moved for hours, and now she was not only moving, but making sounds and seemed to be very excited.

As my eyes re-adjusting to the darkness I could see a little more than shadowy outlines, the wolf was sitting down facing us, and had cocked his head, obviously listening to the baby. He looked more like a dog now that he wasn't showing his teeth. Maybe he wasn't a wolf after all.

"Here boy," I called to him, without lowering my rock-throwing arm. He opened his mouth letting his tongue fall out, stood up and walked up to us with his head lowered, just like my old dog Sam used to do. He was a dog after all. I kneeled down to pet him, letting the rocks fall to the ground beside me, but before I could touch him, the baby, who was still strapped to my chest, reached out and grabbed his ear.

"Oh no!" I uttered, fearing the dog would now become vicious again. However, he just licked the baby's face. She wrinkled up her small nose and released her hold on his ear. I gently put my hand on his head just as a new sound drew my attention. "Oh, oh." I was sure that the men had found where I'd climbed up out of the water and were closing in on me. I looked around, but it seemed to be very dark again and I couldn't see anything. Where the dog had been was blackness, even the baby, who was right in front of my face couldn't be seen. I lifted my hands up to my chest feeling for the baby, but she wasn't there. The baby was gone! Then hands grabbed me by both arms, I fought to break free I had to get away. I had to save the baby!

"Mandy, Mandy, wake up! You're having a nightmare." The voice of my roommate ebbed and flowed through the dense fog that had taken over my head. I struggled to understand the words. What was she saying? A nightmare? It was only a dream? That meant that there was no baby, no men, and no white dog. I opened my eyes to discover that I was still in my room in the dorm with my roommate Jill. Relief flooded over me as I realized that I didn't have the responsibility of saving that baby girl after all. Tears streamed down my face, but it was confusing because even though I was relieved that I didn't have such a responsibility, I was also experiencing a feeling of sadness. During the dream ordeal, I'd become very bonded with the small baby with the bright blue eyes and now that baby was gone leaving a large empty feeling.

Two years later...

"Mandy, your baby is a girl. Mandy, open your eyes and look at your baby," the voice floated in and out of my head. It didn't seem to be real and I didn't have the energy to lift my eyelids, they had become huge lead lined covers for my eyes. The delivery was over and I just wanted to sleep, I felt so tired. No one had told me that having a baby took so much energy. I lay there planning to sleep for a couple of days.

"Mandy, don't you want to see your new baby?" the voice continued. "She's beautiful, lots of blond hair with great big blue eyes. I swear she's studying your face." *What was the wavering voice saying? Blue eyes studying my face?* Somehow that stirred a déjà vu type of memory in my foggy brain. Slowly I forced my eyes open. The lovely face of the baby in my dream floated above my chest, looking straight into my eyes. I could almost feel the water lapping around my body, as it had in that dream so long ago.

I thought new born babies weren't supposed to actually see right away? I thought. It was clear that this baby was definitely able to see and she was calmly looking at me just like she did in the dream. Her eyes even stayed on me as the nurse removed her and walked away to clean her up, I wondered if

I was dreaming again; the baby's calm face, the long swim on my back, the strange man in the car, the white wolf/dog, all flashed through my mind as I briefly relived that very vivid dream experience over again. What did it mean to dream about saving a child from men determined to kill her and then give birth to that same child at a later date? These were my last thoughts just before I faded out of the picture and into the oblivion of an exhausted sleep.

Six months later...

I hadn't realized how much I'd missed running. The muscles in my legs, back and arms were singing the song of freedom. This was even better than eating chocolate. I felt like I was finally ready to get back into full swing, with my exercise, by running in the park and taking the baby along with me. Pushing the stroller, with the three big bicycle wheels, along these smooth blacktop paths was a piece of cake. Hooray for whoever invented this great contraption.

Wearing my favorite navy blue jogging suit with my hair tucked up into a baseball cap, and my well broken-in running shoes felt great. I noticed the groupings of fir trees waving to each other in the breeze, the calm open fields, the well maintained children's play area with happy little faces squealing and laughing, the small lake with its attractive foot bridges and wildlife; birds, ducks, geese, frogs, and others I could only hear.

May, in the Pacific Northwest, is a beautiful time of the year. The sun was shining, but it wasn't hot, so weather-wise, it was very comfortable. *This is as good as it gets*, I thought as I negotiated a sharp left angled turn around a big fir tree that had pushed its roots up through the man made black topped path. This was my first trip around this area and time to head for home. I didn't want to stop, but neither did I want to over do it the first time out and be laid up.

The path gracefully wound around the lake in and out of the trees, past natural wooden benches providing a view that served to calm the nerves while testing the body. I watched the ducks as they swam and bobbed for food, looking so funny standing on their heads with their little tails and feet sticking up out of the water. I could hardly wait for Naja to get old enough to appreciate some of these great natural wonders. Bob would have liked this park and he would have loved watching his daughter play and learn here. Unfortunately, he didn't even know that I was pregnant before he died.

Bob's death still haunts me as being very bizarre. Not only because of the way that he died, but also the timing. How many men say 'I do' at their wedding, walk outside to the parking area and are murdered, by muggers, next to the 'Just Married' sign decorating the car. If we hadn't jumped the gun and slept together the night before the wedding, I wouldn't even have little Naja right now.

Stopping, to take a breather, on the small bridge that allowed foot traffic to cross to the other side without going the entire distance around the lake, I checked on Naja, who was sleeping peacefully and looking like an angel in her pink cap and tucked snugly under the light fleece blanket. These were only a couple of the many lovely things that I'd received from the baby shower given to me by Jill and one of the ladies in the office.

Unfortunately, my immediate family were all dead and gone, and so were any of their families, although, I had heard of a distant cousin who lived in New York somewhere. It had been a rough couple of years, first my dad died suddenly of a heart attack, then eight months later, mom just decided she didn't want to be here anymore without dad, and she died in her sleep, and then Bob was murdered. Thank God little Naja and my job kept my mind occupied and my body busy.

Bob's adopted parents were also gone, leaving no close relatives, but I didn't consider this to be a problem, I tended to be a loner with only a few select friends anyway, and felt that I was doing quite well by myself. I lived in the small house that Bob and I had chosen together before the wedding. After Bob's death I used the insurance money to pay off the house so the baby and I would have the home that Bob had intended us to have. I still had my job and a nice car. Yes, I was doing fine. There wasn't time to feel sorry for myself, and now spring was here and I could enjoy my favorite time of the year.

Leaning against the railing, I stretched my legs one at a time by bending them forward in a lunge, stretching out first one leg and then the other. When I'd finished I looked over the bridge railing and watched the ducks bobbing up and down in the water below. I couldn't help thinking of Bob again and the times that we had run the trail along the Willamette River, in John's Landing, stopping to cool down at a Coffee stand, sipping an iced drink before going home. Now I ran alone here in this park in a residential area, avoiding the river path with its memories.

Slowly I became aware of a tingling at the back of my neck, and then it became all encompassing and focused on my mid section causing a slight feeling of nausea. The sun was warm, the birds were singing, and I could hear ducks quacking and frogs speaking in their ribbet language, but I was definitely becoming uncomfortable.

Turning towards the path I'd just run across I saw a man watching me from the other end of the bridge. I couldn't see his face, because the sun was behind his back, but there was something familiar about his well built but slim, sturdy body shape and his attitude. It was still daylight but I felt a chill followed by a slithering fear traveling up the back of my neck.

Turning back to the stroller I continued my run across the bridge, once on the other side I turned so that I was running along the side of the lake following the path that allowed me to glance over at the bridge without being obvious. The man had moved to the center of the bridge and was standing exactly where I had been resting and he was still watching me sending another chill running its course through my body.

I moved swiftly along the path; my legs moving with determination carrying me out of the area, carrying me away from the bridge and the man, but not carrying me away from the fear that I took with me. The encounter had acted like a shot in the arm, renewing my energy, and as I ran, I tried to remember if I'd seen this man before. Why did he look so familiar? Why did he create such a fearful feeling?

Suddenly, I jerked to a stop, the birds and the breeze in the trees stopped also as I remembered! He looked like the same man in my dream before Naja was born. The same man with the car, the same man who stood with the headlights behind him and this time with the sunlight behind him so that I couldn't see his face. The same man who drove away and left us to be eaten by the wolf! How could he be here? This wasn't a dream! Who was this guy and what did this mean? I could taste the bitter bile flavor of fear in my mouth. My confusion was even greater. What had just happened?

Reaching my blue Honda Prelude in the parking lot, I quickly transferred Naja and her car seat to the back seat, threw the stroller into the trunk, and then jumped into the car and locked the doors, my heart beating fast and furious in my chest. Before starting the engine, I looked back the way I'd come and then for good measure I looked in all directions, but I didn't see the man. He apparently hadn't followed me, or…he was standing somewhere out of sight just watching me at this very moment.

The car roared to life and I backed out of the parking space, turned towards the street and headed in the direction of the mall. I didn't plan to stop and shop, but wasn't going to lead the guy directly to my house either. I drove through the mall parking lot, up and down, in and out, around and out onto a different street than the one I'd come in on. My original plan to stop at

Starbucks on the way home for a cool Frappacino was forgotten. As I turned towards my neighborhood, I watched the rearview mirror after each turn. Finally, I felt certain that no one was following me and only then did I relax my tense muscles and head for home.

Pulling into the garage, I quickly pushed the button to automatically close the large door feeling thankful that I didn't have to park my car out on the street as I had while living in my apartment. The security of getting in and out of the car in a garage had always felt like a luxury, but now it had become more than comfort and luxury.

When we'd chosen this house, in the suburban Multnomah area, we planned to drive into town together to save on gas and leave one of the cars here in the garage, but after Bob's death I'd sold my car, which was smaller and kept Bob's Honda, which had a larger trunk and more room for baby stuff.

I just sat in the car for a few moments regaining my composure and experiencing the feeling of safety as it surrounded me. I allowed the soothing warm feeling to wrap comfortably around me, bringing me back to a normal secure space before opening the car door and gathering up the baby.

I loved this house, it was a small two level with only two bedrooms, but it had a nice comfortable feeling. The garage led into a small kitchen, which was white, making it appear larger than it actually was. A green tile topped table with its white legs and white chairs sat in the center of the room. I'd spent hours at the Saturday Market picking out small glass hanging 'rain drops' of various colors, which I would painstakingly hang at different levels in the garden window in front of the sink. As I walked in from the garage the light sparkling from the drops sent beautiful rainbow colors all around the room and I immediately felt better. Safe and secure in my own little house. I took a deep breath of relief and headed down the hall and up the stairs to the baby's bedroom. There was nothing to fear. That was just some man walking in the park, looking at the ducks and he just happened to remind me of that strange dream I'd had so long ago. Everything was fine.

Day One

Five years later...

Sitting confidently in a comfortable executive chair, I studied the room. It was a typical business meeting room, decorated in a very expensive style. The chairs had wooden frames with fabric and padding on the seats. The walls glowed in a soft peach color, chosen to create peace and tranquility. Flowers appeared to grow from lovely framed pictures with shades that complimented the wall colors. Indirect lighting radiated towards the ceiling and potted plants of various sizes were placed near the corners in Feng Shui style to keep the Chi circulating around the room. It was definitely a warm friendly room designed to get the most out of any meeting.

As I waited for others to join me, I wondered what the agenda was going to be. Meetings had become the main part of my job these last few years, so not knowing the agenda wasn't a problem. I knew that someone would fill me in, and I could wing it if I had to. Patience, however, wasn't my strong suit. Where was everyone? Was everyone else late or was I early? Being a gung ho overachiever was something I'd been accused of many times.

Growing up in Scappoose, a small town outside of Portland, Oregon, I attended a rural school and considered it just short of a miracle that I'd been able to experience higher education at the University of Oregon. My folks were people of modest means and had to struggle to pay for my education cutting back on their own wants and needs to make sure that I could finish school and have a better lifestyle than they'd had. I'd worked two jobs during school to help out with the expenses and I wasn't going to waste their money, their efforts, or their faith in my abilities.

If working hard to get where I was, meant I was an over-achiever, then so be it. I'd always worked hard, in fact, I'd had only taken two vacations in the past five years, one for my honeymoon, that ended up as a mourning period since the wedding day and Bob's death were one and the same, and the other was my maternity leave, when I spent three months at home with Naja. Interesting, how Naja was so much like the man she never knew, the man who never knew her. Her father, Bob, was a handsome blond man, who always commanded attention automatically with his power and his charisma. While

I, on the other hand might be considered attractive, I certainly would not be listed as striking, with my short brown hair, slim athletic figure and no nonsense attitude.

Bob automatically expected to be at the forefront of business. While I had to work at it and didn't brighten a room when I entered as Bob always had, but we'd made a great team at the insurance office where we met. He was the sales specialist, working well directly with clients, while I handled all of the paperwork behind the scenes. We'd decided that we would make just as good a team in our personal lives, so we planned the ill fated wedding, the personal team theory, unfortunately, had been left untested.

I had, however, made advances on my own merit in the insurance business after Bob's death. I still stayed behind the scenes, as far as clients were concerned, but had worked up to a managerial position, holding meetings, and making decisions.

The sound of voices drew my attention to the door across the room just before two people walked in talking in hushed voices. They looked around suspiciously as if this setting was totally unfamiliar, and indeed the room didn't seem to comfortably relate to them.

The attractive blond woman was thirty something and dressed in cut-off jeans and a man's shirt with the sleeves rolled up, as if she'd just come from painting the walls or scrubbing the floors. She looked over the circle of chairs, pushed up a slipping sleeve, and decided upon a chair across the room.

The second woman about the same age had her black oriental hair pulled back in a single long braid and was also dressed very casually. She stood rooted to the spot for a few more moments, seeming confused. She looked behind her, considering a retreat, but then with a sigh took a seat next to the women she'd walked in with.

I studied them and wondered if these people were under-dressed in their casual clothes or if I was over-dressed in my dark green business suit. What type of a meeting could this be?

Before I was able to introduce myself to the women, several more people came into the room, all looking very different. Everyone was wearing a different style of clothing. I was confused; I'd never been to a meeting where the dress code was so random. Twelve people filled twelve chairs, in twelve different types of attire, and obviously from twelve different lifestyles no dress code here, this could be a meeting at the United Nations. No one spoke out loud. Some smiled or nodded and a few exchanged hushed formal greetings.

Sitting there waiting for the meeting to begin, my mind wandered back to Naja. I was surprised when Naja had displayed such efficiency and knowledge of the rules and regulations at her preschool. I started reflecting back…

Entering the school, with its tiny people chairs and tables and the soon to be discovered works of art covering every available wall space, always brought me back to reality. The sincerity and innocence of these little people and how hard they lived and worked together here in their miniature village was such an eye opener.

I'd arrived at exactly three o'clock the designated time to pick up Naja. Only instead of finding her quietly coloring at one of the mini tables, she was standing in the middle of the room giving instructions to the rest of the children. She was explaining that while the teacher was on the phone everyone had to behave, play quietly and not leave this room. Her voice was very emphatic.

Apparently this was the ruling set down by the teacher and Naja was the self appointed sergeant of arms making sure that it was carried out. The teacher, with a phone to her ear, caught my eye as she looked towards Naja and smiled.

Just then Naja became aware of me, and said, "I can't go yet, Mommy. Miss Susan is on the phone." Apparently she took her job as 'crew chief' very seriously, and the other children seemed to accept her leadership without any problem.

As Susan hung up the phone I nodded my head towards Naja and asked quietly, "Is she always this bossy?"

"She's not really bossy, she just learns the rules and makes sure that she sticks to them. She and anyone in her immediate area," she added laughing as she hugged Naja good-bye. "See you on Monday, kiddo." She sang out as we left.

With her soft blue eyes, and her long blond hair Naja looked like a saint, but she definitely wasn't that. She was very assertive and serious natured, always wanting to know why, and it had better be a logical reason. She has a drive for information and challenging mind games rather than physical sports. It must be paying off because for a five year old she was just too smart. She often behaved as if she were the mother and I the daughter. Reminding me to lock the doors, turn off the coffee pot, or pickup the cleaning on the way home. I couldn't help but notice that more and more often, this tiny little child displayed a wisdom that would be considered beyond her years. She is such a serious little thing, perhaps we need to do more fun things, add more laughter and games to our lives. I'd often felt that it was my fault that Naja was maturing too fast and missing out on her youth.

My attention drifted back to the meeting room and the folks sitting around patiently waiting for things to begin. Snatches of conversations were drifting towards me from different areas of the room, and from what I could understand almost everyone was talking about their children. Looking around, I noticed that nearly everyone in the room was of the parenting age. Interesting, perhaps this was a meeting regarding a children's program of some sort.

Well, enough, all ready! Let's get on with the meeting, I thought, impatience getting the best of me. "Does anyone have a copy of the agenda?" I asked, hoping to get things started.

"Agenda?"

"What is the agenda?"

"Why are we here?"

It seemed that I'd opened up a can of worms. Everyone was looking at me and asking questions that they apparently expected me to have the answers to.

"Wait a minute," I told them, holding up both hands to end the barrage of questions. "I'm not the one in charge. I don't know what's going on either." That did end he questions. In fact, it ended everything. The entire group of eleven people just sat there in the circle of chairs and looked at me, still expecting me to give some type of information or assistance.

"Who's heading up this show?" I tried again, looking around the room trying to get things going. "Is the mediator here?"

Others were also looking around the room, expecting someone to finally end their social conversation and tend to the business at hand, but no one did. So they all looked back at me, who in my tailored business suit apparently appeared the most likely candidate to fill in until the person in charge arrived. Okay, I'd certainly had enough experience, but had no idea what the subject was supposed to be.

"Okay, anyone have any idea what the agenda is supposed to be?" No one answered.

"Well, why are you here?" I continued to probe.

"I haven't a clue. Why are you here?" countered the blond woman in the cut off jeans. The room suddenly felt slightly hostile and the energy became close and thick.

"Damned if I know! I must have run off without checking on the subject of this meeting." I explained. "I didn't think that I'd be heading it up." I was stumped. I'd never been faced with a room full of people and not know what the subject was supposed to be. If it were insurance related, I couldn't put a handle on it.

"Doesn't anyone know why we're here?" questioned a woman who was sitting on the edge of her chair, like she didn't plan to stay very long. People looked at the others around them, the confusion they discovered in each other's eyes merged together in one large clash that was almost audible. Discovering that they were all at a meeting and none of them knew why was, indeed, an interesting situation. How did everyone get here? How did they know where this meeting would be held? No one seemed to remember, and my situation was no different, I wondered if I were suffering short-term memory loss already, I remembered how my mother had started forgetting things as she got older, but she was much older before she started that. How utterly confusing this was, I ran my fingers through my short hair as I often did when frustrated.

"Well, if no one shows up to tell us why we're here, we can go home, but in the meantime let's take care of the introductions." I instructed the group and quickly began before anyone could interrupt or object. "My name is Amanda 'Mandy' Minton and I work in the administration department of a large insurance company. I have one child she's 5." I threw in the bit about Naja because I'd heard many of them mention their children and hoped that this would give us some kind of common ground. Then I nodded to the person on my right indicating that she should continue.

The black woman on the right didn't look like a businessperson; she looked like a domestic housewife. No make-up graced her face, her hair was worn in an afro and her clothes consisted of faded blue jeans and a white tee shirt that said *'JUST DO IT!'* Something was strange about this particular gathering of people. Whatever they had in common to bring them together in this meeting certainly wasn't obvious. Perhaps this was an offshoot of the PTA. I mused as I studied the woman speaking.

"My name is Sally Porter. I'm a housewife and mother. I haven't a clue as to why I'm here either, but I do have kids, a 5-year-old and also an 8-year-old." She offered, re crossing her legs, raising her eyebrows and turning her palms up in a questioning gesture.

The next person was a man, his light brown hair was showing signs of balding on top, but he wore it short and didn't try to make up for the receding hair by growing it longer on the sides and the back as some men did. He was dressed in worn blue jeans and sturdy well-worn steel-toed boots.

"Well, ahhh, I sure don't know why I'm here. I ain't no businessman, but I am in the building business." He shifted in his chair and then added, "my name is Bill Bellows. I'm married and have three kids, 4, 6, and 8." He finished, looking like he was glad that was over. I could relate to his discomfort, remembering back when I was new at speaking in a group. It's definitely a learning experience filled alternately with stress and relief.

"Guess I'm next," said a female voice, sitting slightly behind Bill Bellows. Only her long slim legs, starting at the top and crossing at the ankles, could be seen from my position. They were clad in cherry red stretch leggings, and ended with her gold strap sandals.

"My name is Lindy and I'm not finding this meeting, or whatever, very interesting or informative, so I suggest that we call it quits and go back home." She kept her voice firm, and unfaltering, as she remained in her laid back relaxed position in the chair, but I think she felt out of place and uncomfortable.

"That could be the next step, Lindy, but let's finish this first. What do you do and do you have any children?" I smiled at her as she leaned forward and revealed her face. Her features were lovely, her brown hair long and curled slightly at her shoulders, but she looked hard, tough even. I considered Lindy and decided that she'd led a challenging life and had a lot of barriers up, probably for good reasons.

"Yea, I've got a 4-year-old boy, who is the light of my life. I'm a single mom and I'm working in a bar to make enough money so that life well be better for him than it was for me." She threw that information at the group almost as a challenge. She remained stiff and guarded, daring them to judge her.

Well, I had no intention of judging her. I just smiled again, and said, "Good for you, I hope it works." Then I moved on and pointed past her to the blond woman.

"I'm Teri Thompson. I run a nursery school. I also have one child of my own and she's 3." Teri with her blond hair professionally styled in a casual chin length bob was a very self-assured, educated, confident woman. She was comfortable in her cut off jeans, which showed off her shapely tanned legs, and you could tell she wondered about this suited woman who was pushing them to become a group by interacting. I just smiled.

Next to Teri was a man, dressed like a jogger, with dark, angry eyes. His hair was also dark and cut very short, almost in a military style. "Doesn't anyone know what this is all about? I've got better things to do with my time!" he demanded, with a voice as angry as his eyes.

No one answered we all just sat there looking at him. After all, what was there to say? We'd already been through all of this.

"All right! I'm Ron Cole, I work at a fitness center and I also have a preschooler, age 4," he begrudgingly stated before leaning back in his chair to emphasize that he was finished.

"Do you suppose that this is a meeting for some children's group?" asked the young woman next to Ron. "I mean, so far the only thing I can see that we have in common are our small children. I too have a 5-year-old boy. Oh, my name is Cindy Taylor and I'm in retail sales at a department store downtown."

Cindy's retail sales experience showed. Although slightly overweight, she had on clothes that hid her problems, looked flattering on her, and the autumn colors complemented her mounds of auburn red hair.

"She's right. Everyone so far has at least one child between 3 and 8 years old. I have two, one is 4 and the other is 6. My full time job is taking care of them. My name is Hally Dorhn."

This came from the slim, Asian woman with her braided hair. She was dressed in navy blue Bermuda shorts and a white shirt style blouse with anklets and walking shoes. Even though she was casually dressed, her clothes looked expensive; she gave the impression of being fashion conscious, and having some type of professional background.

A very deep voice interrupted my critique of Hally. The voice belonged to a short stocky man of Hispanic descent wearing a very bright red and yellow colored print shirt and well-worn Levi's.

"I'm Ramon Cordova. My daughter is also 3, and very bright for one so young. What a job keeping up with her." His accent was thick so I had to listen closely to be sure that I understood him. I sensed that Ramon hadn't shared his type of work because he was currently unemployed, and was choosing to talk more about his daughter to cover the fact that he wasn't giving a type of work. I had nothing to base this feeling on, but it was the hit I was getting, I decided not to insist that he answer the 'job' question.

Sitting beside Ramon, was a woman who didn't quite fit with the rest of the group, age wise. She was much older than the other parent types that were here. This woman was more in the grandmother age bracket. She was a beautiful woman, with soft white hair, very brown eyes, and light olive skin. She was well-groomed and wearing a 'knock your eye out' diamond ring. She could possibly be Greek, Italian or even Spanish, I thought.

"I'm Rachael DeLeon. I'm retired and my children are grown, but I'm raising my granddaughter, who is 4." She raised her eyebrows and continued with, "*I*, sort of tip the scales towards the small children theory, of why we're here together, don't I?"

She was right. It certainly wasn't fashion, sex, job, or age. So far, small children were the only things we had in common, but it still didn't give a clue as to why we were supposed to be meeting. I was puzzled.

"This is all very interesting, but I don't see that we're getting anywhere," said the next man, as he shifted in his chair. He let out a big sigh, "Okay, I'm Pete Jardin. I own a small convenience store. Yes, I too have a small child. He's 5."

Pete was very impatient, out of his element, and definitely didn't want to be here. His well-groomed hair was parted on the side and combed back, while his white shirt was left open at the neck. His casual short navy blue windbreaker, matched his dark blue slacks.

"Well, looks like I'm last," said a beautiful young woman, who looked to be Persian. Her soft cream-colored sweater showed off her dark hair and eyes. "My name is Shala, my daughter's name is Lisa and she's 4. It looks like it's all about kids. So now what?" she said, looking directly at me with expectation.

Well I guess the ball is back in my court. "So now what?" I repeated the question, to no one in particular. I certainly don't know any more than the rest of you do. "If no one can think of a good reason for us to be here I suggest we chalk this up to a meeting with some very nice parents and call it a day."

"Yeah."

"Good girl."

"It's been different."

"**Wait**... isn't anyone interested in why we are here?" questioned Sally, the black mother, still sitting solidly in her chair, looking determined to stay until she solved the mystery.

"Yes, I am, but I don't know how we're going to find out, since no one here seems to know, and the person in charge didn't show," I answered as I turned and addressed the rest of the group. "Anyone have any guesses?" Some were still sitting and some were already standing ready to make their exit.

"I have another question," came the deep voice of Ramon, the Hispanic father, who was no longer lounging back in his chair, but sitting upright very intent upon what he was about to ask. "How did you know about this meeting?"

At first there was complete silence and then several voices spoke up trying to answer the question, but more questions developed and the confusion only deepened.

"Well I... I don't know."

"I... ahh...Where is this meeting? Where are we?"

"Well, how did you get here? Does anyone remember driving here?" Ramon prodded further, leaning forward now in his intensity.

"No, I only remember walking into the room."

"Me too."

Silence took over the room as both those sitting and those standing went into introspection and searched for answers to these questions. I too was feeling confused and disorientated because I considered myself a very organized person and yet, I didn't seem to know how I knew about this meeting, how I got here, or for that matter... where 'here' was. I recovered from my confusion in time to look around at the other faces in the room. Some were completely blank, as if they had suddenly turned into mannequins. Others wore expressions of surprise their eyes wide, mouths open. While still others seemed confused, questions visibly etched across their faces, and some even looked angry, their brows knitted together in frowns their mouths set tight. Several more minutes went by and no one spoke. Those standing did, however, manage to return to their seats moving more like zombies, showing no emotions, no fluid movements, and seemingly no control over what they were doing.

I was struggling, I felt I should say something, but I didn't have any answers either, what could I say to help this situation? Slowly, one or two at a time, the others started to come out of the shock that they were experiencing and once again turned towards the logical leader.

NO! I thought. I didn't want to be in charge. I didn't know what was going on. I'm as confused as the others with no answers for them. I didn't even have any answers for myself.

"I knew that something strange was going to happen today. I didn't think..." Rachael spoke up, but then let her thought and her sentence drift off, as she fought to regain the control she'd lost during the discovery that she; that none of us, knew where we were, why we were here, or even how we got here.

"Okay, there has to be a simple answer to this. We're just missing it. Let's go over this detail by detail." My training had finally kicked in. This wasn't thinking, I was functioning on automatic. Saying what needed to be said to get things back on track and quiet the others. Actually, my mind was concentrating on how warm it was and how uncomfortable the chair had become. The words coming out of my mouth and my feelings were not in sync. They weren't even in the same energy field, I definitely felt scattered.

"Here's what I know," speaking slowly, letting things drift back into my head a little bit at a time, I began. "My memory begins while I'm sitting in this chair waiting for a meeting to begin. I figured it was a meeting, because this looks like a meeting room to me, and besides I attend a lot of meetings so I'm programmed to think meeting."

They just sat there and waited for me to go on. "That's it. That's the complete extent of what I know about this meeting. Does anyone have anything to add?" I found myself praying that someone would contribute information that would shed some light on this very strange situation. Anything, at this point, would be welcomed, but apparently no one could fix this unknown quality of *where*, *why*, and *how*.

"So, what do you think this means?" Talking to my image in the bathroom mirror would have produced more results. "Well, don't you think that we should communicate a little? Or should we just sit here and look at each other?" I asked them, feeling like I was the only one even trying to solve this unknown and confusing problem.

"She's right," Sally said. "We do need to talk about this. I can't remember this morning. I only remember last night, when I went to bed after watching my favorite TV show."

"I've got news for ya. This ain't mornin, or even daytime. Look out that winda. It's dark. It's nighttime. So we either skipped a whole day, or this is still Friday night." Bill's words hung on the air like a heavy, unpleasant odor.

"I don't understand what you're saying? What day is this meeting?" Ramon asked in his very deep and now confused voice.

Rachael, coughed lightly, and said, "Let's take a poll. What is the very last thing you remember before you found yourself in this room? For me, I was working with my crystal pendant and then I went to bed. That's the last thing that I remember … going to bed."

"I think that's the last thing I remember too."

"Me too."

"Yes, I went in and covered Chad in his bed, then I went to bed myself," Cindy, murmured looking off into space, as if she were going over it in her mind.

26

"So, have we pretty much established that the last thing we remember is going to bed?" I questioned, wondering what the hell this meant.

"I'm confused. Did we miss a day er what?" asked Bill.

"I don't think that we missed a day... I think that we went to bed and we are still there. We're all asleep," said Rachael. Then she folded her hands, and waited for the chaos she obviously knew would be forth coming. She wasn't disappointed.

All hell broke loose. Everyone was talking, shouting, and waving their arms around. The room became charged with confusion, anger, and fear. I glanced around, noticing how the different people were reacting. They were acting just like I was feeling, which was denial, this just wasn't happening. Many were showing signs of being very frightened, their eyes wide their bodies ready to jump up and run, while still others were indignant, acting like this was someone's fault, but certainly not theirs, Rachael, however, just sat it out, and didn't say anything more.

My mind just wasn't able to accept the idea of a common dream with these strangers. There must be another explanation. What Rachael was suggesting just wasn't possible. When the din started to subside, Rachael sat forward in her chair and spoke again.

"Okay, okay. Now that you have that out of your systems, think about it. What other explanations do *you* come up with?" she challenged them.

"Well, I've heard of mass hypnosis, maybe this is kinda like that."

"How could it happen, we weren't all together anywhere?"

"Maybe it was one of those subliminal messages over the TV."

"I haven't watched TV in ages."

"Are you suggesting a form of mass consciousness has taken over our minds and put us together into this meeting... this dream?" asked Lindy, looking at Rachael, her eyes wide, her long cherry red legs no longer lounging and crossed, but drawn up under her chair in a flight position.

"Mass consciousness?"

"I never remember my dreams when I wake up, let alone while I'm having them!"

"Ya know you guys lost me a ways back there."

"Me too, what are you saying?"

"Let me see if I understand this," interrupted Ron, roughly tugging his jogging shirt down in the front in his fear and anger. "You are suggesting that the powers that be, arranged for us to come together in a dream. Get real!" He scoffed at the idea, and at those discussing it, in his abrupt and opinionated style.

"It does seem rather far fetched, I'll admit, but it's the only thing that works," Rachael tried to explain to him, in a soft calm voice.

"Well, it doesn't work for me!" stated Ron scowling at Rachael, and scooting his chair backwards and out of the circle.

Bill apparently wasn't happy with Ron's rude behavior towards the grandmother Rachael, and he directed his words towards him. "Well, if that doesn't work for you, then *you* give us a better answer, and while ye're at it, also come up with *why* we're here?"

Ron made a grunting sound and turned his head and body away, trying to remove himself from the entire situation.

Studying the group I found myself reflecting. These were normal parents with different lifestyles, but all struggling with the same problem, and none coming up with an acceptable answer. Perhaps Rachael was right. Maybe this really was a dream, a dream involving twelve people, but, even if it were possible...why? Why would we be together?

Rachael watched the fear and confusion bounce around the group. "In all of my 65 years, I've never encountered a situation like this and I thought that I'd experienced almost everything." She sighed, settled back in her chair and continued. "I lost my parents early in life and was raised by my grandparents. The fact that I am now raising my grandchild had been 'foreseen,' but I did not understand when I first started to see visions. Until now, I'd considered that to be the strangest thing I'd been faced with." She drew another big sigh. "When I was a little girl, long before I started seeing my own visions, my Grandmother told me, 'Rachael, you are here for a very important mission. You will be involved with children...there will be much danger.'

"I assumed when my daughter and son in law were killed in a traffic accident, and I was left as the only living relative of their infant, that I was seeing my grandmother's prediction come true. Now I'm beginning to see a bigger and more demanding picture forming." She spoke softly to no one in particular, but she had captured everyone's attention.

Although fascinated with her story, I couldn't help wondering what the hell she was talking about and what did it have to do with me?

Day Two

The leaves blowing gently on the tree outside of the window teamed up with the rays of sunshine, and created dancing patterns across my face and pillow. I watched the changing forms for a while before stretching and getting out of bed. Then suddenly I remembered that today is Saturday, my favorite day, because it's the beginning of the two days I spend uninterrupted with Naja.

Slowly I made my way to the bathroom remembering that this morning we were going on a run through the park, stopping off at the swing sets and then doing some shopping before naptime. Naja softly padded into the bathroom while I was brushing my teeth. As usual, she emulated me, first brushing those tiny baby teeth and then brushing her hair, blond hair just like her dad's. We shared the time together, talking about the day that was about to begin.

Naja was excited about seeing the other children, and the shopping trip. She had some definite ideas about what she wanted to buy, and she spent quite a while explaining exactly what she needed for her tiny dollhouse. It was interesting to watch how she arranged the furniture in the different rooms of the doll house. In the early stages things were random, however, with time, observation and practice she started arranging the rooms to look like rooms that she'd seen, starting with ours, then Jill's and sometimes a picture in a book, now she was starting to add a few touches of her own. It was hard to believe the focus that she had for a 5-year-old.

Jill, my college roommate and closest friend, her 7-year-old daughter, and a new mother named Toby and her infant son, usually, joined us on our runs. We'd developed this trio after I'd noticed that strange man in the park several more times throughout the years. He never threatened me or came near, and I still hadn't gotten a good look at him, but he did make me nervous. Then on top of that, lately, we'd started hearing rumors of childnappers, attacks on jogging women, and other negative things as we began to circulate among the regular park goers.

Jill and I decided that the 'safety in numbers' thing was the safest way to enjoy the park, so we formed a 'Park Watch' with some of the other women who regularly ran or visited the park. We developed signals using whistles and many of the women carried cellular phones with some of the other women's cell numbers listed on the backs, Jill and I were some of those women.

It wouldn't be long before I'd be losing my running partner; we'd already pushed it to the limit. Jill's daughter, Samantha, had really outgrown the three-wheeler, and she didn't want to ride 'like a baby' anymore as she put it, but her young body couldn't keep up with us when she was on foot.

As I loaded Naja and JoJo, her favorite stuffed, but unidentifiable animal, the water bottles, and other gear into the large three-wheeled stroller, my thoughts turned to Sami. Even though she was two years older than Naja, she often seemed the same age or even younger. It wasn't that she was dysfunctional or even slow. She was a perfectly normal seven-year-old, but apparently Naja was just a fairly advanced five-year-old.

As I watched Jill explain to Sami for the third time why she had to ride in the three wheeler, I noticed the difference between the two young girls. At first, I'd assumed that I was the typical mother thinking my particular child was smarter than all of the other children, but then people started mentioning Naja's advanced skills. Jill even mentioned it, feeling uncomfortable with what she was noticing. I tried to convince her that it was only because Naja lived in an adult world, with her mother as her main companion, and didn't have an older brother like Sami had, which gave her certain advantages and certainly an adult approach to things rather than the typical five-year-old view. Jill appeared to accept this answer and besides, she knew that Sami was bright enough.

Toby came driving up just at we were ready to start off. It didn't take her long to put her sleeping baby into the stroller and join us. We, with our bigwheeled strollers, ran along the wooded trails enjoying nature's wonders; the birds flitting around, the trees over head, the ducks in the lake. The leaves rustling in the wind sounded like they were calling out a greeting as we ran by. I loved it. It was a comfortable feeling communing with nature.

We'd been jogging for about 20 minutes, when we heard the whistled signal. Three sharp sounds, a hesitation, and then three more sharp sounds. We stopped our strollers, our instincts on full alert and listened. Jill's normally pleasant features were contorted into intenseness as she listened, and waited. Toby, who had dropped a little ways behind stopped beside us, her face showing anxiety. I kept turning my head trying to decide where the signal had come from. Then it came again, from down the hill and to the left.

We all started running, the three wheelers flying along on the black topped path. We no longer noticed the birds or the rustling leaves of the near by trees. The young girls squealed with delight at the fast pace not understanding the situation. Toby and her new baby fell a little behind again.

As we turned the corner, we saw three women standing together. They pointed over a low rise of green grass past where they were standing as they saw us running towards them, and before the strollers had even stopped, the women were yelling that a man had grabbed a small child and run over that hill.

"Jill! Stay with the girls, and call 911!"

"No, don't go alone!" I heard Jill say as I turned and raced down the grassy slope. I didn't plan on tackling the guy just keeping him in sight. That is if I even saw him. Off to the right more whistles sounded I veered in that direction.

Grouped near the water fountain were several more women. When they saw me running towards them, they pointed straight ahead over a grassy slope. One of the women, a young, strong looking gal, wearing a baseball cap with her long dark pony tail swinging back and forth through the hole in the back, broke away from the group and cut down the slope to join me.

"Jeans, blue shirt, blond hair," she managed to communicate as we ran. We'd only run for a short distance when we heard a dreaded sound, the screaming cry of a child. As we rounded a clump of large bushes we saw a child laying on the ground ahead of us and a blue shirted figure ducking behind some fir trees and up a brush covered hill. We stopped when we reached the child. She was our concern; neither of us had any intention of confronting the guy.

The child was scraped and bruised from being thrown to the ground, but didn't seem seriously damaged. As the young woman knelt down, gathered her up and began comforting her, I dialed Jill's cell phone number. I could hardly speak I was so out of breath, but I did manage to tell her that we had the child and the guy ran up towards 7th street. Still gasping for breath, I sat down on the ground beside the woman cradling the crying child. Looking at the little girl, I suddenly realized that she had a striking likeness to Naja. She was about five years old, with blond hair and blue eyes and she was even wearing a red tee shirt similar to the one Naja was wearing today. Even though I was very warm from the exertion of the run, I shivered at the thought that this could have been my own precious daughter.

The young woman carried the child up the hill towards the blacktop path and the waiting women. I followed still looking over my shoulder towards the hillside. The nanny, of the child, was almost hysterical sobbing and muttering in a foreign language.

While waiting for the police, I noticed a bag lady shuffling along the sidewalk keeping a respectful distance from the gathering group of mothers and children. Casually I moved across the walk to intercept her without appearing to be aggressive and startle her.

"Hi."

"What's up?" asked the bag lady nodding her head in the direction of the group of obviously upset women, and not seeming the least bit frightened of me as I had assumed she would be.

"Some guy tried to run off with one of the children."

Her reaction was one of shock and anger. "Here in my park!" She snorted.

"You said 'tried.' Does that mean he failed?"

"Yes, thank God, he failed. I wanted to ask you if you'd seen a man in a blue shirt and jeans running away or hanging around the area."

"No I haven't, but I'll keep my eyes out, I don't want that sort in this here park. Was it your child?"

"No, but it could have been." I was thinking how much the child did look like my own child. "Thanks," I said and turned to go.

"Was that what all that whistling was about?" the bag lady asked, eyeing me with curiosity.

"Yes, we have a signal we use if there's a problem," I explained to her, finding her interest curious.

"What kinda whistles do you use?" she asked a twinkle in her eye. "I'm in the park a lot of the time..." her voice drifted off leaving the rest of the sentence unfinished.

What a great idea! I thought. "This is what we use, just a common whistle." I showed her the whistle and then realized that it might be common to me, but probably this woman wouldn't have a way to obtain one. "Here, take this one. I have another at home," I offered, and pulled the cord over my head and handed it to the woman.

She reached out for the whistle and our eyes met. Her eyes were deep blue and intelligent; she seemed like a very aware person. I found myself wondering if she had children of her own somewhere, and how had she ended up in this type of life? I masked my curiosity and explained the signal system to her and when we used it.

The woman glanced over her shoulder and started moving away. I turned to find a man in a business suit watching us as he talked to Jill.

"What's your name?" I asked as I turned back to the woman, but the woman had moved away and was leaving. "I'm Mandy," I called after the retreating back.

"Call me Alice." The woman tossed the words over her shoulder and rounded the corner and out of sight behind a large rhododendron bush.

"Hi, I'm Lieutenant Adams," the business suited man explained holding out his hand, as I walked across the grass to the group. "Was 'she' bothering you?" he asked nodding his head towards the rhododendron bushes that Alice had disappeared behind.

"No, on the contrary, I made contact with her. I was asking if she'd seen the man who grabbed the little girl. She hadn't, but she seemed willing to keep her eyes open for us. I even gave her a whistle so she could signal if she saw anything wrong."

"Yes, the ladies were telling me about your signal system. It's a good plan, and certainly seemed to work today," he admitted, with a grin. "You ladies seem to be on top of things. However, I also heard that you ran off after this guy. That's not a good idea."

"I didn't plan on confronting him," I said, frowning and looking sideways at Jill. "I just wanted to keep an eye on him until help arrived. As it turned out, I guess he wasn't comfortable with two 'mothers' chasing after him. You know what they say about mother bears and their cubs?" I added with a smile, trying for a lighter feeling.

"Yes, it did work out well, but you must be careful chasing guys in the park."

"NO! Guys must be careful of mothers when grabbing children in the park!" I said in a louder voice than I'd intended. Which immediately drew applause and hoots from the excited women who were standing in small groups and a sly grin from the uniformed officer talking to one of the groups.

The lieutenant stood there with his eyebrows raised, staring at me, while I flushed with embarrassment. "Sorry," I apologized.

"No, I apologize to you. You women have a good system, you used your heads and you saved a little girl from God knows what. Keep up the good work." He flashed a huge grin and turned to leave. Then he turned back and said, "Smart move, incorporating the bag lady. She hangs out in this area and could possibly be of help to you some time." Then he turned and moved to another group of ladies to finish his report.

Jill poked me in the ribs and made a suggestive face.

"What?" I questioned, deliberately choosing not to understand her meaning.

"Whata ya mean, 'What'? You know what! He's an attractive guy and he was interested in you."

"No way. He's just doing his job. Come on let's go to the mall," I said, turning to leave and successfully changing the subject. Jill was always looking to match me up with someone. I was aware that she was watching me as I tucked Naja in and turned the stroller around. I know it makes her uncomfortable to see me going it alone. She has a great husband and is very happy at the domestic life of wife and mother and she wants me to have her idea of a normal happy family life too. I caught her next glance which was directed across the sidewalk towards the Police Lieutenant. *Jeeze Jill, you can't pair me up with every man I talk to*, I thought in frustration.

The shopping trip didn't hold much interest for me; I was still keyed up over the incident in the park. Naja, however, loved it and talked me into several new pieces of furniture for her dollhouse and a very advanced picture puzzle. Jill looked at the puzzle with a question in her eyes, but didn't say a word.

When we finally got home, I was really tired and would have like to just crash, but Naja was fired up and full of energy. She insisted that she would help with the dinner because, as she put it, her mom seemed tired.

I wondered at the perceptiveness of one so small. Naja stood on a stool, reached her small hand into a drawer and pulled out two forks, one regular size and one her size, then she climbed down and took the forks to the table where I had already set the dishes. Next, she painstakingly separated two paper napkins from the others in the holder and set them next to the plates.

Turning to me with a big smile she said, "There, what else do we need?"

"I think that does it partner, let's eat." Only one really ate dinner that night, I just pushed my food around on my plate, while Naja, between bites, talked about the excitement of seeing real policemen, buying new toys and even the food she was eating. I, however, kept thinking of the red tee shirt the other little girl had been wearing and how much she'd looked like Naja.

Later, as I watched fascinated, Naja arranged and rearranged the new furniture in the doll house to look very much like a furniture display Jill and I had stopped to admire in a store window while walking through the mall. *Amazing, maybe she's going to be an interior decorator when she grows up*, I thought.

At last, it was bed time, I had trouble reading the continuing story that I read to Naja each night, because I was all but nodding off. My bed never felt so good.

~

Walking through the door, I experienced stunned surprise, which was followed by a weird feeling of déjà vu. I was looking at the meeting room from the dream last night, a dream that involved 11 other people. "Oh no, here I am again," I said out loud to the empty room.

After standing there for a full minute, I finally decided to make the best of it and took a few steps into the room. Maybe I could find out exactly where this meeting was being held. I continued to stand there looking around the beautifully decorated meeting room for a reception area or the name of the building. This definitely wasn't the building that I worked in or had ever been to a business meeting in. For one thing, it was much neater than any I'd seen.

As I turned around and gazed back towards the door I found that Sally Porter, the black woman, and Rachael De Leon, the grandmother, were standing in the doorway staring at me, they both had their mouths open almost as wide as their eyes. A movement from the left drew my attention, turning in that direction, I saw Ron Cole, Mr. Fitness, walking towards us from the hallway.

"What the hell!" he expressed out loud as he realized where he was.

"Well put!" I said feeling that he'd taken the words right out of my mouth.

The four of us stood there staring at the room where we'd spent last nights dream, but no one made a move to move forward. I had the feeling that the room was calling to me, inviting me in. It wasn't a bad feeling. In fact, it was a feeling of welcome. So I took the plunge and stepped completely into the circle of chairs.

The energy in the room was not the turbulent feeling that was felt last night as everyone wanted to leave, it was more positive and had a fairly calming aura about it.

Deliberately I walked to the middle of the circle and turned around to face the others, holding out my arms. "It didn't hurt a bit." The other three were still motionless by the door. My voice must have stimulated them into movement because they walked towards the chairs, in the middle of the room just as Bill Bellows, convenience store, Lindy, red leggings and then Cindy Taylor, with her red hair, came into view behind them. I turned away smiling at the visual associations I'd subconsciously attached to each of the people and also because I didn't want to see the total look of shock that I knew would be on their faces.

Walking around the room, I looked for anything that might be a clue as to where we were, where this building was located, who owned or managed it, or who was pulling the strings to this strange occurrence? There were no desks, no memos, and no phones. Even the wastebaskets were empty. Not a clue as to where we were, or why we were here.

"Well ladies and gentlemen," I said as I picked out a comfortable looking chair and sat down, "it would appear that we meet again." This was not a happy group of people. All I got for my weak effort in humor, were frowns, scowls and under the breath mutterings. So... I sat and waited, along with the rest of those present.

Eventually, everyone from the night before was back. None excited about the circumstances. After some milling around, and a lot of grumbling under their breath, everyone took a seat and then looked straight at me. I decided to say nothing and just wait. After all it wasn't my show. I studied my nails, picked at some invisible lint on my skirt and just waited.

"Okay, okay, what's going on?" asked Lindy looking directly at me. Lindy didn't seem like a person who was big on playing games. Obviously her life had been full of hard knocks. She had all the signs of having been abused, probably as a child and as a wife and mother. Usually that type of experience made a woman stronger and more independent or they gave up and became complete slaves to their situation. I sensed that Lindy wasn't in the slave category and that she wasn't in the mood for bullshit, she felt that I knew something more than I was sharing, and she wanted to know what it was.

Well, I didn't, so I just ignored the question and looked around the room with a questioning look on my face. What I did notice was that everyone was wearing the same clothes tonight that they were wearing last night, even me, although, this is not what I wore today.

"Guess you'd better pick out your favorite outfit the first time you attend one of these shindigs, if you get advance warning, that is," I sarcastically mused to no one in particular.

No one spoke up, just as I knew they wouldn't. I leaned back in my chair and waited. I just didn't feel like being the leader of a bunch of angry rude people this wasn't my party.

As I tried to look mentally occupied I felt a pull coming from across the room, a tug that demanded my attention, and when I looked up, Rachael was studying me with a smile on her face. I just smiled back, nodded, re-crossed my legs, and studied my shoe, still not taking on the responsibility of heading up this group.

"I've been thinking," Rachael said in a voice that sounded like she was still thinking only now it was out loud. She unconsciously fingered a crystal pendant hanging around her neck, stroking and turning it around in her fingers sending out sparks of brilliant colors as it caught the light. "We are like a group of people who were directed into a life boat, then set a drift," she continued. "We don't have a food, exposure or shark problem, but we certainly can't just sit here waiting to be rescued. We need to take some responsibility. Not necessarily for our situation that seems to be a done deal, but for trying to figure out what is happening, why it's happening, and most importantly, what we are going to do about it." Her energy enveloped everyone like a cloud. It drifted into every corner of the room, and softly covered everyone in a pink hued blanket.

I knew I liked this woman, I thought. *She's a survivor and has a logical head on her shoulders.*

I notice that others started to relate to her also, their body language and the expressions on their faces all began to soften. Her age not only set her apart, but also worked well for her. She looked and sounded like 'mother wisdom' herself. She didn't represent a threat to anyone, and actually seemed to radiate comfort.

"Yeah she's right, I don't wanna be here, but I also don't wanna just sit here staring at the floor," Bill Bellows said, looking seriously at each of the faces around the room. "I'm a doer not a sitter."

I'd seen his kind before, he's a driven man and just hanging around with a bunch of strangers with no logical outcome wasn't comfortable for him, I speculated as I watched him fidget in his chair.

"Yes, let's figure this out."

"How? This is insane!"

"I still don't believe that we're asleep. There has to be another explanation."

"Well, it sure comes under the heading of weird in my book."

The brief statements were a beginning. They were starting to loosen up. I glanced at Rachael, catching her eye; I smiled again, remembering her background. There was a lot of knowledge and understanding of people behind those dark eyes and that Mona Lisa smile.

"Okay, where do we begin?"

"Who knows anything about dreams?"

"I don't think this is like your standard type of dream."

"No kidding!"

Glancing across the room, I noticed Rachael was again looking at me with a peaceful, knowing smile. *Damn!* I thought as I took a controlled breath, and said out loud, but continued looking straight at Rachael. "Perhaps we should get organized and try to get as much out of this time as possible."

Rachael continued her serene smile and slightly nodded her head up and down. She seemed to know that I had the training to carry this off. She was probably a manager who was an expert at delegating when she was in the working world. Subtler than any I'd encountered, but she does get the job done.

Before looking around the room at the other faces, I felt my body do an automatic shift; a slight stiffening, bracing for rejection and preparing for rudeness and hostility again, instinctively protecting my own feelings from the pain other people inflict with their lack of sensitivity. Every face was turned towards me as I spoke and now they just waited for me to go on. Okay…so maybe they were over the resisting and blaming period. I relaxed a little and took a deep breath of fresh air, untainted and devoid of fear.

"Let's start with dreams. I've heard that some dreams are a form of receiving information and that often, our personal angels, spirit guides, higher self or even God *herself,* is sending us messages while we sleep." Having laid out my personal theory, I waited for them to totally reject the ideas of receiving messages while asleep, angels, spirit guides, higher selves and certainly God being a she. However, no one batted an eye; they just waited for me to go on. Apparently at this stage these suggestions weren't as far out as they might have seemed before this dream thing happened.

"Let me tell you a story." I began. "Once upon a time, there was a young woman who dreamed that she was rescuing an infant from men who wanted to kill the child. She and the child were saved by a large white wolf/dog. Then years later, this same young woman, gave birth to that very same child that she had dreamed about years before."

Looking around the room at the faces I tried to get in touch with their reaction to the story, but the only one who showed any expression was Rachael. She sat there, with a serious look on her face, nodding her head up and down. She looked deep in thought.

"Did you dream the birth of the child too, or is that real?" asked Lindy, dressed in her red leggings and oversized black sweater. She looked serious and was leaning forward, her arms resting on her knees, waiting for an answer.

Obviously, it was pretty clear that I was the girl in the story. I smiled and said, "Naja is real." Hesitating, I then added, "But the point of my story is that dreams can be very strange and still work to your advantage. You can gain information and insight from them or you can find them completely strange and totally incomprehensible. This one for example seems to fall into the latter category."

At the confused look on some of the faces, I added, "Meeting with strangers in a dream seems completely strange and totally incomprehensible to me."

Ignoring that statement, Sally asked, "So you don't understand why you dreamed about your child in danger before you even conceived her?" She and most of the others were very intent on my personal dream. They were more interested in that dream than the one they were now involved in. I guess it's easier to relate to someone else's dream or problem than your own.

I wonder what they'd think if they knew that I'd also seen the same man that was in my very first dream. Only this time, he was real. "No, I haven't figured that out yet," I answered. "However, I do feel that at some time I will understand the reason for that dream."

"It had to be to warn you of a danger to Naja," suggested Cindy, looking very sympathetic.

"Yes, but the child in the dream, was a baby. Her daughter is now five years old. Maybe she's gotten past the danger," Shala pointed out, pushing for the positive outlook.

"Actually, that's exactly what I've been thinking. However, I have seen one of the men from the dream. He follows me around the park from time to time. It started when Naja was six months old." Well, so much for keeping that to myself.

Several of the women gasped and there was a general fluttering of hands and a definite change in the energy field, within the room, as fear coupled with the feelings of mothers protecting their babies flashed about like small lightning bolts.

I managed a smile and said, "He never came very close and I haven't seen him now for 6 or 8 months. Although, I do watch every shadow, but nothing has happened, so I think that Shala is right. The danger, whatever it was, is probably passed."

Even as I reassured them the picture of the little girl, who looked like Naja, crying in the park after the man had grabbed her, flashed through my mind. A shiver ran up my back and down my arms, and as the last fingers of fear chased each other off of my body and scurried away I became aware of Rachael watching me again. What is it about this lady? She seemed to have a super sense for tuning into what I'm experiencing or thinking. I avoided making eye contact letting the moment pass.

"Tell me... what did the man look like? The man in your dream who followed you around the park," Hally asked, twisting the end of her braid in a nervous gesture. Her face was expressionless, but her eyes were two turbulent pools of fear.

Watching her closely I described the man the best that I could explaining that I'd never seen his face because he always seemed to have the light behind him. Hally's face went white and for a moment it looked like she was going to faint.

A sniff drew my attention, looking past Hally, I saw Teri, the nursery school gal, she had tears streaming down her face. Then silence took over the room. Maybe it wasn't the silence that I noticed maybe it was the complete lack of energy. It was like a giant vacuum had sucked up every bit of energy, every bit of feeling, every bit of life, from the room and had left it in a void.

"Whaat?" I uttered breaking the silence and the void. Looking at each face I saw fear, raw naked fear. This fear wasn't just on one or two faces. It was on every face even Rachael, the wise one.

"Okay, what's going on? Let's have it! What's happening here?" I demanded. Not understanding what these people were experiencing or even understanding why they were experiencing it. No one spoke. They appeared to be slowly recovering from shock apparently brought on by their fear, but fear of what?

Finally, Bill Bellows with a strangely shaky voice said, "I can't speak for the others, but I too have seen that fellow that you mentioned. He's been watching my youngest girl Yolanda. I've even called the police."

"Me too, I've seen him hanging around Jasmine," said Sally weakly her fear still hanging on to her and draining her energy.

"Yeah, I've even chased him, but never even got close," Ron added.

"Wait, wait! Are you telling me that all of you have seen this guy?" I asked in disbelief. "How could you possibly think that it's the same guy? I didn't even see his face."

"I didn't see his face either. He always had the light behind him or was in the shadows, but he fits the description you gave perfectly," explained Pete.

"That's right. Never saw his face."

"Yea, that's what makes it so scary...."

I was completely astounded. How could this be? I'd figured that this dream meeting had something to do with children, but never anything like this! My mind was racing remembering each detail of the dream, each detail of the man on the bridge, each detail of the 'almost child snatching' in the park. "Well, there's more. Today... a child was grabbed in the park..."

Several people gasped and someone moaned softly. "No, it's okay, we got her back all right, but the really scary thing is that the little girl involved looked like and was dressed just like my Naja. However, the guy that grabbed her was not the guy in my dream!"

"Are you sure?"

"I'm absolutely sure! It was not the same guy."

"Maybe we need to be on the look out for more than one guy. Perhaps it's a child napping ring."

"Oh God," a female voice whispered.

"Is the person related to the child in the park today here also?"

"Any of you use a foreign speaking nanny? No? Then no, she is not. So what does that mean?"

"Different man different situation perhaps?"

"Maybe he grabbed the wrong kid."

There it was. The thought that I'd not actually allowed to take form, brought out into the open by a complete stranger. I still didn't want to acknowledge this idea. Why would this guy be after Naja? I didn't have any money. I wasn't in a position of power where I could benefit anyone if threatened.

Looking around again, I still could not believe what was developing. As I looked at these people, I noticed that everyone seemed to be thinking and remembering, just as I had. Then I heard what was in the back of my mind. What was probably in the back of everyone's mind.

"Do you suppose that's why we are together here in this meeting? Because we've all seen this particular man near our children?" Rachael asked, looking thoughtful, as she fingered the crystal around her neck again. "And if so... why our children?"

Once again, the air vacated the room and we sat there not even breathing, we sat there in complete emptiness. The question, *"Why our children?"* hanging in the airless room.

Day Three

Sunday was another day of fun and games with Naja. I'd planned a short trip to the park for another run, a little swinging, a little teeter tottering, a little sliding, and a little jungle gym stuff. After all of that, I expected to be exhausted and ready for Naja's nap. The problem was, Naja was beginning to outgrow her nap, and was objecting to taking it. So today, I changed the plan a bit. Today, after the park run, we were going to take in a Disney movie with Jill and Samantha as an added treat. Toby had decided that the park was becoming too dangerous and had informed Jill that she wouldn't be joining us anymore. That's a shame, people shouldn't have to hide in their homes to feel safe, and I didn't plan to allow anyone to force me into such a lifestyle.

We arrived at the park like a gust of wind on a stormy day, the car rushing into the parking space. The door popped open and I jumped out, scurrying around the car to let a squealing Naja out of her confinement. Naja was wired and I had been moving fast to reach this destination of treed bliss so I could stretch out these legs, and relax. I always felt good after a run. Naja even seemed to relax after a couple of turns in the park.

Looking around I didn't see Jill, but that wasn't really surprising, we'd arrived a little early. I guesstimated that we could probably make one complete circle around the lake before Jill and Sami arrived at the park.

Naja quickly climbed into the 'Wheeler,' as we'd started calling her transportation vehicle, and I swung it around and headed towards the path to the lake, but before I actually got started my cell phone rang. It was Sunday, so I wasn't expecting any business calls, this must be Jill.

"Hi. Aren't you coming?" I answered assuming that Jill was either running late, or that she was canceling.

"Don't run by the lake today," said a low, whispering voice. The voice was so husky that I couldn't tell for sure, if it was a man or a woman.

"What? Jill is that you?" There was no response to my question. "Who is this?" I asked in a stronger tone, feeling the beginnings of fear fluttering in my stomach.

"The lake is a dangerous place today," said the voice ignoring my questions.

Quickly I raised my eyes, slowly scanning the park and the streets that I could see, as I asked, "For everyone or just for me?" Instead of an answer I heard the line go dead. I couldn't see anyone suspicious lurking around the area. Who had warned me? What was the warning about? Should I let this voice scare me off and not go into the park today? YOU BET! Suddenly the friendly trees and the inviting paths turned into menacing shapes and dark avenues of no return.

"Who was it, Mommy? Are Auntie Jill and Sami going to be late?" Naja asked, leaning out of the stroller and looking back. *Oh God, that innocent face. Pull it together ...don't scare her*, I cautioned myself.

"No honey, it wasn't her." *Oh Jeeze, I've got to call Jill and head her off.*

Quickly dialing Jill's home phone number I listened as it rang and rang and then clicked onto the message machine. I punched in Jill's cell number, but it apparently wasn't turned on yet. Now what? Had she left already or was she just involved in something at home?

"Okay Naja, we're going to wait here for Auntie Jill and Sami. Let's get back into the car." Without a word, Naja gathered up her JoJo critter and her blanket and walked over to the car. She looked back as if to say, 'What are you waiting for?' No complaints, no questions, just cooperation.

When Jill arrived I quickly got out of the car to talk to her in the street without the kids listening. Ignoring Jill's attempt to explain why they were late, I rushed on and told her about the phone call and suggested that we bag the park trip today.

Jill had a scared look behind her eyes. Then she said, "Wait. Listen to me. As I started to back out of my garage this morning I discovered that a large delivery truck was blocking the driveway. No one was in the truck. I was looking for keys in the cab when, Herb, the retired widower who lives across the street noticed. He told me that he'd seen a man stop the truck, get out and get into a car about 20 minutes earlier. The truck was empty and there were no keys."

"What'd you do? How'd you get here?" I asked.

"Well Herb used to be in the motor pool in the army, so he hot wired it."

"No way!"

"Yea, he pulled it out of the way and said he'd call the rental company to come and get it. He was so excited, said he hadn't done that in years. Made his day I think."

"So what's going on?"

"Yea, what is going on?"

"Well I don't know, but we're sure as hell not going into that park today."

"Right." Jill put on a happy face and broke the news to Sami that we had decided to go for brunch and the movie and skip the park. Sami was delighted, she didn't like the three-wheeler anyway.

"I'll follow you to the mall."

Brunch with the two girls was interesting to say the least, they laughed and played throughout the entire meal. Jill glanced at me from time to time, but there wasn't a chance to really discuss the events before heading out to the theater.

Kids' movies in the middle of the day are a challenge, the theater quickly filled to the brim with children of a variety of ages and manners scampering over everything like monkeys, but the girls loved the outing. Although it didn't completely take my mind off of the park thing and Jill's strange abandoned truck. Was there a connection? How could there be, but if there was, what was it?

Near the end of the movie, I was overwhelmed by an uncomfortable feeling. I felt very strange. Jill and the girls were enjoying the movie, but the uncomfortable feeling grew stronger, so that now I was actually shifting around in my seat unable to sit still. Finally I started looking around the theater. I even turned around and looked behind me, all I saw were animated faces watching the movie, until my eyes swept the area further back in the theater, the area at the top of the long main aisle. There stood a figure in the open doorway that led down the aisle. The light outlined the slight strong figure of a man. The figure was familiar; in fact, it looked just like the man in my dream and the man on the bridge.

As I watched he started walking slowly down the aisle towards us, the light following him like his own private aura highlighting his body, but shielding his face. Just then, the movie ended in a big flurry of music, and a dozen kids and parents poured out of their seats and flooded the aisle, blocking the man halfway between the door and our position. I grabbed Naja's hand and spoke quickly to Jill.

"Get out quick! Other door!" Jill took one look at my face, grabbed Sami by the hand and ran to the front of the theater, dodging seats and kids, heading directly for the emergency exit on the far side with Naja and me right behind her.

Outside Jill looked at the girls, with a smile on her lips, and said, "Wow, wasn't that fun? We beat the entire crowd." The eyes that met mine over the top of the laughing girls, however, were very serious. "We need to talk," she said between her smiling lips.

"Right!" I agreed. "I'll call you tonight after the girls are in bed."

I dawdled through dinner and the dishes, lost in thoughts of what to say to Jill. After finally getting Naja settled in for the night, I reluctantly headed for the phone. Explaining to Jill wasn't going to be easy. I didn't want to scare her to death, but she certainly deserved to be aware of the dangers. We'd been friends since college and had been through some rough times together.

Jill was there with me at the wedding when Bob died and for the delivery of Naja. She'd even handled the thing about my dreaming about Naja and then giving birth to her, very well, but there was no way I could tell her about the dream meetings. I'm still having trouble with that myself. With a sigh, I picked up the phone and dialed Jill's number. Jill wasn't going to like the idea of Naja and I being stalked by this guy.

"Hi Jill, I hope you're sitting down," I said as I nervously twisted the phone cord around my finger, dreading the next few minutes, knowing that I had to put some distance between us. Jill and Sami's safety were more important than having company in the park. I ended up telling her about everything except the dreams.

"Listen Mandy, something is very wrong here. Why would anyone be stalking you?"

"I really haven't a clue, but I plan to be very careful."

"Right, like chasing him in the park?"

"Jill, I hadn't planned to catch or confront that guy in the park."

"Right! You hadn't planned on it! Just what would you have done if he'd stopped and challenged you?"

"Ahhh, well...I hadn't even thought about that, besides that other gal joined me."

"What if she hadn't?"

"Jill!"

"I'm serious, Mandy. If that guy had stopped and confronted you, would you have walked away and let him have that child?"

"Well of course not!"

"That's right, you'd have fought like a tiger for that child, and she wasn't even yours."

"Okay, okay, I get your point. I will be careful."

This was not good enough for Jill, she wanted to call the police right away. I explained that I'd never really seen him and couldn't recognize the voice on the phone. Jill insisted and we debated the pros and cons for a half hour. Finally, I agreed that I'd file a report, just to calm Jill down, and that we'd skip the park runs for a while, but would meet for other fun things like lunch or movies.

Thank God that Jill and Sami had Fred, and weren't living alone. Fred was a big guy, a great husband and father and very protective, so I wouldn't worry about them as long as they stay away from me...that is.

I tossed around in my bed, unable to fall asleep. I really didn't want to skip the runs in the park, and I really didn't like someone else directing my life, but I knew that Jill was right. I rolled the problem and its alternatives over and over in my mind without finding a solution, before eventually falling into a fitful sleep.

~

Walking through the door of the meeting room I found that everyone was already there, however, the energy in the room seemed to be standing still. There was no conversation going on. No one greeted me. However, every face turned to watch as I walked across the room and sat in the one remaining chair. I didn't say a word either; I didn't meet anyone's eyes. I didn't want to be here. I didn't want to share my experiences with these people. I didn't like not having a choice. Lately it seemed more and more of my choices were being limited; the park runs, the dream meetings, what would be next?

After a few moments, Sally Porter who was sitting next to me, reached over and put her black hand over my white one. I took a deep breath and smiled, but still didn't meet Sally's eyes. I could feel the pressure of the unanswered question that was shared by eleven people.

"Sorry to be late," I finally said without looking at anyone in particular. Now I had to apologize to a group of people I didn't even know for being late to a meeting I didn't want to attend, while I was asleep. This would be funny if I wasn't feeling so angry and depressed.

"What'd I miss?" No one said a word, the room remained silent. However, this silence was not quiet. I could hear the unasked questions bombarding me from all directions.

"Mandy, what's wrong?" Rachael finally asked, in her comfortable nurturing voice.

Oh great! Am I so transparent that this entire group of strangers can read me? I fumed feeling even more depressed and dejected. I wanted to go to bed curl up in the fetal position, pull the covers up over my head and escape.

"We have some things to share with you, but perhaps you'd like to talk to us first," Rachael continued.

"No," I sighed, "go ahead, did you discover the answer to the question we ended with last night? What sets our kids apart?" I muttered, feeling myself slipping further and further into a gloomy depression. It pulled at me like quicksand threatening to suck me into oblivion.

I watched, feeling more distanced with each moment that passed, as Rachael nodded to Teri, the nursery school teacher. Teri turned toward me and said, "No, but I did something else. I checked with the parents of the children in my school, to see if any of them had noticed this 'man' that we've seen."

This got my attention. Looking up from my chair, I started dragging myself back from the quick sand, using my interest in Teri's words as a lifeline.

"Not one of them has ever seen him," she explained, "even though, at least once, he showed up right after the parents had picked up their kids. I told them that I 'thought' that I might have seen a man hanging around the area. I wanted to start a 'watch,' kinda like you did in the park where you go. The parents were all for it and are going to keep their eyes open and some are even going to drive by, at different times of the day, to scope things out."

I shot out of 'mud hole three' in a flash sitting up straighter and feeling like I'd just had a B12 shot. "That's great, Teri! What a good idea!" I exclaimed with enthusiasm.

"Now that's modesty," laughed Bill, "to show such excitement for your own idea." He laughed again and others laughed with him. I gave up feeling sorry for myself and joined the laughter feeling more alive again. Rachael watched me as I came out of my depression, I could feel her eyes on me, assessing my attitude, trying to read me. Her instincts were very good she didn't miss a thing.

"Mandy, it seems to me that you may be the unknowing catalyst to this situation. I feel that it's important that we all share any information that pertains to our children and this problem. We can help each other this way and maybe even discover what it is about our children that has brought us together." Rachael explained her feelings on this situation, looking around the room and ending by focusing back directly on me.

What was it about this woman? She seems capable of tapping right in to me. I knew that Rachael was very much aware that I was holding something back.

"Okay, Rachael," I said with another sigh and a smile as I met her gaze. "I did have a problem today." Quickly I told them about the phone call and the 'man' in the movie house. "I'm feeling traumatized. At first I was angry at this guy, but now I'm feeling depressed." I felt myself starting to slip backwards again.

"He's wearing you down. Don't let him do that!" Lindy quickly spoke up. "I've had that experience before! He'll keep at ya til your will is gone. You absolutely must stay mad, if that's what will keep you from giving up."

"Si, don't forget he's after your Nina," added Ramon in his deep accented voice. "I'd like to get my hands on this guy!"

A sudden thought occurred to me. "Did anyone else see this guy today?"

"Yes honey, I saw him too. He was standing on the corner, with the sun on his back, when I came out of the store with Bobby," Lindy contributed.

"Me too, I saw him out of the window of my car. He watched me drive by with Chad."

I quickly interrupted her. "Did you see his face?" I asked, hoping that we might finally have a better description of him.

"Nope his face was not visible, because like with Lindy, the sun was behind him."

"Anyone else see him today? No? Well, I guess he can't get around to all 12 of us each day. Let's keep a record of who he visits each day so we can track him." I suggested, feeling better when I was doing something.

"Good idea."

"Yeah, maybe we can figure out where he's going to be next and lay in wait for him and then beat the hell out of him," Ron stated in his typically aggressive manner. The other three guys agreed with him, and started talking about how they planned to tear him limb from limb.

I glanced around the room for something to write on. To my surprise lying on the desk, very neatly waiting for me, was a yellow legal pad and a freshly sharpened pencil. I stared at the pad and pencil. Why was it there? It wasn't there last night when I was looking around for a name or a location clue. It was as if it were there because it knew that I was going to use it tonight. I felt the feathery touch of goose bumps move up the back of my arms, run up the back of my neck and into my hairline.

"Did you find something to write on?" the soft voice of Rachael asked. Even though her voice ended with a question, I had the strangest feeling that she already knew that I'd found something and exactly what it was. I turned to look at Rachael before answering. Her face looked innocent enough, but her eyes looked all knowing.

"Yes, someone conveniently left a note pad and a pencil," I said as I stood up and retrieved the pad and pencil from the desk. Rachael smiled sweetly, not showing the surprise that I was feeling. I noticed that the only one who apparently witnessed the exchange was Shala. Shala was so quiet that you hardly remembered she was around. Rachael had looked away, but Shala was watching her with open curiosity written across her face, but not any more than I was feeling. Rachael was definitely an interesting lady.

I wrote the date, the names and times, of those who had seen the... 'Boogie Man.' As I decided to dub him, yeah, I like that. It gives him an aura of something that's scary, but not actually real. Like visualizing someone who intimidates you, while they're in their underwear, softening the fear factor rather than enhancing it. I sat there grinning at this visualization, until I noticed the silence creeping towards me. Glancing up I discovered that everyone was watching me again.

"Well, you sure look better than when you came in. So what are you grinning at?" the voice of Cindy was heard, sitting across from me.

"Just give a business woman a pencil and a legal pad and she's happy," quipped Pete with a frown on his face, he obviously was one of those who had problems with women in business.

"Oh, it's just silly...I... named the 'man' that we see, the Boogie Man. It takes away some of his reality. Well, I guess that's not exactly what I was grinning at. I was taught that if there's someone who intimidates you, you're supposed to visualize him in his underwear or sitting on the toilet. You know, something that takes away the power that you've given him in your mind. I guess I was visualizing."

Several people laughed, some smiled and some just looked like they thought I'd lost my mind. Guess you can't please all of the people all of the time. One of those who didn't appreciate the humor was Hally, the Asian woman.

"I don't see any humor in making him seem unreal. He's very real and very dangerous to our children!" She was so upset it looked as if she was going to cry.

"How do you know he's real? Is this dream real? Or maybe it's not real when we're awake. Maybe it's this dream that is real," said Ron, in his angry and abrupt manner and confusing things completely.

"Whoa, whoa, whoa," I said, holding up my hands. "First of all, Halley's right, he definitely is dangerous, but so is fear. We need to be prepared and alert where he or any other stranger is concerned, but we cannot run scared.

You lose your power when you give in to fear. Bringing this guy down off of his fearful pedestal is important. In fact, he seems to deliberately promote fear more than action." I explained these new ideas as they came unexpectedly into my head. Interesting how talking out loud brought out ideas I didn't even know I had floating around in my head.

"That's right. That's why he keeps the light behind him, kinda like shining a flashlight under your chin, and also why he just shows himself and doesn't actually do anything," added Cindy.

"Right, if we respond the way he wants us to, we'll panic and do the damage ourselves."

There was silence as this thought flowed around the room, moving in and out of the different minds, changing form with each encounter.

"Let's talk about the kids, like why these particular kids?" Pete questioned, studying each face as if he thought we had information that he didn't have and were holding back.

"That's a good question. What sets them apart in this Boogie Man's mind? They aren't all the same age. They aren't all the same sex. They aren't all the same nationality. What then?" Sally laid out the differences and ended with frustration written clearly across her face.

"In fact, that seems to be the only thing that they do have in common....the fact that they are all different nationalities."

"But there are lots of other nationalities than ours who aren't here," Shala said quietly.

"Yeah, that can't be it."

"Okay, what about abilities? Do they all like to do something that most other kids don't?"

"Wait," I said, suddenly getting an idea, "try to be unbiased, and tell me about the mentality of your child. Not the typical proud mom and dad stuff, but what's different about *their* way of thinking?" The faces directly in front of me went wide-eyed and startled. I looked around at the other faces. Everyone was, in some form or other, showing a great deal of surprise and knowing all at the same time.

"Ah ha!" I said out loud. "That's it! They think differently." It was noticeable in the problem solving abilities and the leadership qualities of these kids. The knowledge was sinking into each parent and they were now looking at each other, gaining confirmation just from the expressions on the other faces. Then bedlam reigned. Everyone started talking at once, to each other, to themselves, comparing situations, stories things said and done by the children. It felt good to find others with similar situations to share with.

Rachael stood up. She waited for those around her to notice. Finally, everyone was looking at her. She not only had their attention, but their silence as well. She cleared her throat and said, as she sat back down, "This morning I woke and my entire bedroom was bathed in the color of Indigo. Later when I got Dina up, her aura was Indigo. It stayed that way throughout breakfast and lunch. I started calling her my little Indigo girl. When she went down for her nap I meditated, thinking of a possible reason for this Indigo color to be around my granddaughter. The message I got was that she has come here to change and ultimately save this world."

No one spoke, no one even moved. Rachael continued, "I believe now, that these are a generation of children that have indeed come here to help save us from the chaos that we have created for our world."

Someone muttered, "She sees Auras?"

Another questioned, "She got a message?"

As Rachael sat there silent, Shala spoke up. "This rings true for me. Not because my child is involved, in fact, I wish that she weren't, this is not going to be easy, but because I can 'feel' that this is so. It puts a lot of unanswered questions about my child into perspective."

"This is an interesting idea all right," added Bill. "I'm not sure that I'm completely sold on it, but Yolanda is so different. I have two other children and they definitely are not here to save anything, probably more like destroy as much as they possibly can. The difference between them is very noticeable."

Hally spoke up and confirmed that she too had one child that seemed different than her other child.

Sally, the other mom that had two children, stated that there was an absolute difference between her kids. Not so much in what they did, but how they did it and the way that they thought about things. She stated that Jasmine definitely seemed more aware than the others.

"Aware is a good word. It really describes the difference."

"Yeah, very quick to catch on."

Teri, who had an entire nursery school to compare with, had been very quiet. Now she spoke up and said. "I can't believe this. Of course I'd noticed the difference between Jami and the other kids, but I'd convinced myself that Jami was maybe gifted, because the other kids are no dummies. Jami is only three, but she learned all of the rules, the programs I use, even the procedures... she could almost run the school already. I've actually had to give her jobs to keep her busy, so that she doesn't challenge me for my job, while the other older kids could care less."

"So Rachael... these Indigo children, just what is it they are going to be doing to save our world?" asked Pete, looking like he'd rather bite his tongue than ask this question, or even be a part of this idea.

"I don't know, but you can bet I'll be following up on this idea in my future meditations," she said in her soft voice.

"You don't actually believe she gets information from beyond? Do you?" Ron directed his question to Pete, hoping for an ally in his effort to deny this entire idea.

"I believe it's possible and further, I believe it's about time we started getting help in this world. We've been struggling along fighting a losing battle for too long!" Lindy threw her challenge right in Ron's face, daring him to respond. Ron just shrugged his shoulders and sat back in his chair, not wanting to take on Lindy.

I sat there listening to and observing the discussions going on between Rachael and several of the other parents. This was certainly very interesting, but children born especially to change the world? Didn't that seemed a bit much? Then... so did this dream thing. I tried to keep an open mind, but this entire situation was so strange.

My focus turned to wondering about Rachael. She was certainly a mysterious woman and now she says that she sees auras in color and gets messages from... somewhere. I do believe in the Spiritual or Mystical world, and have read quite a bit about it, but I've never known anyone who actually applied it. Although, I have used my intuition to help me through a lot of sticky situations, but intuition is just a woman thing. Certainly not like getting a message from beyond. I was the one who originally introduced the Angel, and/or Spirit Guide thing into this group, but actually I really don't know much about the subject.

Then, without regard to others that were talking I said, "Rachael, what about this message thing? How do you receive this message? Do you hear voices?" I couldn't help myself, I just had to know more about how this message was obtained, and from the looks on some of the faces, I guess I'd just asked the question that was on several minds.

"I wondered if anyone was going to ask that question." Rachael smiled, and then looking around the room, as if she were making sure everyone was paying attention, she continued, "I do hear a voice, but many people who receive messages do not. Some see a symbolic message, or feel the answer. Others just have a knowing. We all have Angels that guide and help us, and if you ask they will give you information. However, you do have to be open to receive."

There was a rude snort from Ron.

Ignoring him Sally asked, "What do you mean be open to receive?"

"Well, for example, if you ask a question, you have to believe that you will receive the information, and then expect and wait for the answer. Many folks will ask a question, but not believe that they are really going to get an answer. They asked, and then shut the door so the answer can't come through. Or, they are focusing on 'hearing' an answer when they're really not an audio person, so they miss the visual, feeling, or the intuitive thought."

"Intuitive thought? I was under the impression that being intuitive was just a woman thing, not an angel communication," I commented out loud, but was really thinking to myself. Thinking of all the times I *knew* when something was going to happen. Like the fear and nausea I experienced just after Bob left the church, to bring the car around following the ceremony. I thought it was just nerves, but now it looks like it could have actually been intuition.

"Women have developed it more than men, but it's certainly not exclusive," Rachael explained.

"Are you telling us that we can ask questions, like you did, and get answers?" demanded Pete with a confused expression contorting his face.

"Yes sir, that's just what I'm telling you. However, it does take a little practice, because most people have shut down the psychic powers that they were born with."

"Born with? We were born with these powers?" Lindy looked very excited, leaning forward.

"Why would we shut them down?" Ron asked.

"Why indeed. By the age of 5 or 6, most children have lost contact with their psychic abilities, because they are programmed that none of that is real. I'll bet that each one of you has contributed to your child's losing this very natural power. For example, how many times have you told your child to stop making up stories, or talking to imaginary friends?"

No one spoke, the wheels were going around inside of their heads, remembering the times they had squelched their child's imagination. Their psychic powers!

The reaction of the parents or maybe their expressions must have been apparent, because Rachael said, "Don't feel bad, you did exactly what you were programmed to do. You did what was done to you." Still no one spoke.

They were feeling the guilt. I was feeling positively devastated. I'd prided myself on keeping an open mind and allowing Naja to think freely, yet I knew that I too had, at times, suppressed her expressions and thoughts.

Rachael chuckled. "Not to worry, it's not permanent damage. They can recapture these lost abilities, just as you can. Actually, these Indigo kids probably didn't really let it go anyway, and if they did, they won't have any problem getting it back. I believe that they are very advanced. Or at least have more awareness than any of the rest of us."

"What about this awareness? How does this give them an advantage?"

"It probably makes it easier for them to learn and understand. They will pick things up very rapidly and actually put what they have learned into action, and I don't think they can be intimidated by guilt as most of us can and are."

"Yes, I see that happening."

"Me too."

"That's exactly what's happening."

"I, for one, need more information."

"Me too, can you teach us how to tune in to our Angels?" Sally asked in a hushed voice.

It was obvious that Rachael was surprised and pleased that these people, although dubious and tentative, were opening up and breaking away from their limited thinking.

"Now, this is new to you, but I've been practicing metaphysical thinking for more years that I care to remember. My mother, my grandmother and her mother before her had been 'healers' and 'prophets' in our culture. It was, of course, not understood then, just as it isn't completely understood or accepted now. The main difference being that today people who practice this form of activities are no longer burned as witches, and therefore no longer have to keep their abilities hidden away in the closet."

I quickly looked around the room to see how many were feeling as Sally was. I was surprise to see that almost everyone seemed to be in a positive, receptive mood. Ron Cole and Pete Jardin were the only two who looked dubious. The other two men, Bill and Ramon, and all of the women appeared to be receptive to this new idea that involved their kids.

"Do you think that contacting their angels is one of the methods our Indigo kids will use to accomplish their goal?" Bill asked the absolutely silent room, in his very serious voice. The group and the energy in the room seemed to wait expectantly for the reply.

"Yes, of course," Rachael obliged them.

"Then I think we need to help them. We need to be able to use our lost abilities or at least understand how they work if we're going to be of any help to the kids," he explained to the others.

"Yes..." began Lindy before I cut her off by jumping up and saying in an anxious voice, **"What's that?!"** The next thing I knew, I was standing in darkness, I couldn't see a thing. I stood very still, scarcely breathing. Who had turn out the lights? I couldn't hear the others in the room. I held my breath trying to hear even a tiny sound, finally I detected the sound of breathing, soft rhythmic breathing, I stood very still, waiting. As I stood there, it dawned on me that I was standing in Naja's room, and that it was Naja's breathing that I was listening to Naja was sleeping in the small bed to my right. Why was I here? What was wrong?

I continued to stand very still for a full minute, but didn't hear anything unusual. As my eyes slowly adjusted to the darkness I could see the light colored walls, with the brightly colored pictures of Mickey and Minnie Mouse dancing around with their cartoon friends. The lamp on the small end table near the bed was outlined in front of the window. The book I'd read to Naja before tucking her in still lay on the table. Naja's form was visible in the bed and as usual, she'd kicked the covers off.

I moved towards her and covered the small body with the blanket. Then I walked to the window and peeked out of the blinds. The bedrooms were on the second floor and from this vantage point the night seemed quiet and peaceful, the world outside seemed to be sleeping peacefully. Well, now I know how sleep walkers feel when they suddenly wake up somewhere else, after walking in their sleep.

Just as I started to turn away I saw something white move quickly across the grass and along the fence line. Peering closer, I saw nothing unusual; perhaps it was just a flash of light from a passing car. I did, however, go downstairs and check every window and every door just to be sure the locks were in place, even though I was positive that I'd locked everything earlier. Something had disturbed me and brought me back from the dream meeting. What could it have been? Maybe Naja had made a noise in her sleep.

I retraced my steps back up the stairs in the dark, thinking that it was time to call in a favor. One of Bob's grateful clients had told me if I ever needed any security systems in my house to let him know. Now seemed like the time to take him up on that offer.

I started making mental notes of what I'd need; door and window alarms and motion sensor lights attached outside were a must. Walking into my bedroom, I wondered if the alarm system would solve all of my current problems. Like the mysterious dreams, or the 'Boogie Man' I guess that would be wishful thinking, it definitely wouldn't be that easy, but it was a start. I'd call him in the morning and try to arrange to be squeezed into the schedule for an emergency hook up.

Day Four

I love my little step saving kitchen with its sparkling white background and the green accents that I've added a few at a time, along with the crystal rain drops. The garden window faces east and each morning, when it isn't raining, granted that isn't often here in Portland, but on nice days, I'm able to fix breakfast to the dancing light shapes on the cabinets as the morning sun shines through all of the colored glass and crystal. This was one of those mornings. I loved it! Unlike the sunshine states, we always appreciate the sun and never have a chance to get bored with it.

As I fixed Naja's breakfast this morning I wondered what happened at the dream meeting after I'd left so abruptly. My speculations were interrupted when I heard Naja say, "Mommy, are you listening?"

"Oh, no honey I guess not, what did you say?"

"I was asking you about the white dog that was in my room last night. Did you let him in? He was so soft and he licked my face."

I froze in mid movement holding the glass in one hand and the milk container in the other. My legs became rubbery and my head began to spin, I felt like I was on the verge of fainting. Reaching for the top of the counter I carefully set the glass and the milk carton down, and then gripped the edge of the counter and hung on. I considered putting my head between my knees, but knew I couldn't let go of the counter and the chair was too far away.

Finally, my head came back from wherever it had gone, but it brought with it a lot of pressure and noise. As I struggled to regained control of my body, I realized that I was drenched in sweat and my fingers hurt from hanging on to the counter so tight.

"Where's my milk?" Naja interrupted the survey of my body's reaction. I poured the milk and set it in front of Naja, with a shaky hand and then headed for the sink. I ran my hands under cold water, particularly the under side of my wrists, where the blood vessels were close to the skin, trying to cool down my body temperature.

"Naja, did you say that you dreamed about a white dog?" I asked and then belatedly thought about what Rachael had said about programming children's thoughts. However, Naja wasn't to be programmed so easily.

"No, I didn't dream it. He was really there. Didn't you see him?" she asked her voice taking on a slight edge of confusion. *Damn, I don't want her to be afraid.*

"No, I didn't see him, but I don't always see everything you do," I said as I sat down beside her at the table. "Did he scare you?" I asked casually, not looking at her.

"Oh no, I love him," she stated without hesitation.

"Well that's good. We'd better hurry or we'll be late," I said, quickly changing the subject because I didn't know where to go from there, but I wasn't able to change the strange feeling in the pit of my stomach. Was this the wolf/dog from my pre-Naja dream? How could that be? Well the Boogie Man was here, so why not the dog? Then I remembered the flash of white I'd seen as I looked out of the upstairs window last night. Could it have been the dog?

The doorbell rang, a sound heard so seldom that I jumped a foot and just sat there with my cup half way to my mouth.

"That's the door bell, Mommy," said the wise little voice from across the table.

"Yes, I know." Setting the cup down I stood up and moved to the front of the house. Peering out of the peephole, I watched a man in a business suit, as he glanced up and down the street, and then studied his fingernails. Looking past him I searched for his car. Sometimes you could tell a lot about a person by the type of car they drove and the shoes they wore, or so my mother always said. No car in sight and his shoes were certainly out of viewing range.

He rang the bell again.

I turned the dead bolt and opened the door. "Yes?" I studied his face and then glanced down at his dark non-fashionable, but well polished shoes. He was about mid thirty, brown hair, brown eyes, smiling mouth, but with a tough hard look about him, and except for the suit, I would have put him down as military, rather than as a businessman, even his shoes had that spit polished look. My mother would have been so pleased with my observation.

"Good morning, sorry to bother you so early," he said, as he casually glanced around the area, behind me. I shifted my weight to block his line of vision, but said nothing. He looked into my face with his mouth still holding its smile. Too bad that smile didn't extend to his eyes.

Standing my ground I used the noncommittal expression I'd learned, watching Bob in the business world. I automatically did not like this man.

He didn't feel right, and I didn't trust him, I pulled the door closer to me, closing the opening even further. He must have realized that I was becoming defensive, because he suddenly changed his tactics and said, in a very stern business like voice, "Are you Amanda Minton?"

I didn't answer immediately, but instead, looked directly into his eyes, using my own methods of controlling a meeting. When the silence began to strain, I leaned back on my heels, like I had everything under control and said, "I am." He seemed a bit disturbed by my reaction. He was undoubtedly expecting to be in control. *Did he think I was just going to invite him in for coffee...or what?*

"Ahh well, you must be the widow of Robert Minton then." He watched me closely for a softening at the mention of my dead husband, but I gave him none.

"Yes, I am," I said without altering my attitude.

"May I come in? I have business to discuss, regarding your late husband's estate." He didn't move his feet, but his body contracted in preparation for forward movement. This time I moved quickly, stepping forward in a deliberate blocking maneuver.

"I don't think so. If you'll give me your card I'll forward it to my attorney."

He looked startled and moved back a step. Then he said, "I'm sorry if I've caught you at a bad time," indicating that I was having a problem. "I'll call for an appointment."

"Not a bad time at all. I just don't do business with strangers in my home without prior arrangement." That should let him know I wasn't intimidated by his 'bad time' comment.

"Certainly, I understand," he muttered as he turned and quickly moved down the walk, motioning to a large black car, which appeared from out of my viewing range, and moved quietly forward. I watched him climb in and the car smoothly gain momentum as it drove away. I couldn't see past the dark tinted windows, but I had the impression that there was more than the driver and the man, who had just left, inside of the large car.

"Well, I wonder what that was all about," I said out loud, as I closed and re-bolted the door. Turning, I headed for the phone it was definitely time to add a security system.

The woman that I used for baby-sitting only sat for a small number of children and her house was practically a fortress. She had a security door on the front, the yard that the kids played in was square and visible from every angle and it had a high chain link fence around it. She even had locks on the gates. She said that she didn't want any of the kids escaping down the street. I remembered thinking that her security was overkill when I first saw it, but now I was certainly grateful for it. I was still feeling vulnerable, for myself and for Naja.

Waving goodbye to Naja I felt confident that this would be a safe place for her, while I spent the biggest part of the day cooped up inside of my office. I'd always loved the job and my office, but lately it was difficult to get through the day my mind just wasn't in it. I kept rolling the dream meetings and Indigo kids over and over in my mind, and now I had to worry about men in big black cars with tinted windows. I headed back home to let the security system people into the house.

Mr. Graf, who looked older than dirt, said that Bob was the best man he'd met since coming from the 'old country.' He'd been very upset when he learned of Bob's death and didn't like the idea of his leaving a wife and child unprotected, "It wasn't right." He'd told me many times over the 5 years, and now to be able to help out Bob's widow, was something that pleased him very much, and it certainly worked for me.

He'd even come to oversee his crew and he assured me that it was his pleasure to do this for me in double quick time, and I'd be snug and secure by lunchtime. Then he walked me through the entire system, showing me everything and giving me the code for the alarm before I left. He would personally lock up before he left. What a nice man, too bad there weren't more like him around. As we progress forward, and become more citified, I guess something's become lost, like helping others because it's the right thing to do.

Our office building was in one of the attractive brick strip malls along Barbur Boulevard, just short of being included in the crowded downtown area. It was easy to drive to and had ample parking for the employees, which many of the business didn't have.

"Good Morning Pat," I greeted the receptionist as I entered through the double glass doors. The lobby was decorated with white walls, light gray carpet, glass tables, and dark gray overstuffed chairs. It had a comfortable, cozy feel even though it was very contemporary in design. Pat, holding the phone to her ear, looked up and smiled.

I moved across the lobby to my office on the far left side. As I entered, my phone started its chirping type of ring, and I sighed, knowing that my workday had begun.

The day finally ended without much productivity on my part, and I felt guilty at having come in late and for not living up to my usual output of work. Naja, however, did live up to her usual output of energy and distracted me on the drive home.

Our first order of priority was to become familiar with the security system. I talked out loud to Naja, giving her a very basic description of the alarm system. Like never opening the door when the red light's blinking or a very loud siren would go off. She just looked at me with her eye brows arched.

Dinner was next and then thank God it was bed time. "Okay Little One, it's time," I said, but I was thinking it was really past time for me. I could have gone to bed much sooner, but that wouldn't have been fair to Naja, so I'd watched puzzles become pictures, read stories, and tried to act interested.

I had to admit, I did feel much better with an alarm system and motion lights. I'd opted not to have the motion alarm inside the house, Naja might get up in the middle of the night and set off the alarm. Then just as I was heading to my room, one of the outside lights snapped on. I peek out of the window just in time to witness eight of the nine years of life being scared off of the neighbor's cat. Well, now maybe that cat will stop using my flower beds as a toilet, I chuckled.

~

Arriving at the dream meeting, I hurried to a chair, anxious to begin and share my experiences with the others. Not everyone had arrived, so I had to wait, because I wanted everyone's input to the strange appearance of the White Dog. How different from before, when I didn't want to share with these strangers.

Several of the others were looking at me sideways, but not saying anything. They were obviously waiting for me to offer the reason for the rapid disappearance the night before. I felt excited and agitated at the same time. Why wasn't everyone here? I wanted to get on with it! Apparently my feelings were showing, because once again Sally comforted me by reaching over and patting my hand as she said, "Take a few deep breathes dear, it'll relax you."

I took the deep breaths, grinned and said loud enough for everyone to hear, "Thanks Sally, I guess I haven't settled down yet, even if I am asleep." A few chuckles could be heard from the other side of the room. "I know about struggling with and subduing emotions; holding back and keeping things in check. I spent the early years of my life dealing with prejudice and hate, while holding back my desire to fight and lash out. Now as a mature woman and mother I can look back, using hindsight to see things differently. My father was a victim of a hate crime when I was still in grade school, my mother never recovered from his murder. We, my two brothers and one sister, grew up on welfare and basically had to take care of each other, plus our mother," she shared quietly, just as the two remaining people came through the doorway.

"Hi, sorry to be late," Halley apologized as she came hustling in. She didn't offer an explanation, but quickly took a seat.

Teri followed her in and said, "Yeah, me too, did we miss anything? Like what happened to you last night?" she said looking directly at me, catching me by surprise. I was still thinking about Sally and her childhood.

"No, I've been saving that information until you two got here," I told them, squeezing Sally's hand. When they were seated I looked around the room and noticed that I definitely had the entire group's attention everyone seemed to be waiting for me to begin.

When I hesitated, Teri said, "You scared the hell out of us! One minute you were standing in front of your chair saying 'What's that?' and the next you were gone. Just gone. I've never seen anyone disappear before," she explained, eyes wide.

"Yea, that was something!"

"You mean I just went up in smoke? Poof?" I asked. Then before anyone could answer, I added, "So it's not like when we arrive and walk from nowhere, through a door, into this dream meeting."

"Nope, apparently if there's some kind of emergency or you wake up quickly, you're just gone."

"Yes, that's exactly what happened. I found myself standing in the dark, but thought that I was still here for a few minutes. Actually, I was in my daughter's room." At that several voices murmured. I quickly continued, "She was okay, but something took me there. I must have heard something with my conscious body, but everything seemed okay. The interesting thing was... the next morning Naja asked me if I had let the big White Dog into the house."

"What?!"

"Do you mean the wolf dog in your dream before your daughter was even born?"

"Oh my God!"

"Did you see him?"

"I'm not sure, I may have seen him. When I looked out of the window, I saw a flash of white move across the lawn. It could have been a car's headlights and I didn't really see or hear anything out of the ordinary, but there must have been something that woke me."

"Why was the dog there? Did he leave because you came back?" asked Rachael, looking serious.

I looked at her without really seeing her, without really hearing the murmuring around me. I was back in Naja's bedroom the night before. Nothing.

I don't think I've overlooked anything. I focused back on Rachael, who was still sitting there with her question hanging between us.

"I don't know. I wasn't aware of him at all, but he obviously left when I came back," I told her, still thinking about why he was there.

"Naja must have seen him, was she afraid?" asked Shala, leaning towards me, in her interest.

"Well, I nearly freaked, but she said she loved him and wasn't afraid. What I'm curious about is, why was he there?"

"How did he get in?"

"And out?"

"Good questions, I went immediately downstairs and checked all of the doors and windows. Everything was fine," I told them, feeling very confused. "Maybe, he was in her dream after all."

"That would make more sense." I heard the comment, and had thought that myself.

Rachael was tapping her fingers on the arm of her chair and looking very thoughtful. Then she said, "Sense is not what we're dealing with here. Take this meeting for example." She hesitated to let her words sink in. "The real question here is, like Mandy said, why was he there?" Turning towards me, she said, "Have you ever seen this dog before or after that first dream?"

"No, I haven't and I didn't actually see him this time. Naja just told me about him, and she had absolutely no way of knowing about him. I've told no one but you people about that dog, not even my best friend." As I explained, I realized that the more we discussed this the more confusing it became.

"I think that the White Dog is Naja's protector. Her Guardian Angel, if you will," Rachael said in earnest.

I felt the pressure in the room increase, the hot breath of fear had entered through the very walls. I heard the intake of air as it rushed through the mouths of several people and saw faces that reflected my own thoughts back to me. Guardian Angel! Naja has a Guardian Angel? After the fear, my next reaction was relief and it flooded over me, this was good. I liked the idea of an angel guarding Naja. However, the next reaction was, why did Naja 'need' a guardian. Is she in danger?

I looked at Rachael and then at the others around me. The sympathy in their faces showed that they apparently had come to the same conclusion that I had. Why did she need a guardian to be showing up now?

"Okay, do you have any ideas on why she needs a Guardian Angel?" I asked, looking at Rachael. Rachael didn't answer right away, so I turned and asked, "Anybody?"

"You did have a symbolic dream of danger for her before she was even born, and the White Dog appeared when she was threatened, and now he has appeared again. We can only assume that she is in some type of danger. However, she does have 'divine intervention,' so I would have to say that whatever her mission is here on earth it must be very important," Rachael said in a low, controlled voice, "and that the rest of our Indigo children are somehow connected to her. Perhaps she is going to be a leader of some type and these other kids are part of the team."

What had been a fairly quiet room suddenly became alive. People were shuffling around, voices were murmuring, energy was darting in every direction. The words 'Divine Intervention' were still vibrating around inside of my head, but everyone else was caught up in the part that involved their own children and any possible danger to them.

"What kind of team?"

"I don't like this."

"Considering that nothing we are doing makes any sense, this does fit in somehow," Lindy said, spreading her hands out in front of her, in a hopeless gesture.

"Wait a minute! Wait a minute!" I said, standing up and circling behind my chair. "Let's do this right. I think that we are all somehow involved in whatever the hell is going on, so we need to include every bit of input that we can." I paced in the small space behind my chair and the peach colored wall. The flowers in the pictures seemed to be alertly waiting for me to go on. Waiting to hear, the rest of the story.

Most of the group settled back into their chairs and seemed to be willing to delve into this in an organized way. I continued to pace, my thinking was always better when I was in motion.

"Okay, let's use this scenario. Suppose that these kids were all born at this time to perform something beneficial to mankind." I stopped briefly.

This was like creating a fairy tale. I shoved those feelings of foolishness away and continued, "Suppose further that for some reason, someone or something, didn't want this to happen..."

"Cutting off the head of the snake stops the entire project," Ron stated bluntly, interrupting me.

"Jeeze, Ron!"

"Good God! What a thing to say."

Ron looked embarrassed and for the first time, lost his arrogant attitude. "I'm sorry Mandy; I didn't mean your daughter was..."

"Never mind, I know what you meant and that pretty much is what I was getting at," I answered him as I sat back down in my chair.

"So, this guy has sized up all of our kids, following them around and such, and has concluded that stopping Naja will end the project," Cindy restated the general idea *Reader's Digest* style.

"So, how can... how do... I don't understand this at all," Ramon finished in confusion. I started to explain the scenario again and he said, "No, no, I understand that part. I don't understand how these kids decided to be born for a certain reason."

"Yeah, I've been having a little problem with that too, but then I've been having a little problem with this whole thing. Including the fact that we are sitting here talking to each other right now," added Bill.

Well, you know fellas," I explained, "We don't have the answers either, so we're just kinda going with the flow and making this up as we go along..."

"Yea I know, it's one of those female things," interjected Pete with a sigh.

"Let me," said Rachael, taking the lead. "Perhaps we should start at the beginning. We all appear to be of different faiths, religions, beliefs and programming. I think it will be much easier to function if we are all in tune, so to speak, regarding our knowledge on life, death and what's beyond." She looked around the room, studying each face before going on. She frowned as if she were having a problem trying to decide how to continue with what she was going to say.

Finally, she made her decision and used the same approach that I had used. "Suppose we assume that everyone gets to choose their experience here on earth before they are born." A feeling surged through the room, a thick warm feeling. It wasn't negative and it wasn't exactly positive, it was just a reaction. "Suppose further, that we also have access to information that well help us decide which parents to choose. Parents who, based on their gene pool, DNA, lifestyle, and such, can help us to accomplish this experience.

"In this case these Souls, with their 'over all' view of life and how it's going, decided to come down in a loose group, team up and fix things. However, in order to do this... they needed to be together, or at least in contact. So they or someone or something, arranged to have us, their parents or guardians, be brought together in this dream meeting." She finished with a rush looking very pleased.

Everyone just sat there staring at her. This idea wasn't totally a new concept to me, my folks believed in souls coming to earth to 'experience' life, but this presentation including my role certainly was. Some of the others sat there with absolutely no expression on their faces, while a couple had their mouths hanging open in their surprise. Sally and Lindy, however, were looking very interested and even nodding their heads in agreement.

"This works well with the idea we discussed last night, you know, the kids being able to contact their Angel Guides to help them accomplish their mission," Sally added nodding her head up and down again.

"Yeah, yer right. If they can decide and get the parents they want, they sure ought to be able to talk to guides," Lindy emphasized. Both of these women were totally into this, accepting the entire concept without the doubt that the rest were struggling with.

Suddenly I remembered the original question and turned to look at Ramon. If he was confused before what kind of condition was he in now? He was sitting very still his eyes cast down studying his hands.

"Ramon?" I spoke his name quietly, so as not to make him the center of attention.

"Si?" he answered, looking up and meeting my eyes. He seemed to be almost teary. Turning to Rachael he said, "I don't understand how what you said can happen, but I do know that my Nina, who is only three, talks about choosing me. I had no idea what she was talking about." He stopped with a catch in his throat.

"Lisa has told me many times that she must find her friends. I thought she was talking about her imaginary friends," Shala almost whispered.

"This is just too absurd!" Pete stated. "You don't really expect me to go along with this charade, do you?" He stood up and walked across the room.

"And what has your Indigo child done that fits into this supposition?" Lindy asked.

He stopped dead in his tracks. Finally he turned around and said. "Jon is a very imaginative child and he says a lot of strange things, but certainly nothing that validates anything in this wild story." He then walked back to his chair and sat down with his back partially turned toward her. Obviously he was still in denial and did not want to be convinced.

"I have three kids, but my 4-year-old Yolanda is the only one that has ever acted like she is on a mission. I swear she is gathering information for a project. So, even though this idea is a wild one, it definitely fits," contributed Bill, glancing at Ron.

"Well, I've got an entire nursery school full of kids," Teri spoke up, "but Jami is the only one of the bunch that acts like she has something important to do with her life and she's only 3. She is very impatient with the other kids, who are all older, when things have to be repeated again and again. She wants to move on to new projects. I think she too is information gathering."

"Yes. Does your Jami ask questions about the detailed workings of everything new?" Hally asked, directing her question to Teri.

Nodding her head, Teri was about to elaborate, when a new voice was heard.

"Mine too. Jasmine wants to understand how everything works, and then turns around and explains it to her sister and anyone else who will listen," Sally added with excitement.

Lindy was perched on the edge of her chair, nodding her head like crazy. "Yes! Bobby does all of those things too."

I stopped the flow by asking, "So I still have an unanswered question bouncing around in my head. It sounds like all of the kids have the same advancement, the same quest for learning about things; the same quickness for catching on to things, the same leadership qualities, and the same independence. So, why will heading Naja off, stop the project?" The question acted like a cold-water shower on the excitement the others were experiencing at finding children similar to their own.

The room went silent. No one wanted to meet my eyes, until I looked towards Rachael. Calmly she looked right at me and said. "There is always a leader in every project. They probably decided before they came here who would, for whatever reason, be the chosen leader." I sat there considering her explanation. It made sense, well, as much sense as any of the rest of this, but I didn't like it. I didn't want Naja to be in a position that put her in danger.

Lindy interrupted my thoughts, "I know exactly what you're thinking and I would be feeling the same way. You're a mother, and it's natural. But, we don't seem to be in control here. It looks like our *kids* have already made their plans and we were the instruments to get them here."

Rachael cleared her throat and said, "Sort of. Actually, I believe that it's more than that. I think that we all agreed to take this job. In other words, we too are a part of the project, and you Mandy even tuned in to your part, in a dream, before Naja was born. Our part was to bring them in or be there for them immediately after arrival, and also to provide an atmosphere of understanding to accept their differences and to aid them towards their goal.

"Just like we would with any of our children, but in their case, being aware on some level of where these particular children are headed. Further, *we*, without even being consciously aware of how, when or why, are also going to prepare the way for them." Rachael hesitated and then continued her theory, "we have probably been living the exact lives we needed to live, and experiencing the experiences we needed to experience to prepare us for this very job."

Well, her little speech was just as effective in cooling things off as my splash of cold water had been earlier. Everyone sat there trying to digest what she had just said. Even Ron was in deep thought. Rachael in her wisdom didn't try to convince anyone by overstating her case. She just sat there and calmly watched the internal turmoil and the stretching of past beliefs and ideas each and every person was actively involved in.

After mulling this idea over and deciding it was certainly every bit as plausible as anything else, my mind came back to the beginning. *Naja picked me. The dream that I had before she was born wasn't a chance happening.* Slowly I realized that my life was more than just raising a child. First and most immediate I am to keep Naja alive and well. Secondly I am to provide her with all of the information that she needs to fulfill her job, plus I have to pave the way for her to lead a group of Indigos to save the world. *Well hell! Did I volunteer for a big job or what?!*

Belatedly I considered Bob. Why had he been killed before he even saw his child?

"Rachael? Why do you think Naja's father isn't here to help me with this? What was his role?"

"Have you talked to him about this?"

"My husband was murdered on our wedding day. He never even knew that I was pregnant."

"Oh no."

"My God, murdered?"

"How? What happened?"

I explained the circumstances of my wedding day and Bob's death to a

stunned group. I watched as they listened to the story, as their faces showed
how they were reliving that tragic day right along with me.

"Did they ever find out who killed him?"

"What did the police think?"

"They never found the killers and the police chalked it up to a mugging
with bad results." I slowly turned to look at Rachael as I asked, "Any hit on
this?" I wasn't really expecting an answer, but this question had been in my
mind for six years and some day I hoped to find an answer, a closure. A
mugging with bad results just didn't seem to make it.

"Considering the direction that our conversation has been going, it is
entirely possible that whoever has enough information to want to stop the
Indigo kids from their mission must also have known of the prearranged
team and who the leader would be and tried to stop Naja from being born by
killing the intended father." Rachael spoke in a soft comforting voice.
However her information was anything but comforting.

"Are you suggesting that Bob's murder was premeditated? That he was
deliberately stalked and killed?" I whispered, feeling the room begin to close
in on me. The walls marched closer, the air in the room became warmer,
while the faces looking at me began to blur.

"Mandy?"

"Mandy!"

"Are you all right?!"

"Mandy!"

I heard many voices speaking trying to break through the fog. Then
someone grabbed my arm with such force that it hurt. The pain brought me
back from the slow drift towards blackness.

My eyes focused on Rachael's face, which was very close and the grip on
my arm that I would have thought beyond the ability of someone Rachael's
age. Other faces also hovered around mine, all of them wearing concerned
expressions.

"I'm okay," I managed to stammer, as I pulled away from Rachael's vice
like grip.

"Whew. Honey, you had us scared," said Lindy from somewhere behind
me.

"Are you sure you're okay?" Cindy asked, looking at me with a very
concerned expression.

"Yes, I think it was just a shock. I mean I've always felt that there was
more to Bob's death than it seemed, but of course, I didn't dream of this. I

think the shock is that it fits. It really fits," I explained in a shaky voice, as I gathered my wits back together. "My God! Someone has been after my Naja since before she was even born, and Bob died because of it!"

Everyone was quiet as they returned to their seats. "Why would killing Bob have stopped Naja from being born? What if I hadn't slept with Bob before he was killed and what if I went on to marry someone else? Naja still could have been conceived."

"Wow, that's right."

"Yeah, was it only Bob that was involved with Naja before she was born?"

"Naw, don't yew remember, Mandy had a dream about Naja while still in college," Bill reminded us.

"I think I have a possible answer," Rachael said, stopping the speculation. "The Soul of Naja probably needed the exact combination of Mandy and Bob to be set up for her current role. Her parents had already been preestablished, even though they hadn't even met."

"Yes! That's it! Didn't you say that you conceived Naja the night before the wedding?" Lindy asked.

I nodded in the affirmative.

"Yeah, the killers couldn't have known that."

"They probably didn't even know why they were killing him. They were probably just hired hit men."

I felt my stomach turning over and hoped I wouldn't be sick. Fortunately no one noticed my discomfort in their excitement.

"That's right! Even the Boogie Man, who probably did know, didn't have time to change things," said Teri. "Oh my God! If he'd had the time, Mandy would have been the one killed instead of Bob!"

All eyes suddenly turned towards me. All minds suddenly remembered me as the person they were talking about. I read the sympathy in their faces.

"It's okay," I said, waving my hand in the air. "It's good to finally know what happened, and to know what could have happened." Several heads nodded in agreement, although, many couldn't meet my eyes.

Then Shala broke the stretching silence by saying, "I wonder when they discovered that killing your husband didn't stop the conception of your daughter?"

"Well, she said that the 'Boogie Man' started following her six months after the baby was born," Pete reminded us.

"Oh, oh," I suddenly murmured out loud.

"What!" Lindy quickly questioned.

"He didn't seem too serious about stalking us until after this group started to meet. He'd just sorta check us out once in a while." I stopped talking and looked around the room. "That's when the bogus insurance man came too."

"What bogus insurance man?" Ron stated as he turned to face me looking very serious as he pulled his body up straight and stiff.

"Honey, I think you'd better tell us everything," Lindy said as she pulled her chair in closer.

"That's right. You're not in this alone anymore. We're all involved now." This came from Teri, who looked like she was explaining a situation to a student.

"Yeah, involved through our kids," stated Bill, his face flushed with emotion.

"What happens to you and Naja can have a direct effect on us and our children," Shala added looking directly into my eyes and emphasizing the point by reaching out her hand to touch my arm.

These people were strangers, yet here I was completely involved with them in possibly the most important issue of my life, of Naja's life. I didn't want to share with them I'd always been a loner, taking care of my own problems. However, they were right, we seemed to be in this together whether we liked it or not. We had to depend on each other for our children's sake.

I told them about the man in the dark business suit that tried to bluff his way into my house claiming to have information about Bob's insurance. I explained that I'd known instinctively that he was not who he said he was. I glanced at Rachael and said, "Intuition?" Rachael confirmed it with a smile and a nod.

"Intuition! Rachael, you were going to teach us how to use our physic abilities," Sally suddenly remembered.

"We'll get around to that. Go on, Mandy."

"When I reported the situation to my lawyer, he said that he had heard from no one and told me that it was probably someone wanting to sell me something. I 'felt' it was more than that, but what could that man have wanted?" I finished by asking the group who were all sitting in a close circle around me listening intently.

"What did the man who grabbed the little girl in the park that looked like Naja want?" asked the soft accented voice of Ramon.

"Mandy, I know that this is very difficult for you. I understand what you're feeling, but we must try to understand what's going on in order to be safe. In order to keep Naja and our children safe," Rachael explained.

"I know, but we're talking about people wanting to *kill* my daughter. That's just very hard to accept. Whatever happened to our civilized world?" A tear escaped and began a slow slide down my cheek. The room was silent. Everyone was looking at anything but me and no one had an answer. They too were feeling frustration and fear. My entire world was tilting sideways, and I felt like I was sliding off the edge.

"Mandy?" Ron said quietly. "Although I never talk about it, I spent time in prison as a youth. I'd come from a lower income neighborhood and had fallen in with a gang, who preyed upon helpless people, intimidating, robbing and even beating some. One night things went very wrong and an old man died. We were all caught and locked up.

"After my release, I met a girl that I never dreamed would give me the time of day, but she did and I turned over a new leaf and stayed straight. I've learned that life wasn't as bad as I originally thought it was. Now, with this, I have fear that somehow I'll lose everything I've found; my wife, my child, my respectable life.

"We all have that fear and we are all in this together. Hang in there. We'll pool our knowledge and our experiences to help each other. You'd be surprised at what I learned while in prison. I would never in a million years have thought that experience would be a possible benefit to me, or maybe even all of us."

"Thanks Ron, thanks you guys," I said lifting my head. No one was there. The room was dark, there were tears on my face and the moon light was shining through my bedroom window. I wasn't alone anymore. I didn't have to face the Boogie Man and his henchmen by myself. I took a deep breath as I turned over and closed my eyes.

Day Five

Naja sat there eating her breakfast with her usual enthusiasm, while I studied her with a completely new view. She wasn't 'just' my very own wonderful Naja. She was a little person with a big project in front of her. I understood projects from my own business background, but I'd never had any that equaled the size of the one in front of Naja. Then it occurred to me, that I too had a big project. I had to keep my daughter safe, so that she could fulfill her destiny. Of course, all parents take on that type of job. However, the difference here is that not all parents have someone or maybe several someone's wanting to intercept her, and possibly wanting to kill her. However, I did have an advantage; I had been forewarned and apparently had a large White Dog ready to help out, not to mention eleven other people to confide in.

I started feeling better about the situation, certainly better than I had last night. I was over the shock and fear that accompanied the realization of the circumstances. This was definitely not how I had visualized my life. I wondered, *Whatever happened to the fairy tale family of four, the cute little house, with the picket fence, a dog, a cat and minor little issues like how to send a balanced meal in a lunch box?*

As I poured Naja a second glass of milk, I wondered if I could convince the dog to come and live with us. Wouldn't that be great! Naja would love it and I'd sure feel better.

"Better hurry, honey," I called out, as I gathered my papers together from the table where I'd been sorting them and stuffed them into my briefcase preparing for another workday in the real world. Naja came bounding in acting like any typical 5-year-old. She loved her preschool, and apparently was already displaying signs of leadership. Either that or they were signs of bossiness, I thought with a chuckle, as we made our way to the car, setting the alarm from the garage.

At the school, Naja darted off to join the other kids, but as I turned to leave, Miss Susan said, "Do you have a large White Dog?" I stopped dead in my tracks her words coming as a complete surprise. When I didn't answer right away, she continued with, "Yesterday there was a dog, actually a large

White Dog that looked more wolf than dog, hanging around the play area. Naja said that he sleeps with her. So I wondered if he followed you here." I still stood there staring at her. What should I say? Why was he here?

"Ahh... he's a friend of ours, but we don't own him. Some animals just aren't owned." I smiled, evading the questions.

"Shall I let him into the yard?" she asked, and then belatedly said, "Is he friendly with other children?" I was still stuck on why was he here and how had he found her.

"No, leave him on the outside, that way he can go home if he wants to," I finally suggested as I turned and headed for the door that I knew was there, but couldn't see. The White Dog at Naja's school. What did this mean, and did Miss Susan say 'sleeps' with her, as in more than once?

The day was moving much too slowly, it was all I could do to stay in my office and not run out the door and drive to the pre-school. I got through the paper work, and was waiting until the lunch hour when I planned to drive by the school, but to my frustration, I discovered that I had a lunch meeting scheduled. I had to give up and put my focus on my job, it was clear that I couldn't keep doing my work with my mind on Naja, the dog, the dream meeting and the Boogie Man.

Later that afternoon, as I pulled up in front of the Day Care my eyes automatically scanned the area for the White Dog. I didn't really expect to see him, but I looked anyway.

"Let's hurry, Sweetie. I was hoping to get in a run at the park before dinner. What do ya say, are you up to it?" I asked Naja as we headed for home. I really needed a run. I was wired tight. Naja nodded her head furiously.

"Okay, we still have enough daylight for a couple of turns around the park, let's get going," I stated as I bundled her and JoJo into the 'wheeler.' Ignoring the nagging guilty feeling I was experiencing, because I'd told Jill that I wouldn't run in the park for a while, but I couldn't let some jerk run my life.

"Let's go fast. I love it when you go fast," Naja stated peering back at me.

"You've got it," was my answer, I just had to stretch out my legs. We started off to the left, which was not the usual pattern, but I just felt like I needed a change.

The run was good. I kept an even pace, taking time to notice the natural elements around me, trying to relax into the setting. This park was beautiful and well kept up with no over flowing garbage cans or litter along the paths.

Suddenly there was the piercing sound of a whistle. I slowed the threewheeler and stopped at a path intersection, holding my breath so I could hear better.

"Wasn't that the whistle, Mommy?"

"It sure sounded like it, but I couldn't tell where it came from." I couldn't decide what to do, or which way to go. Who was in trouble? Suddenly, it occurred to me that "we" were the ones in trouble. Quickly I turned around and headed back the way I'd just come. At least I knew what was in that direction.

As we rounded a blind shrubbery filled corner, I saw a large figure moving towards us from across the grass. Clothing flapped about the body as it lurched forward. It was the bag lady, what was her name? Alice. Yes it was Alice and from her hand dangled the whistle that I'd given her.

"Say, this really works. You really responded quickly," she gasped out the words as she came lumbering closer.

"Was this a test?"

"No Miss. There are slick looking guys parked in a big black car down by the lower parking lot. The one you usually run by first."

How did she know which way I usually ran? "Why is that important to me?" I asked her, wondering about guys in a big black car.

"I have a place that I hang out up above." She nodded her head to the hill that overlooks the park. "I watched that big car follow you in, watch you and then turn towards the lower parking while you were getting the little one set up." She looked at Naja and smiled. Jeeze, I hoped it didn't scare Naja because her smile was more of a grimace, but Naja returned her smile without a flinch.

"I wasn't sure you'd even hear the whistle and I wasn't sure what you'd do if you did hear it. You could have gone charging off to save someone else," she told me with a grin. "What made you turn around?"

"I don't know, I suddenly felt like the warning was for me."

"Yeah, I was sending you a message all the way down the hill."

I stood there staring at her. This woman had sent a mental message and I'd gotten it?!

"It's amazing what you can pick up on when your senses are alerted," said Alice who was grinning like a Cheshire cat.

"Alice, how can I thank you? I shutter to think of what could have happened."

"No problem dearie. I told ya I don't cotton to trouble in my park." She'd turned and was looking over her shoulder, across the grassy area. "I think that you'd better git moving now."

I looked out towards the grass and strained to hear anything, but heard nothing. Then suddenly from nowhere, the Boogie Man stepped slowly out from behind a tree, just off to the side of where Alice had been looking. The low-lying branches threw a mottled shadow across his face. I heard Alice gasp.

"So... he's involved," she muttered as she turned and looked at me with a strange expression on her face. She looked at Naja and then back at me. "Show no fear!" she quietly said. "Let's walk together up this path. Ignore him."

We turned and walked together up the path towards my car, not looking behind us. When we reached the car I got Naja into the car and started folding up the stroller.

"Alice, why don't you come with us for dinner? We can stop at that fast food place near here."

"Naw Honey, you don't need to do that."

"Alice, I'm not driving off and leaving you here, with all of those guys around," I stated firmly as I opened the passenger door and stood my ground.

Alice looked me in the eyes and then climbed inside without any further argument, although, she did mutter something that sounded like, "Never have been able to resist logic."

Alice did, however, insist that we use the drive thru window and after we'd gotten the order, she gave directions to a street that led to a secluded place above the park. There she gathered up her food and got out of the car. "See ya," she said over her shoulder and was gone.

A shutter went through me as I thought of what might have happened if Alice hadn't signaled me. Remembering what Alice said as she spotted the Boogie Man, I wondered what she meant by 'So he's involved'? She seemed to know him. Glancing in the rear view mirror as I turned the car around, I saw Alice unwrap her hamburger and take a hefty bite, then, looking all around her, she ambled off the sidewalk and across the grass.

So much for a run, Damn. "Let's go to the zoo," I said over my shoulder to Naja in the back seat.

"Yea, let's go to the zoo," she sang out.

Portland has a very nice zoo, up above the West Hills and even though it wouldn't be a run, it would be a lot of walking up and down the rolling hillside. Come to think of it, there are walking trails up there too; however, I remembered they'd be way too narrow and steep for a stroller, besides, they go off into the wooded area with lots of trees and fewer people. Probably not a good choice.

The animals in the springtime are so lively and cute, we fed almost everyone from the 'special' foods prepared and sold for the animals. Naja loved it. The trip to the monkey area was short. They are just a little too lively and romantic in the spring. I had no intention of trying to explain their activity to a 5-year-old.

We sat on the grassy hill and watched a "Birds of Prey Show," which was interesting and a little scary for the young children. The birds were shown on a stage, with all sorts of descriptions and information about each one. Then the trainers would turn one of them loose into the air and it would fly over our heads to another trainer behind us. Some of them swooped down low causing squeals and cries from children and moms as well. Naja watched, very interested in everything they did. She was fascinated to see such huge birds fly so close, but she didn't seem afraid, just fascinated.

It turned out to be a very tiring day even though we didn't get to complete our run. Naja fell asleep in the car on the way home and struggled through the bedtime snack. That, of course, could have been due to all of the junk food she ate at the zoo. One package for the animals and they all had their own package and one package for us.

Naja actually went to bed early and without a fuss, I guess she needs to do more walking and not just always riding in the stroller. It was time to change my exercise habit, I thought as I sat down to watch the TV for the first time in days. Flipping through the local news channels, I caught a flash of a familiar face. There in the background of a group of people, at the end result of a car chase, was Lieutenant Adams listening to a couple of guys while he wrote in his small note book. He was nice looking, in a basic, strong silent type sorta way. *I wonder if he is married. Jill would probably know*, I mused. *She probably checked out his ring finger first thing.* I chuckled, thinking of Jill and her motherly attention to me. You don't get many friends like Jill. In fact, I didn't have many friends at all. I wonder why some people seem to have a friend for every day of the week and some of us have one or two...or only just one.

~

I sat in the meeting room, legal pad on my lap. It was on my chair as I came through the door. It was also the same one that I'd used the night before last. The list of those who had seen the Boogie Man the night before last was still listed on the page.

"Hello," a cheerful voice called out. It was Sally, looking more chipper than I'd seen her so far. Even though she generally was pretty positive and up, tonight there was something different about her.

"Hi, you look happy, what's going on?" I questioned with a smile that matched hers, but before she could answer, several more of the group came through the door, all talking and laughing together. What was happening, why was everyone so cheery tonight? I wondered if I'd missed something. I leaned back and watched as others came in with bright outlooks, even Ron the abrupt, sour guy, seemed to be a lot friendlier than usual.

Finally everyone had arrived and they were settling in their chairs. As they relaxed into the meeting mode, they all looked at me, and I realized that I was still the unofficial leader of this bizarre gathering. Then my mind immediately went to Naja, who would be in a similar position one day. The unofficial leader of a group…this group's kids!

"How are you tonight, Mandy? You look like you may have gotten over your shock after last night's discoveries," Sally questioned gently, lest she set me off again.

"Thanks, I think I've got a handle on it now." I smiled as I answered her.

"And, isn't this a happy group of sleep walkers?" I said to the group, still wondering why they were so happy. Then it hit me. They believed in their kids enough to accept the circumstances in this weird dream meeting. *That's an interesting reaction*, I thought as I shifted gears to begin yet another meeting with this group of strange people.

"Last night, we forgot to list the names of those who saw the Boogie Man, so let's begin with that and then add today's names to the list, before we forget again," I suggested.

"So, who saw him yesterday?" I asked looking around the room. Everyone else was looking around the room too. "No one? Humm. Well I saw him today after day care, who else saw him today?"

"I saw him today too," Shala offered. "He watched us this morning at the grocery store. No, I didn't see his face," she added, anticipating the question.

"Yeah me too, as far as I know, he doesn't even have a face just a menacing body shape," Ramon stated in a disgruntled voice. "I still want to get close enough to jump on him and beat up that invisible face. I came from a large family of boys in Mexico and we fought and worked hard all of our life and I worked even harder to get my family into the United States and I'm not going to let some strange gringo spoil it. Keeping my family safe and getting a new job so my wife won't have to work so hard cleaning rooms at that hotel are my two main goals in life. This guy's not going to scare me!"

"I almost saw his face. I walked away from him and then quickly turned to see what he was doing. He had moved out of the shadows and I saw the lower part of his face, then he leaned back quickly, when he saw me turn," Sally told them, with excitement.

The group got into a discussion about his face, as I wondered why no one had seen him yesterday. Then a piece of the puzzle fell into place with a loud crash. I could feel the energy as it fell from the sky, past me and lodged itself into place right along side of the White Dog 'guarding' Naja at preschool yesterday. He was watching Naja, or trying to, that's why no one else saw him. The fact that people had seen him today and that the dog was not seen at the preschool, according to Miss Susan, confirmed it.

My thoughts were interrupted when I heard, "So what do you think, Mandy?" I just looked at them, not fully recovered from the puzzle discovery. "Sorry, I guess I wasn't paying attention. Think about what?"

"Think about why he wasn't seen yesterday?" explained Lindy, who suddenly looked like a light went on in her head, as she connected with me.

I had already discovered the answer to that question, but didn't want to share it just yet. I still wasn't used to including these people into my personal life and thoughts. So I quickly said, "It's anybody's guess, we haven't established a pattern yet." Lindy's eyes didn't leave my face, she knew something was up, but she didn't say anything.

Changing tactics again, I laid the legal pad down and said, "I think it's time to start sharing some of our kids' attributes and see if we can figure out where this is going, and if we should be contributing anything or heading in any particular direction to help out."

Several heads were nodding up and down, but Rachel's wasn't one of them. She sat there looking at me and said, "I have something to share with all of you." I had the distinct impression that she was sending a message to me. A message that said, that 'I' should be the one sharing. Probably that impression was only guilt since I knew that I was holding back.

"I saw Indigo color again last night in my meditation. Not the kid's in particular, but the color of Indigo. It was like the color itself was trying to send me a message." She had the group spellbound. Not a person moved, everyone was holding their breath, waiting for the message.

"The Indigo color was challenged by a dark muddy color and they appeared to be in a struggle. Then the Indigo color began to intensify and spread until it completely blotted out the muddy color, and shown as completely pure, bright and strong." She stopped and looked around at the group of listening people. We all just sat there looking back at her wondering what this information meant.

"I wasn't sure what this meant, at first, either," she said, reading the question written on the faces circled around her, "but as I thought about it, it became very clear to me. The color Indigo represents the kids; the muddy color is, obviously, the Boogie Man and any other negative influences. The muddy color tried to merge with the Indigo color to dilute its strength by muddying it, but the Indigo was too strong and kept the color pure. Thus winning the battle, don't you see?" She looked at us with a question on her face and her hands spread out in front of her, willing us to understand.

"Actually, I do see. I think that your interpretation is exactly right," Hally stated, speaking very strongly and looking like she always saw colors fighting. Others were a little slower to accept or understand the symbolism of the colors.

"Well, I'm not into interpreting visions, but it does seem to fit," added Bill. Slowly the others seemed to accept the idea too.

"I like the idea that the Indigos won."

"Yeah me too."

"I liked the way the Indigos became strong and overwhelmed the muddy color," stated Ron.

"I found it interesting that the Indigo worked as a whole. A team, a family," Ramon added.

"With the fact that the Indigo worked strongly as a whole," interrupted Rachael, "I think we should do as Mandy suggested and compare notes. What do these children have in common? What do they have that makes them a team?"

"Yeah, a team that they aren't even aware that they're on."

"Let me begin," said Rachael. "Let me tell you a story," She began, "One day, my granddaughter and I were discussing a rather large bruise on her face. I asked her how she had hurt her face. Dina, who is four-years-old, told me that while she was playing next door with Amy, her friend, hit her on the face with a toy box.

"'Oh, that's too bad Dina, did you cry?' I asked her.

"'Yes, I cried a lot.' Then she explained that Amy's father came in and told her she could have a piece of candy and that Amy didn't get any candy.

"'How did you feel about that?' I asked.

"'She didn't say she was sorry,' Dina said seriously. 'So, the fact that you got candy and Amy didn't get candy because she hit you, didn't make you feel better?'

"Dina looked at me and repeated, 'She didn't say she was sorry. She just cried because she didn't get candy.' She dug around in her pocket and produced a paper wrapped piece of candy, which she held out in her small hand. 'I didn't eat the candy.'

"Then she leaned back, looked up at me and said, 'What would you have done, Grandma?'

"Looking down at her I asked, 'Do you mean about saving the candy?'

"She pulled away from me, looked very serious, put her hand to her bruised face and said, 'No. About Amy?'

"I realized that even at the age of four she understood that this situation had been treated differently than we would have handled it. I said to her, 'I would have explained to Amy that hitting someone hurts them and that you never want to hurt your friends. Then I would have asked her to tell you she was sorry for hurting you.'

"Dina stood there looking at me, but her eyes were distant, she was once again next door reliving the scene. 'Yes,' she finally said, nodding her head. 'The candy wasn't a good way.'

"Now, the interesting thing about this story," Rachael said coming back to the present, "is that she understood the difference in how the situation was handled, but didn't know exactly how it could have been done differently. So she asked, she computed it, and then she was satisfied."

"Yes!" exclaimed Cindy, "that's exactly what Chad does. He's always asking me questions about different situations and then I can actually see him thinking it over and filing it away in his little 5-year-old head. He's like a little computerized robot, collecting information and data on the different ways things can be accomplished."

Many heads were nodding up and down as parents recognized these traits in their own little people. Some were deeper in thought obviously remembering similar situations with their own Indigos kids.

"Lisa even takes it a step further," said Shala. "I've heard her relating some of the information she's gathered to her friends. Not as in sharing, but as in being in charge." She grinned as she added, "She is a very bossy child, and does things her own way. She doesn't like to stand in lines and wait. In fact, she doesn't seem to relate to the rules and regulations that we grew up with at all."

Many agreed that their kids were the same as they laughed together. I thought of Naja directing the children in her preschool while the teacher was on the phone. She seemed bossy too, and definitely didn't follow the old rules that I'd grown up with, but she was also practicing being a leader. She had a different agenda and apparently knew it, at least on some level.

"Perhaps they aren't really bossy as we think of bossy. I mean, maybe it's more like they have unconscious knowledge that they sense. They know that they know, and they display it to their peers in the only way that they know how."

"I think that they display it to more than just their peers," laughed Sally.

"You know," began Cindy, "maybe my Chad isn't really an Indigo, he's very quiet. Not out going at all, in fact, you hardly even know he's around. He even seems a little timid."

"How old is he?"

"He's five."

"Maybe it's one of your other kids that's the Indigo."

"He's my only one."

"The very fact that you're here indicates that he must be an Indigo. Besides being an Indigo doesn't mean that they are all *exactly* alike. They are still going to have their own individual personalities. Your son is just quieter about it, and apparently cautious too. I'll bet if you watch him closely you'll find that he is doing the same things as the others only doing it in a quieter more careful fashion," Rachael explained to Cindy, as she looked around the room to include any others who might have similar feelings. Watching Hally I noticed that she was relating to this explanation. Her boy must also be a quiet one.

As the others continued to discuss quiet verses out going, my memory took me back to when Naja was three. She was even information gathering then. "You know," I said out loud, but still thinking about the past, "when Naja was too young to have a grasp of what questions to ask to get the information she wanted for her information gathering process, she used to pick arguments with me to see how I would deal with the situation. It took me a while to figure out that she really wasn't as argumentative as she was appearing to be. She was actually acting out a scenario, because she didn't know how to put together the question. I remember, at the time, thinking it was strange, because in some of the debates she would take a stance against something that I knew that she had formerly been for."

"So, in acting this out, did she get the information she was after?" asked Ramon.

"Actually, I think she did, because as I remember, she continued on after it even when I told her that this was not something to argue about. She was like a dog with a bone; she wouldn't let go of it. At the time, I didn't understand what was going on and I'd be the one getting upset, she was very methodical about the entire thing."

"I think that's what Carman is doing now! She's three and gets me into some of the most loco arguments," Ramon exclaimed, his eyes bright. "She's getting answers without knowing how to ask the questions!"

"Well, I guess this gives us parents an entirely different slant on why our kids argue," Bill said, looking like he'd just made a big discovery.

"But does it give them a common thread?" asked Pete, who had been fairly quiet during the meeting. "I mean a lot of this just sounds like kids, any kids. What constitutes an Indigo team? Working together for a common goal, Right? Well these kids don't even know each other much less understand that they have a common goal." He suddenly noticed how he had thrown cold water on the entire group and their idea of a progressive project, "I'm sorry, but..."

"It's okay," I interrupted his apology. "You're right, a lot of this is typically kid stuff, and the kids don't know each other or what a goal or teamwork even is. But if you add in our situation; the fact that we, a group of complete strangers, are being brought together while we sleep each night, plus the fact that the very only thing that we have in common is our kids, it..."

"Don't forget that we've all seen the same Boogie Man that too is a common thread for us," Sally interjected, pointing her finger for emphasis.

"Right," I acknowledged her input, "and I think it's safe to say that a lot of the things that our Indigos are doing are also things that other regular children do, however... as we progress and discover more of the traits our kids have we are also going to discover that the 'other kids' don't do 'all' of the same things."

"You mean, one kid here and there will have one of the traits, another will have a different or similar trait and so on, but none will have all of the same traits that the Indigos do?" asked Cindy.

"Yeah, I get it," stated Pete, smiling and looking like things had just slid into place inside of his questioning mind.

I happened to glance at Rachael and noticed that she was studying me. I smiled but she just continued her inspection. *Okay, I guess it's time to share,*

I thought, feeling that Rachael already knew I wasn't telling everything. I'd hate to meet her across the table during a big merger meeting, I decided as I formulated my thoughts.

"I have some information that's off of this particular subject, but it's something you might find interesting." I re-crossed my legs and prepared to tell them about the dog. "The reason none of you saw the White Dog yesterday is because he spent the day outside of Naja's preschool." I didn't add my thoughts on why the dog had been there, I wanted their input.

"I knew it!" said Lindy. "I knew something was up as soon as I saw you."

"Practicing your intuition were you?" I responded with a grin. Then I looked at Rachael who was silent but had a knowing look on her face.

"What do you think that means?" asked Bill with a serious frown taking over his face.

"Is this school safe? What kind of security is there?" Teri questioned, thinking of her own school.

"So... the Boogie Man was watching Naja, and the White Dog was running interference," Shala almost whispered. "Just like he's done since before she was even born."

A long silence followed her statement; a silence full of unanswered questions, full of fear, and full of relief, relief that it wasn't their child being stalked by the Boogie Man. That they didn't need a large White Dog to stand guard over their Indigo child. I didn't blame them, it was certainly very natural for parents to want the safest life possible for their children.

Cindy, reading the silence, said, "This man would like to cut off the head of snake, as Ron put it," Ron flushed and looked down at his hands, "but what do you do if you can't reach the head of a snake?" she stopped and looked around the room.

"Oh, my God!" whimpered Hally. "You chop it wherever you can!"

"Oh no..."

"She's right," Ramon stated. "None of us are out of these woods."

"*We* don't have a White Dog guarding our kids!" Shala said with a catch in her voice.

"No!" I spoke loudly over the confusion and turmoil that had taken over the room. **"Don't let this man create fear!** Fear is as big an enemy as this Boogie Man is." I lowered my voice as they quieted down. "Remember the Guardian Angels? All of our kids have Guardian Angels watching over them. They are here for a very special purpose do you think that these souls would come here, as wee defenseless children, without providing some sort of protection for themselves?"

The fear was drifting away from the center of the room remaining only in tiny tendrils along the outskirts and in the far corners. Everyone was silent, but they weren't idle, they were searching their minds for some fragment of proof to validate this idea. They wanted desperately to believe their children were safe. They were searching their memories for any shred of evidence that a guardian Angel was watching over their child.

Shala was fighting to keep her emotions in control, then she said quietly, "I know fear, I know what it's like to be intimidated, threatened, and much worse. In Afghanistan I've lived that life already and after the death of my husband, I took the first opportunity to flee to a safer environment to raise my child. I didn't want that kind of life for my daughter. I'll fight to the end to protect her and the new life that I've established here in the U.S. I can't go backwards."

Everyone was silent, thinking of the conditions that females are subjected to in the third world. Shala was quiet, but she must be a fighter to have taken the step away from that life and into this new one. I was thinking that compared to what she'd been forced to live, 'we' certainly could do this.

Then out loud I said, "Okay, listen, we can do this. Let's continue. The White Dog didn't show up until Naja was close to being in real trouble. As long as I was doing my job of protecting her, the dog stayed away. It was only when I was not around or would not be able to cope with the situation that the dog appeared." Remembering today at the park, I hoped that they'd feel more at ease as I explained. "The Guardian doesn't need to show up for your children, as long as the main focus stays on Naja."

"She's right, and don't forget it probably won't be a big White Dog," added Rachael, leaning back in her chair and again fingering the crystal around her neck.

"Well, I'd like a dog. In fact, that's not a bad idea. I think that I'd like to buy a dog, but I guess that wouldn't work in an apartment," Lindy said, looking disappointed.

"A dog is good as a warning device, but they aren't all into protecting anything except their food dish," Ron stated looking like the very idea of owning a dog was distasteful, and he apparently didn't seem to think much of their ability to protect. However, I was remembering how formidable the White Dog appeared in his protection stance against the Boogie Man in my dream.

As the group continued debating the pros and cons of owning a dog, I was considering how fortunate that Naja was to have the White Dog for protection, but would the two of us; the dog and I be enough? Could I do my part, was I up to the challenge?

Day Six

Naja must have sensed that I was experiencing an emotional problem this morning. I felt her staring at me, and as I looked up she said. "What's wrong, Mommy? Are you having a bad day?" I looked at this little person, who was much wiser than I was when I was five, and wondered where this was all going to lead.

"No, honey, I'm just tired." Actually, I was feeling guilty even though I'd explained to the others last night at the dream meeting, that their kids didn't need protection at this stage. I was left feeling like Naja was safe and the others were vulnerable. I couldn't help feeling a responsibility to keep all of the other kids as safe as Naja.

"Don't worry about it, Mommy, it'll all be okay." Naja's words broke into my thoughts sounding like she knew just what I was thinking. I studied the top of her head as she ate her cereal. Why had she said that? I tried to shake off the odd feeling in the middle of my stomach. I was sure that I was getting paranoid, attaching significant meanings to innocent words.

Moving a little slower today, I cleaned up the kitchen, gathered up Naja's and my things and headed for the garage. Setting the alarm, I backed the car out of the garage and we headed up the street. As we turned the corner towards the main street, I suddenly remembered that even though I'd moved slower and been more organized, I'd left a document on the kitchen counter. Turning at the next street I headed back towards the house from the opposite direction.

"What are you doing, Mommy?" Asked the curious little voice of Naja, from her car seat in the back of the car, as she realized we were going in the wrong direction.

"I forgot my paper in the kitchen," I explained as I maneuvered around a kid on a bicycle and then tried to negotiate around a parked garbage truck. As I tried to swing out around the truck I saw a small gray panel truck that had been in front of the garbage truck, pull across the street and stop in front of my house. Two men hopped out and approached my door. Quickly I braked the car and remained behind the cover of the large truck.

One of the men looked like the bogus insurance adjuster from the other day. I edged the car slightly out just enough to see the truck in front of my house. As I did, the two men came running from the house jumped into the truck and it surged ahead driving down the street in a big hurry. It wasn't until I pulled out around the garbage truck and drove closer to my house that I heard the alarm.

I stopped and called 911 on my cell phone. The dispatcher said that a patrol car would be there in 5 minutes. Which was just enough time to explain to Naja that since the alarm was going off we'd better get some help in shutting it off.

Sure enough, a patrol car pulled up in exactly 5 minutes. Wow, such service was impressive. I entered the code and stopped the alarm's annoying sound. The patrolmen discovered that someone had forced the front window, just behind the large evergreen bush, setting off the alarm. I told them that I'd just left and had returned for a paper that I'd forgotten.

"They must have been watching you and struck right after you left. Strange they didn't know you had an alarm, must have been random and unprofessional, because usually burglars case a place, they check to see if there's an alarm in place, and they usually go around to the back of the house," the officer said, pulling off his hat and scratching his head, in puzzlement.

"Well, I just had the alarm put in yesterday and the gates to the back are locked from the inside," I informed him, thinking about the man who kept looking past me at the inside of the house, I couldn't help grinning. "Guess he got fooled, didn't he?"

"Yep, you probably threw a monkey wrench into his day." The officer grinned back. "We're going to check around your house maybe we'll get lucky and find something of interest. But don't count on it," he informed me as he headed back to the porch.

Yeah lucky I pulled those strings and had the house wired and the alarm system installed yesterday, I was thinking. Wonder why they wanted in? I was climbing back into the car to explain to Naja, when I heard someone calling. Walking down the street, tugging at her dog, was the neighbor, who lived two houses down and on the opposite side of the street. I had seen her, but didn't know her name, or any of my neighbor's names for that matter.

This was one of the areas that had been developed by one builder, so the houses, although nice, lacked in originality. Four different plans had been used so about every fourth house was different than its next door neighbor, some one level and some two and some had the floor plans reversed to add a little more difference. The streets were mostly a straight shot, but now and then a curve was added, again striving for a individual look, but basically it was a 'cookie cutter' project of upper modest homes.

It was a working neighborhood, everyone was off to his or her jobs by at least 8:00 AM each weekday. This particular lady was a bit older than the rest of the neighbors, lived alone and didn't seem to have a job outside of the home.

"Hi," I greeted her, knowing what her curiosity must be.

"What's goin' on?" she asked without bothering with a greeting.

Her face had a curious, but not a fearful look. Strange, most women living alone would feel frightened at seeing police attending to a house where an alarm was going off.

Before I had a chance to answer her, the officer called out. "Hi Mary, I didn't know you lived around here."

Mary called back to him and then she turned back to me. "Break in?" she asked. She seemed to be a person of few words.

"Yes, and I was only gone for a few minutes. I'd turned around and came back for something," I explained.

"Was it the guys in the black car?" she asked without preliminaries.

"You've seen the black car?" I questioned in surprised. "No it was a gray panel truck."

"Any advertising or writing on the side?" she questioned further.

"No...now that I think about it, it was just gray."

"Okay, let me have a word with Jimmy there," she said nodding towards the officer and headed towards the porch. Telling Naja to stay quiet in the car for just another minute I too headed for Jimmy. What the Hell was going on?

"Mary, here, tells me that a black car has been hanging around here lately. She said that the men in it looked like they were in business suits, but acted like they were on a military assignment. Know anything about it?" he questioned me as soon as I approached. Mary stood silently and watched my every response.

"As a matter of fact, a man who was wearing a business suit, but acting like a professional military man came to my door the other day. He wanted to come in and talk to me about my husband's death. I told him to see my attorney and he left. And...one of the men in the truck looked like that man."

Both Officer Jimmy and Mary stood there looking at me. I could sense the wheels going around in their heads, but didn't have any idea what they were thinking about.

"Did he?" Mary asked.

"Excuse me?" I uttered, not following the question.

"Did he contact your attorney?" she explained.

"Ah... No. I called my attorney later and he hasn't heard from anyone."

"What was your impression? Did you think that he was on the up and up?" she asked in her abrupt style.

"Actually, I did not. I didn't feel comfortable with him. I all but shut the door in his face. Not, however, before he got a good look inside of the hallway and living room."

Mary and Jimmy exchanged glances and then Jimmy said, "Maybe you'd better fill out a complete report on this down at the station. Could you come down later today?"

"Of course, how about after lunch?"

I watched as Mary turned to leave, dragging her little dog with her. Did that dog have legs? His stomach seemed to be touching the sidewalk. "Mary!" I called before she'd gone too far. "Mary, thanks for your help. I had completely forgotten about that man's visit."

Mary gave me a glance that either said, *You're too stupid or you're lying.* My guilt said she suspected the lie. She turned to leave, but then stopped and asked, "What'd you're husband die of?"

I was startled, but answered, "He was killed, about 6 years ago." Her attitude softened slightly as she asked. "How did he die, was he in the military?"

Military. She must be trying to make a connection between these military-looking guys and Bob. "No, he wasn't in the military he was killed during a mugging in a parking lot."

She stood there looking at me, but not really seeing me. She was deep in thought.

"Mommy, come on, we're gonna be late for school," Naja's called from the car.

We both looked towards the car and at the concerned little face in the window.

"Well, guess I have to go. School is very important you know," I said smiling, and calling to Naja. "Be right there."

"Sure wasn't when I went!" came the response from Mary, and she turned up the sidewalk towards her house, still dragging the little dog along beside her.

I returned to Officer Jimmy and asked if they could secure the window until I could get back and have it repaired. He said they would, but the alarm wouldn't be able to be reactivated until the window was fixed.

"I guess that's okay. Surely they wouldn't come back so soon?"

"Not likely, but we'll alert the patrol unit in this area."

As I turned to leave, I asked him, "How do you know Mary? She seems to be a very alert person."

He laughed and answered, "She should be, she was a detective for 25 years. Then just decided she'd had enough and retired. She still does some computer programs for us, but she calls her own schedule."

"Well, I think I like having her as a neighbor," I said.

He laughed again and added. "Don't count on coffee klatches, she's not the chummy type."

"That suits me," and I turned and ran to the car.

I immediately looked up a window glass company close to my home and arranged to meet them there later in the afternoon. It took threats and extra money to get such speedy service, but they finally 'squeezed me in,' as the gal making the appointments told me.

Somehow I managed to get through the morning meetings and then headed to the police station. Apparently I was expected and was ushered into an office. A man in a suit came in a few seconds later and indicated I should take a chair. I chose the nearest one and when I looked up I was staring into two surprised brown eyes. "Hey, aren't you the detective I met in the park?" I asked, just as surprised as he was.

"Yes, so we meet again," he said as he sat down and leaned back in his swivel chair. "Sorry, I didn't connect the name. So, you had a burglar set off your alarm," he said matter of factly.

"Yes. You've talked to Mary haven't you?" I questioned him not knowing how I knew, but it felt obvious. He looked startled at first.

"I can never figure out how you women do that," he said smiling from ear to ear.

"It's called intuition, and it's fairly well developed in mothers," I informed him with a smile.

He laughed and said, "Oh yes, you're the one that thinks Childnappers in the park need to watch out for Mothers." Then he sat forward in his chair his hands folded on top of his desk. "Let's hear your story."

I told him all that I knew, which wasn't much. He seemed interested in Bob's murder, and wanted to know if they had ever caught the muggers. When I told him no, he clicked a button on a machine sitting on the desk and asked for the six-year-old file on Robert Minton.

"Had you ever seen or noticed these men before the visit to your house?"

"No..." I hesitated suddenly thinking of the Boogie Man, but he wasn't one of those guys. Noticing the silence I glanced up to discover that he was studying me. "No. I'd never noticed them before," I said quickly knowing that he was wondering why I'd hesitated. I certainly couldn't tell him about the Boogie Man. He was in my dreams. Well, he had started to appear during the day too. He was still silently studying me, which I decided was a technique used to make people nervous so that they would talk more, and it was working. It did make me feel nervous, and of course, that was because I was hiding something. Suddenly I started speaking quickly, before I changed my mind.

"I have, however, noticed another man, who seems to be around too often for comfort." He still sat looking at me, not saying anything. Why would he? It was working, I was talking. I knew it and couldn't stop. Actually I wanted to tell him. I wanted someone to take over some of this responsibility, someone to get some of these strange men out of my life.

"...and what about that guy in the park?" I continued. I was on a role and couldn't seem to quit. "Did you know that the child he grabbed looked just like my daughter? She was even wearing the same type and color of clothes!"

I knew that I was becoming over emotional. *Breathe*, I told myself. Loosening my grip on the chair arms I leaned back and consciously took in the relaxing breaths.

"Was it the same man that came to your door?" he asked, breaking his silence.

I knew he was going to ask that question. The people in the dream had already asked me that. "No. They are two different men." *Three counting the Boogie Man*, I silently counted. "All looking completely different from each other." All frightening, it felt good to tell someone who had some power, someone who could maybe help.

"Well, we have the description of the man in the park, such as it is, and we have the description of the man in the car, such as it is. Is that it?" he asked, raising his eyebrows in question.

"Well...there is one more..."

He glanced up at me, his eyebrows rising even higher. "One more man?" he asked.

I nodded my head.

"What kind of description do you have of this third man?" he asked, as he again leaned back in his chair and smiled.

I tried to explain that I'd never seen his face, but always knew it was the same guy. He just nodded his head and wrote on his note pad. Then the meeting ended with... "If you remember anything else or you see any of these men again, or get a better description, call me."

Was he thinking I was some kind of hysterical mother, seeing danger in every man that I saw? Damn! I felt like a complete fool as I left his office and made my way down the stairs and out of the police station. I still had a window to repair, so that all of these imaginary men couldn't get into my house.

The window repair men were just driving up as I pulled the car into the garage. Pretty good timing I thought.

"Say Lady, what'd you say to Diane?"

"What?"

"Diane said we'd better be here on time or all hell was going to break loose."

I grinned and said, "Friends in high places." Actually, I don't remember exactly what I told her, but it was something about the police being involved, and they were...sort of.

These glass men were experts and worked fast. They were finished before I expected them to be. I decided to pick up Naja and then stop at the grocery store. She did love to shop.

For two people, we had a large stash of food in that cart, but it was mostly packaged and canned, so it'd keep. The fresh stuff was something I'd have to make many stops for during the week.

Naja decided on Noodle O's, for dinner while I opted for a small pork steak and a small baked potato. We shared cabbage coleslaw. Not her favorite, but I love it. We made a deal that if she'd eat some of the things that I liked, I'd eat some of the things that she liked. I'm still not sure who made out best in the deal. Little 'O' shaped noodles swimming in diluted tomato soup is strictly for kids.

After cleaning up the dishes, we decided to check out the flower beds in the back yard.

Sure enough, they needed water. It had been a dry spring for this area, which usually didn't require watering out of doors until summer. After getting more on us than on the flower beds, we headed for the house.

"Bath time, get those wet socks off down here and then scoot upstairs, I'll be right behind you." I set the alarm, gathered up the wet clothes and headed upstairs.

~

Once again I reached the meeting before the others. I sat there holding the legal pad on my lap and prayed that every one of the Indigo kids was okay. When I'd picked Naja up from school, Miss Susan assured me that there had been no White Dog around. So... did that mean that the Boogie Man was stalking someone else? Was he really dangerous, or was he just toying with us? Did he get his kicks out of watching people react to fear? Watching as they lost their cool demeanor; finding a perverse enjoyment as they began to sweat, delighting as they displayed symptoms of losing control of their emotions.

"So Boogie Man...I think you are a very sick person," I said out loud, as I realized that he was in the room. I hadn't seen or heard him, but I could feel him, the thick, unyielding form of his personality, and the heavy dark energy field that surrounded him. I didn't look up right away, but allowed a second or two to pass and then slowly raised my head, allowing my eyes to lift last. A dramatic action that I hoped would display casualness and *absolutely no fear*.

Sure enough, he was leaning against the wall in the corner, to the backside of the door, his arms folded across his chest, a shadow partially covering his face. As I studied him I had an overwhelming desire to laugh. Not at the situation, but at a thought that had flitted through my mind... He always has the advantage of a shadow shielding his identify. *Does he have to scan out a place first to find the right shadow in the right spot and at the right height? Or, does he bring the shadows with him?* Maybe like that fellow in the funny papers, the one who always had a rain cloud hanging over his head.

That did it; I laughed out loud, much to the Boogie Man's surprise. He came off of the wall and stood straight up, the gray shadow not living up to its job, didn't follow him. There he was with a full-unveiled face.

"You're not bad looking, you shouldn't stay hidden in the shadows," I said, smiling at him, delighted with myself for startling him into an uncontrolled action.

Several of the dream members came bursting through the door talking very excitedly; they marched right into the middle of the room before stopping. I, however, was looking past them at the back of the man, as he was leaving the room. Lindy, who was one of the group turned to look behind her, when she saw me staring, but she was only in time to fleetingly get an impression of movement before he'd turned down the hall and was gone.

"Who's leaving?" she asked, looking back at me. The others quickly looked at the door, but were too late to see the strongly built back of their tormentor.

"Was that you laughing in here just before we came in? Who's with you?" Sally questioned, looking around the room.

Just then several more of the group came in, interrupting the question and There was general confusion until everyone had arrived and finally settled into their chairs. No one looked devastated and everyone was here, so I guessed that all of the kids were okay, and breathed a deep sign of relief. Lindy was watching me closely, still curious about the visitor. I wondered if Lindy had guessed who he was, but decided that she had not, because she wouldn't be sitting there so silent if she suspected the visitor to have been the Boogie Man.

"Well, you're all looking well, no encounters today?" I asked casually looking around at the now familiar faces. What a different group they seemed since the first night, or even the second or third night, I thought as I waited for a response.

"I saw him. He followed Takezo and me home from the grocery store, but I remembered what we talked about and acted just like I had a dozen Guardian Angels walking along beside us. As soon as I thought about being surrounded by Angels, he stopped at the corner and I didn't see him anymore." Hally smiled, nodded her head and looked extremely pleased with herself.

"What time was that?" asked Pete, leaning forward in his chair.

"It was in the afternoon, after 3:00."

"Okay, so he was at my place before that, about noon. He never gets very close, but I always see him. He's not very careful."

"I think he wants to be seen. He can't scare anyone if they don't see him. He probably keeps a more discreet distance with the men, than he does with the women, but I'm sure that he makes sure that he's seen," added Rachael, playing with the crystal around her neck., as usual.

"So," I said, writing on the legal pad, "that's three that saw him today and one that saw him here tonight." I kept my head down and waited to hear a reaction. When I heard nothing from the group, I looked up. Everyone was sitting very still and very silent, without any emotion or even any sign that they had even heard me. In fact, it was as if they had suddenly turned to stone and were frozen in place.

Rachael had her head lowered and her hand was holding her Crystal out about two inches from her body. She was holding it very still, the fingers looking like they had stopped in the middle of caressing the stone.

Teri, with her hand just about to reach the blond curl that had fallen across her forehead, sat absolutely stone still. Cindy, Hally and Ron all faced me their eyes not truly focused, just looking straight ahead.

Sally's very still head was turned away towards Shala who was staring at her with an open expression of question written across her face. Beyond them Ramon had his hand, which was curled into a fist, up to his mouth as if he were going to cough, but the cough was apparently frozen in his throat also. Pete, Bill and Lindy were also as still as statues.

I studied their faces wondering if I was the only one still in the dream? Had they gone off somewhere else and left their bodies just sitting here? I remembered seeing a movie where everyone except the main characters, had been frozen in place. Besides being awake in a dream, was I now the only one functional?

"Hellooo. Is anybody out there?" I called out, looking for some signs of life.

Lindy moved first. She closed her mouth, which had been slightly open, lifted her hand and pointed a finger toward me for several seconds before she was able to say, "It was him... He was the one I saw leaving." Still no one else moved. It was just the two of us. Again I glanced at the others, this time for signs of breathing. Lindy went on, "I knew there was something familiar about that feeling I got! Why was he here? What did he want? What did he say?"

As I turned my focus on Lindy and her questions, I became aware of the revived energy around me. Glancing quickly about, I noticed that the rest of the group had quietly become living, breathing, blinking people again. "So what'd you guys do, go home and check on your kids?" I flung at them, feeling angry at not knowing what had happened and at not being a part of it.

They ignored my question, as if I hadn't spoken. While Lindy pressed for answers. "Tell us. What happened?"

I was having a difficult time concentrating on the question. My mind was screaming. *What just happened?! Does shock react in a more dramatic style in a dream?* I wondered.

"Ahh... I was just sitting here...ahhh, and there he was. He didn't say anything, but I did see his face," I told them, regaining control of my confusion. "He let you see his face?"

"Well, it wasn't intentional. He accidentally stepped out of the shadow and there it was. He's not bad looking, high cheek bones and blue eyes," I told them remembering the penetrating look that came out of those blue eyes.

"He beat cleats as soon as the first group came in."

"What? He was here when we came in?"

"Yes, he was standing over there, against that far wall, almost behind the door. No one even noticed him, until Lindy saw me watching him leave."

"Yeah, I didn't actually see him, but I knew someone was headin' down the hall."

"Why was he here?"

"Yeah, what's goin on now?"

"Well, I wish I could answer your questions, but I haven't a clue as to why he was here," I told them, tapping the pencil on the yellow legal pad on my lap, feeling unsettled. Today had been full of surprises.

The rest of the group was busy trying to discover what the Boogie Man was doing here and what it meant that I'd seen his face. I, however, was going over some of the details of the attempted break-in this morning. That alarm system certainly saved the day. However, I was still wondering what those men wanted in my house, not for a minute did I believe that they were just common burglars.

"You know, you may have made him mad, by seeing his face," Shala, said peering out from behind the shiny black hair that had fallen partially across her frightened face.

"What? Oh. Well, he looked more startled than mad," I answered, dragging myself away from today's earlier events and back to the group. "It was funny though. I mean seeing him lose his cool," I told them, smiling.

"Is that why you were laughing when we came in?"

"Well, I was actually laughing because seeing him in the shadow again, made me think of 'Sad Sack.' You know, that comic character who walks around under a rain cloud all of the time."

All of the faces were silently watching me, but none of them seemed to share my humor.

"Are you saying that you were laughing 'at' him? Did he know that you were laughing at him?" asked Ron, with a startled look running across his serious face.

"Well, I don't know, I guess so, that's when he accidentally stepped out of the shadow, but it's hard to tell with him, he doesn't show much emotion. He didn't even flinch when I called him sick."

"Wait a minute! You called him *'sick'* **and** laughed at him?" someone asked.

"Oh boy," another commented.

"Mandy! What have you done?" asked Sally, her black face blanched several shades lighter.

I watched as fear raced across the faces in front of me. What were they so afraid of? So what if I did offend the Boogie Man? So what?! Why should I tippy toe around him and his intimidating tactics? My daddy didn't raise me to cow tow to anyone, especially some rude jerk.

"You guys are doing exactly what he wants you to do. Experiencing *fear*!"

I looked each one of them in the face. "Get a grip! Besides, it was me not you that challenged him." Silence followed my statement. I just waited, thinking that it was a good thing it wasn't any of their kids that had chosen to be the leader.

"She's right," Rachael spoke softly, nodding her head up and down. "This man *is fear*, it's his job to instill fear. It's our job as the parents and guardians of these Indigo kids, to not allow this to happen. We must not let fear deter us from our jobs."

"That's right! We need to remember that we have Guardian Angels helping us," Hally added in a much firmer voice than her face showed that she was feeling.

"Well, Mandy must be using hers full time."

"Yeah."

"Okay, let's think Guardian Angels."

"Thinking Guardian Angels is good, but that doesn't solve the entire problem. They are here to help you, not to take over the project. You can't just sit back and think that they will carry the ball for you," Ramon stated with feeling and much more savvy than I'd given him credit for.

"Of course, he's right," stated Rachael looking pleased. "You folks are getting the idea. We might pull this off yet." She reached for her crystal and said, "I'm going to balance the energy around this entire group, and then include the energy in the entire room. We can use all of the help we can get."

The others were silent for a few minutes. Probably wondering, as I was, what Rachael was talking about now.

"Mandy... I still can't believe that you called him sick and laughed at him!" Lindy seemed stuck on that aspect. Then suddenly she started laughing. She laughed so hard she almost fell off of her chair. "Boy, would I have loved to have seen that!" she sputtered just before bursting into another fit of uncontrolled laughter.

I've heard that laughter is contagious and it must be true, because several others started to chuckle and then laugh. Soon everyone was laughing uproariously except me. As I stared at them I had the uneasy feeling that they just might have crossed over the edge and were actually hysterical.

"It's okay, honey," Lindy said as she wiped her eyes. "It's okay, just a little good ole fashion stress release." She smiled and winked her eye.

"Yeah, right," I said cautiously, watching as the rest of them made their way back from their laughing binge. Boy, these people must really be uptight to react like that. 'Cause it just wasn't *that* funny.

"Sorry, Mandy."

"Yeah, but I wish that I'd seen it too."

"Well, since you're all in such a jovial mood, I have more news." I hesitated, looking around. "This morning the bogus Insurance man and friend tried to break into my house."

"What!?"

"NO!"

"Mandy, what did you do?"

"Wait, wait." I held my hands up to quiet them. "I wasn't home at the time." I told them everything, including the fact that I had a former detective for a neighbor.

"Mandy, what do you think they wanted in your house?"

"I can't even guess, but I'm sure it wasn't to steal something," I told them. "I've thought about it a lot, but I just don't know why. I don't even know what they wanted in the first place. I'm feeling very confused," I answered and then I giggled and then started laughing, while the rest of the group took a turn carefully watching me. "Confused! Is that an understatement... or what?" I managed to say between spurts of my own laughter.

Several concerned expressions changed to smiles, then to cautious laughter. Others started to chuckle. Soon the entire group was laughing in complete abandonment for the second time tonight, tears rolling down their cheeks, heads thrown back. The sound of laughter rocked the room.

Silently a shadow moved slowly across the open doorway, Hesitated, and then moved forward slightly, just enough to see, but not be seen. I felt a chill ripple through my body, bringing me back to my normally composed self.

Sensing that his form was hovering at the edge of the light. I sent him a silent message, a visualization of a glove tossed onto the floor in front of him. *Even he can't miss this challenge*, I thought smiling. "Give it your best shot!" I muttered quietly. The shadowy form silently withdrew....

Day Seven

"Mommy, Mommy! It's time to get up." The small voice made its way through my deep sleep as I struggled to make my way back to consciousness. I could hear the alarm clock buzzing in the background. When I finally opened my eyes I was looking right into Naja's face, which was about two inches from mine.

"Good morning. Can you turn the alarm off for me?" Wow, I certainly was sleeping sound.

"Mommy, look who's here," said the excited small voice as she scrambled to the night stand and shut off the alarm.

Who's here? Who could be here? I reopened my eyes to see Naja looking over her shoulder, towards the bedroom door. There sat the White Dog his tongue hanging out and looking just like he belonged. I sat up so fast that I nearly dumped Naja off of the bed. "Where did he come from?" I said out loud to no one in particular, since I knew that Naja didn't know, and the dog wasn't telling.

"He was in my room when I woke up. Isn't he neat?"

"Yes, he's neat," I answered, a tendril of fear creeping into my chest as I climbed out of the bed, scanning the room. Why was he here? Is Naja in danger? He didn't look upset, or 'on guard.' My heart was pounding as I jerked my robe on over my nightgown.

"Can we keep him, Mommy, can we?"

"Well, he can sure stay if he wants to," I said, looking directly at the dog, hoping that he would accept the invitation. My mouth fell open as he wagged his tail and lay down with a grunt. Was that a yes? He certainly looked like he was settling in. A wonderful feeling washed the fear away. I'd have help guarding Naja. Was that why he was here? Were things escalating? Was the danger more now than before? As these thoughts followed each other through the maze of my mind, Naja joined the dog on the floor. They looked just like any kid and her pet dog. She was petting him, and he had his paw on her chest and his tongue on her face, and she was squealing with joy.

Stepping over them I checked out the hallway, I didn't actually expect to find anything or anyone. The dog wouldn't be so laid back if there were a problem, but it was something the mother in me had to do. I definitely felt the need to check out the entire house.

The alarm system was on, and nothing seemed amiss. How did the dog get in? Well, I guess doors, windows, or alarm systems don't hamper Guardian Angels. Then it struck me! It probably wouldn't stop the Boogie Man, since he wasn't from this plane either. The alarm system wouldn't stop him any more than it had the dog! That must be why the dog was here.

"Mommy, we don't have any dog food," said Naja, from behind me, "and I think he's hungry."

Dog food? What kind of dog food do Guardian Angel Dogs eat? "What makes you think that he's hungry?" I asked her as I followed the pair into the kitchen still looking around and checking behind each door.

"Well, I'm hungry, so he must be too," she explained logically.

"I hope he eats scrambled eggs, 'cause that's what we're serving this morning." I turned and looked at the dog, who was happily wagging his tail. *Okay! Scrambled eggs it is.*

"Naja, stop playing with the dog and get ready for school," I called to her for the third time. I was wondering what was going to happen when we got into the car for the drive to the school, was the dog going too? Maybe he was going to stay at the house, or maybe he was going to go up in a poof of smoke.

"Okay let's get into the car," I said, opening the back seat door, waiting to see if the dog would follow Naja into the car.

Naja turned to the dog, gave him a hug and said, "Bye, I'll see you later."

Then she climbed into the car. The dog glanced at me turned and trotted out of the garage and around the corner of the Rhododendron bush.

Well! Apparently 'they' had it all worked out between them.

After dropping Naja off at the school, I decided to stop by the police station and give the lieutenant the complete description of the Boogie Man. Once again, he seemed surprised to see me.

"I have a description of the Boogie Man... ah the third man," I said as I lowered my head and quickly sat down in a chair. *Damn, I hadn't meant to call him that to the lieutenant.*

"What'd you call him, The Boogie Man?" he asked, smiling broadly.

"Well, that's what he acts like, always creeping around and trying to scare me!" I said in defense.

"Okay, give me the description," he said struggling to keep from laughing out loud.

"He's medium height, well built and strong looking. He has blond hair, and piercing blue eyes. He..." I never got to finish the description, because, the chair that Lieutenant Adams had been leaning back in suddenly came forward the legs hitting the floor with a loud crash. His face had the expression of someone who had just been hit in the stomach.

I nearly jumped out of my chair. "Are you all right? Do you know him?"

He just sat there staring at me with his mouth open.

"Lieutenant Adams?"

His mouth closed, and then opened as he licked his lips. He blinked a couple of times and said, "Maybe. He does sound like someone I've had dealings with before."

How strange. Weren't professionals supposed to show no emotion? This man was really shocked by the description of the Boogie Man. I couldn't help wondering what his reaction would be if I told him that I also see this guy in a dream. A dream I have each night with eleven other people.

He didn't explain his reaction, but he did regain his composure and changed the subject. He explained that he was still looking into my husband's file as a matter of routine and that he'd get back to me. When I left his office, he still had a strange look on his face, and as the door was closing, I heard him say, "My God!"

Mechanically I got through the day, dealing with business problems that didn't seem to be very important compared to the problems that now haunted my private life. I couldn't wait to pick up Naja. I didn't feel comfortable anymore when Naja was out of my sight; however, I forced myself to stay to the very end of the workday.

I was driving down Barbur Boulevard and had almost reached the day care center when a small tan car cut me off so abruptly that I had to swing wide to the left to miss him. This put me in the lane that went on to the ramp that headed directly on to the freeway the opposite direction. I braked lightly looking into the rear mirror. Another car was coming up behind me fast. Pumping the brake lights and pulled to the left as far as I could I hoping the approaching car would go around me.

The big car behind me wasn't cooperating, it pulled up behind me staying close, and forcing me to move forward on to the freeway ramp. "Damn!" I muttered as I was forced to merge with the late afternoon traffic. I stayed in the right lane planning to get off at the next exit. The big car behind me suddenly whipped around and pulled into the lane in front of me and then immediately slowed down.

"What the Hell..." I angrily spoke out loud. Then I felt a chill run up my arms and into my hairline. Something was wrong here. *Naja! This is a stall to keep me from picking up Naja on time.* I scrambled for my cell phone and punched in the day care number. It rang busy. *Lieutenant Adams! Where did I put his card?* Quickly, I dug the card out of my suit coat pocket. He answered as if he were tired and ready to call it a day.

"Lieutenant Adams, this is Mandy Minton." I spoke fast not taking time for formalities. "I've been forced onto the freeway, I can't reach the day care center by phone and I'm worried about my daughter." I finished all in one breath.

"What's the address?" was his reply, without wasting time on unimportant words. I gave it to him and he said. "What's your cell number?" I gave that to him also. Then he said, "Are you in danger?"

"I'm fine, although there is a big car in front of me that seems determined to keep me on this freeway."

"Where are you?"

I gave him the location and where I planned to exit.

"Watch yourself. **DO NOT STOP,** for any reason. I'll meet you at the day care." The line went dead as I watched the car in front of me suddenly pull smoothly away. *The driver probably noticed me on the phone and thought I was reporting him. The license plate!* I glanced at the bumper but discovered that the plate was covered with brown mud; I couldn't even see its color. Another chill went through me. I increased my speed, heading for the next exit, and it was then that I noticed the police car passing by in the middle lane. The two officers were talking and didn't even glance in my direction or notice that mud covered license plate turning onto the ramp that led off of the freeway. Well now I knew why the big car left so abruptly, it wasn't me on the phone at all.

When I reached the top of the ramp, the other car was gone. I turned to the left and then back onto the freeway heading back the way I'd just come. As I pulled up in front of the day care center, I saw a black and white police car pulling away, but was greeted by the smiling face of Lieutenant Adams. His smile was encouraging, Naja must be okay.

As I jumped out of the car and started to rush towards him, he used his hand to signal me to slow down, his face was still smiling. His eyes, however, darted towards the house. There in the window was the small face of Naja and Miss Susan. I smiled and waved at them and then I smiled at the lieutenant as I walked at a normal pace towards him. Well, not only was he a man of few words and quick actions, but apparently he was also thoughtful enough to not scare a little girl.

"It looks like everything must be all right," I said as I approached him. "I'm sorry..." I started, but he held up his hand and said, "You did exactly the right thing, quick thinking too. I want to talk to you more about this, can I drop by your house later?"

I was startled, but quickly agreed to his request. "What do they know?" I asked as I nodded slightly towards the house.

He displayed an attractive smile that I hadn't noticed before and said, "Well, you're gonna have some explaining to do. That's one smart little girl. I'm still not sure, but I think she interrogated me. She even remembered seeing me at the park after that attempted snatch. I took my cue from that and said we were doing some follow up."

Naja chattered like a magpie the entire drive home. She was very interested in the police visit. "The first policeman asked for me," she said feeling her own importance. "The other man... is he a real policeman? He didn't have the right clothes on. He told me they just wanted to know if I had any information for them about that deal in the park, you know, when you ran off and brought back that little girl who was crying. Then he asked if I had noticed any strangers around."

"And did you?" I asked playing along.

"Yes," she answered, causing me to nearly run over the curb as I turned the corner.

"You did? Who?"

"I saw that man with the dark shadow. He was talking to someone in a big black car," she answered matter of factly.

The blood left my head and I thought I was going to black out. Pulling quickly over to the curb, I asked. "Naja, what are you saying? What man with the dark shadow?" I asked dreading the answer. Was my tiny little daughter aware of the Boogie Man?

"Oh you know that man who lives around here he seems to always have a dark shadow around him. The dog doesn't like him though. I don't think I do either he doesn't seem very happy, but I smile at him anyway, just to be nice."

Oh My God! She has seen the Boogie Man, and he was close enough to smile at! "Where do you see him?"

"He walks by the school sometimes. He used to stop and watch me, but the dog won't let him close to the fence now. I really like that dog. Can we keep him?" Her innocent face looked up at me with a hopeful expression.

"He's not ours to keep, but he can sure stay anytime he wants to. Tell me about this man, does he scare you?"

"Oh no, he just looks. He even smiled at me," she said as she turned and looked out the window at a kid on a bike.

Thank Heaven she'd turned away, because the shock on my face was obvious and it might have frighten her. I regained control and said, "He smiled at you! You've seen his face?"

Naja turned her head and looked in surprise. "Of course, he was looking at me," she answered looking like she thought I'd lost it.

Changing the focus I asked, "I wonder why the dog doesn't like him?"

The small face formed into a frown as she said, "I don't know, but they aren't friends, the man is afraid of the White Dog."

Then I remembered the car. "You said that he was talking to someone in a black car, when was that?"

"Today. Just before the police car drove up. Then the man left and the car drove away."

A new thought pushed through my muddled brain. "Naja, tell me, was the man there before the car or did they come together? And where were you that you saw all of this?" I questioned trying to understand.

"Well..." she started, obviously enjoying being the center of the conversation, "...I was on the playground. Recess was just over when I saw the White Dog, I ran over to the fence to say hello to him and that's when I saw the man across the street. Then the car drove up and they talked. When the police car came they all left."

They *were* after Naja! My mind screamed, and the Boogie Man does work with the military types, who probably aren't as afraid of a dog, angel or not, as the Boogie Man is. It's one group, not two. I pulled the car back out onto the street and made my way home, pulling into the garage and quickly closing the large door almost before the car was completely inside.

We had just finished dinner and were clearing the dishes away when the doorbell rang for the second time this week. Sure enough, it was the lieutenant. I set Naja up in front of the TV, letting her watch the cartoons that were only allowed occasionally.

"So Lieutenant, let's adjourn to the kitchen and have some coffee," I said as I glanced over at Naja and led the way into the kitchen. When I'd finished pouring the mugs of coffee, I said, "Okay, what's up?"

"I'm not sure why, but I do feel that your daughter could be in very real danger. I think you were set up today and a snatch was in the works. What I can't figure out is why? Do you have any idea why someone would want to grab your daughter?"

"No," I answered briefly. I could hardly tell him the theory that the dream group had come up with, that she was the ringleader of a group of Indigo kids that were going to change the world.

He studied me over the rim of his coffee mug for a second and then said. "Mrs. Minton, there seems to be a lot more going on here than is obvious. So we really need to do some serious brainstorming."

"I agree, and call me Mandy."

"Okay, Mandy," he said smiling. Then his expression abruptly turned serious. "Here's what I understand. Your husband was killed on your wedding day. Three different men have been stalking you and two attempted grabs have possibly been made on your daughter. You're not wealthy, you don't have powerful connections and no known enemies." He stopped talking and looked into my eyes, silently asking me for some type of explanation.

Actually, it was three possible grabs if you count the park incident *yesterday that the bag lady interfered with,* I thought. However, I held my hands out, palms up and said, "It's strange, isn't it?" That was certainly true, if he only knew how strange.

"Okay, let me ask some questions," he said, relaxing his attitude and settling back into his chair.

"Fire away."

"How well did you know your husband before you married him?"

"Well... we met at work. We'd worked together on projects for about a year before we became involved. He wasn't from this area originally, and I don't know much about his background. He was adopted as an infant, and now his adopted family is all gone too."

"Did he know that you were pregnant?"

"No, I didn't even know until after he'd died."

"He wasn't in the military, but did he have any friends or connections with the military?"

"Mary asked me that. I really don't think so, certainly none that I knew of."

"Mommy, I need a drink," came the wee voice from the hallway.

"Excuse me," I said, standing up and heading for the fridge.

"Are you talking to my mommy about those men at the school?" I heard from behind me, as Naja came into the room.

"Yes, I sure am," came the answer. "Do you think she has any information for me?" he asked her with a twinkle in his eye.

"Nope. Too bad dogs can't talk, 'cause my dog doesn't like those men. I'll bet he could tell you all about them. Dogs know things," she said, climbing up onto a chair, like she was planning to stay for a while.

"Oh Naja, why don't you take your juice into the other room so we can talk?" I said trying to head her off. How was I going to explain about the dog?

"What kind of a dog do you have?" he asked her completely ignoring my request.

"He's big and he sleeps with me sometimes."

"How do you know he doesn't like these men?" he questioned further.

Oh, oh, here it comes, I thought, bracing myself. *The Guardian Angel Dog is about to be exposed, and I'm about to appear as a nut case when I try to explain.*

Suddenly there was a squeal from Naja and she slid off of the chair, grabbed her glass on the way, "There's my favorite cartoon!" and she headed out of the room, the music drawing her into never, never land.

Saved by the TV. Pouring more coffee into the cups, I used the action to create a diversion away from the dog conversation, hoping the dog subject would just dissolve into space. I sat down in my chair and immediately said, "What shall I do? How can I keep her safe?" Trying to change the subject.

He looked squarely into my eyes and asked, "Is the dog a large white shepherd?"

I sat there completely stunned, just holding my cup and looking at him.

"Mandy?"

"Why yes, he is. Did you see him at the school?" I asked, trying to act natural.

He just sat there holding his cup and looking at me. Then he took a deep breath, looked down into his cup, sighed and said, "This is very serious, Mandy." As he lifted his eyes to meet mine he asked, "How many people are in your dream? Twelve?"

My mouth fell open and the cup fell from my fingers. The sturdy mug bounced off of the table, throwing coffee everywhere. We both reacted instinctively, pushing our chairs back at the same time and almost, but not quite, avoiding the hot liquid.

"Jeeze! I'm sorry." I reached for the towel and the sponge on the counter behind me. I tossed him the towel and put the sponge to work on the spill.

"What a team!" I said as we cleaned up the last of the coffee. I turned back toward the table only to find that he hadn't moved away. He was standing so close that I could feel the warmth from his body. I started to step back when he grabbed my hand.

"I'm sorry, Mandy. I startled you. I should have known better. I should have moved slower, but this time is different. This time a beautiful little girl's life is in danger."

"What are you talking about? What do you mean 'this time'? I demanded rooted to the floor. What was going on? How did he know about the dog and the dream group? I pulled away, totally confused.

"Here, sit down," he said as he retrieved both mugs and refilled them, and then sat down across from me. "Mandy, I know this is very confusing, but we really don't have time to drag this out and play games. Naja *is* in danger, so bear with me. Okay?"

I nodded my head numbly not knowing what was going on, but understanding that this was important to Naja.

"You do meet with others in a dream each night, right?" he continued without waiting for me to reply. "You have the blue eyed man, the Boogie Man as you call him, stalking you and Naja, and the White Dog runs interference between Naja and the Boogie Man, right?"

How could he know this? My mind was whirling.

He went on, "Now... this is important. Does the dog appear to run interference between you and the man also?" This time he stopped talking studying me intently, while waiting for an answer. Somehow I managed to pull my mind out of the quicksand that it had been sinking into and it slowly started to clear and function again.

"Mandy?"

I could hear him, but could I trust a man who knew things that no one could know? Was he working with the Boogie Man? Was this like the 'Good Cop/Bad Cop' routine? Was he trying to gain my trust so that he could use it to help the Boogie Man and the others get Naja? NO! I didn't let them get her way back in that first dream and they aren't going to get her now!

I met his eyes trying to read his motives. All I saw was a man waiting intently for my silent lips to answer.

"You know what? I haven't a clue as to what you're talking about and it's time for me to get Naja ready for bed." I stood up gathered the mugs and set them in the sink.

He sat very still for a couple of seconds and then as he stood up he said, "I know that this is very scary stuff, I've been there. I too have been involved in dream meetings. My group also had to deal with the blue eyed man *and* we also had help from the White Dog."

I had my back towards him as he spoke standing very still wondering if this was a ploy. Could I trust him? Naja was at risk. The other children were also at risk. In fact, the entire world may be at risk. Everything was depending upon my decision. *GOD! What should I do?*

Suddenly Naja came bursting into the room. "Mommy, Mommy! The White Dog is here!"

I jerked around to face her, just as the White Dog walked into the room. He ignored Naja and walked straight over to Lieutenant Adams, his head bowed and his tail wagging slightly. There was absolutely no question that he not only knew this man, but that he also accepted him.

"Well, hello. Glad to see that you're on duty here," the lieutenant said as he leaned down and patted Naja's Guardian Angel on the head.

"Thank you, God," I whispered. This seemed to answer my question.

Naja was on her knees hugging the dog as I met the lieutenant's eyes above their heads. The energy that flowed between us was strong, comfortable and finally completely without fear. The dog's stamp of approval gave me the confidence to trust this unknown man.

"Okay Naja, five more minutes and then it's off to bed." She squealed and dashed for the TV room the dog hot on her heels.

I turned to face the lieutenant. "Okay, yes. Everything you said is true. I'm sorry, I..."

He held up a hand. "It's okay, you did the right thing. You don't know me. We definitely need to get together and talk, but it's getting late for the little one. There is one thing you need to know before I go and that is, you and Naja are involved in something very important. I don't know what, but it does involve Naja. Something is different this time, he usually works alone." This last he muttered to himself withdrawing into deep thought.

Silently I studied him as he wrestled with this problem. When he became aware of my silent observation he flushed slightly and smiled. "Good night, Mandy. We have some serious talking to do *tomorrow*." He emphasized the word tomorrow.

"What time?" I asked without hesitation.

His smile was warm, starting on his lips and finishing in his eyes, as he said, "How about I pick you up at 11:30 for lunch?"

"It's a deal." I smiled back, feeling warmth spreading through my body, as I wrote my office address and phone number on the note pad.

"Here's my home phone. Call me if there's a problem at odd hours. Oh and by the way, my first name is Frank," he told me as he jotted his number on the back of his card.

"Bye Miss Naja and you too dog," he called into the room with the squealing child and the barking dog.

After I'd let him out the front door, I turned back towards the TV area only to find Naja standing in the hall, her small hand hidden in the deep white coat on the back of this huge dog that had come to help us. I had to fight to control the tears that threatened to spill down my face; my relief in finding someone to help us was overwhelming.

"We're ready for bed now," Naja said as they started up the stairs. What a surprise. Naja never went to bed without a fuss. That dog is definitely a keeper. I followed them up the stairs wondering how I could get him to stay after this was all over.

~

I was the last one at the meeting, as I stepped through the doorway. I stopped to observe the group in front of me. They were chatting socially, and didn't notice my entrance. What a different group of people they were from that first night that we'd all met.

Rachael must have sensed my presence, because she slowly turned her head. "There you are. Come on in we've been waiting for you," she said smiling the smile of one friend to another.

"Hey! Are you okay? You're late," Lindy commented. Heads turned and there was not a frown or negative face in the bunch. I was receiving a positive welcome from this group, and it felt good; a policeman who understood and knew something about this confusing situation, and a group of friendly people. Things were definitely looking up.

"Sorry. I had trouble getting to sleep. My mind was working overtime, and have I got news!" I told them barely able to contain my excitement.

"News? What news?"

"Let's hear it."

"Yeah, we could use some news. Good I hope."

"Wait. I'll bet none of you saw the Boogie Man this afternoon, did you?" Heads shook, and muttered "No's", confirming what I already knew.

"That's because he **and** the military guys with the black car guys were trying to grab Naja! They're working together." All Hell broke loose with my announcement.

Everyone was talking, some were waving their arms, many were leaning forward all were looking concerned and excited at the news. "It doesn't look like they got too close to her. You're too happy," Ron said, breaking through the bedlam. Things quieted down, with all of the excitement contained within, so that they could hear the rest of the story.

I related the entire story, beginning with the car forcing me onto the freeway. I did leave out the feelings I was struggling with regarding Frank, but told them what he'd told me about having been in a dream group, the dog accepting him and about the meeting tomorrow when I would have the opportunity to pick his brain.

Instead of cheers, the room was silent. "What?" I asked looking around from face to face.

"Oh, Honey, this is great news. You're making progress in this strange situation, but..." Lindy broke off and looked down at her sandals.

"What is it?" I asked again, confused.

"Well, I think what we're all wondering..." Shala began.

"Mandy." Sally picked up the thought. "What will happen to our kids now that they've missed so many times on yours? We're happy they missed Naja but does that mean that since they can't seem to get the head that they will now go after the rest of the snake?" Sally finished with a sad and serious expression on her face.

"Hold on! How selfish can we be? Mandy has been dealing with this problem all by herself all this time and now we're telling her 'poor us, our kids may be next'?" Ramon reprimanded. There was a strained and guilty silence for about a minute following Ramon's statement.

"That's right! We're all in this together. Her kid is our kid and our kids are her kids. The kids set it up that way before they were born," Lindy stated firmly, throwing off her personal feelings.

"Yea, they're right. Sorry, Mandy."

"Yes, it's just the protective parents losing focus."

"Do you think we should bring these kids together?" asked Teri, tactfully changing the subject. "We could use my day care facility."

"Now there's an idea!"

They were discussing the details of getting together, but I was still reeling from the previous statements. They had a right to be concerned if these guys couldn't get Naja they may turn their efforts towards another child. I'd worried about that before, but what could I do?

"Mandy?" Rachael's voice speaking very softly interrupted my thoughts.

I turned and smiled at her. "I'm okay, but you know, they weren't wrong. The other kids could now be at greater risk."

"There's always been that possibility. We have to continue to work together and trust that this problem has been foreseen and we will receive the help that we need," she explained gently, like a mother would explain to a child. Our eyes met and we bonded as the others continued their discussion about getting the kids together.

"Rachael, how is it you are so wise?" I asked, curious about this woman and her wisdom.

She chuckled softly. "Age for one thing. Age is a wonderful educator if you learn from the experiences that you have during your life. However, if you mean the psychic stuff, don't forget, it's in my blood. My mother was a seer and her mother was a healer in the old country."

"What old country are you from?"

"Oh, I'm first generation here in the US, but my people originally came from Spain."

"You're Spanish then."

"Actually, I'm Sephardi, which means a Jew from Spain. My people left Spain back in 1492, while Columbus was sailing his ocean blue. That was the time of the Inquisition and the Jews were the victims, so most of them left and migrated all over the world. My particular linage traveled across the Mediterranean, through France, Italy, Greece, and Turkey, and eventually here to the U.S. and then the Pacific Northwest."

"Thanks to your mother and grandmother for keeping the psychic senses active. It's certainly helped us all to understand much quicker in this situation," I told her.

"There are no accidents, you know. This is probably why I was chosen to raise Dina and be included into this group."

"Well," I said with a big sigh, "perhaps I can get more answers that will help us, when I meet with the lieutenant tomorrow."

Rachael smiled and nodded her head, but she didn't look as positive as I was feeling. In fact, she looked like she thought the worst wasn't over yet. I looked back at the group and then glanced back at Rachael in time to see her fold her hand, close her eyes, and bow her head. Her lips appeared to be moving as if in a whispered prayer.

What were her psychic abilities telling her that she hadn't shared? I released a big sigh, briefly closed my eyes and added my energy to her prayer.

Day Eight

I was awake before the alarm went off, laying there studying the ceiling. Energy was flowing through my body and I felt alive and well. I was thinking about my lunch meeting and the questions I would ask and the answers I would finally get.

I checked on Naja and the dog, but only found Naja sleeping in her room. The dog had disappeared as mysteriously as he had arrived. Apparently his duties were over for a while.

I found myself humming a little song as I got ready for work. Naja noticed, giving me a smile, but said nothing. I really hadn't felt this good in a very long time.

Before going downstairs I retrieved Frank's card from the nightstand. I'd kept it close by during the night...just in case. I read the name on the front 'Lieutenant Frank Adams,' nice name, nice man. I placed the card in my pocket. There's something different about him. He just doesn't seem like most of the policemen I'd met.

Of course, I hadn't really met many policemen. At least not since Bob's death and I certainly wasn't in any frame of mind to even notice those men. That day was such a mixture of good and bad, I'll never forget standing next to Bob during the informal ceremony, surrounded by a handful of friends. The smell of roses from the flowers I held wrapped its scent around us binding us together as much as the vows we spoke.

It was one of the happiest days of my life. We had spent the night before; consummating our relationship, and then we talked until dawn discussing our future. As we said, "I do," we were ready to take those new steps together.

Then the entire day turned into a nightmare, as Joe, Bob's friend and best man, went out to see what was taking Bob so long to get the car. The look on his face as he came rushing back into the church is one I have never been able to forget. He was as white as a ghost, his eyes almost bugging out of his head, and his mouth didn't seem to function. It kept opening and shutting, similar to a fish out of water. He finally managed to point toward the door and gurgled something that sounded a little like 'Bob.'

The rest of that day was a blur. I remember people screaming, people crying, faces I didn't recognize helping me. Snapping myself out of those memories I shook off the feelings and prepared for today, today and lunch with Frank.

I took Naja into the school and left quickly, avoiding Miss Susan's questioning look. I definitely needed to give her some information, but I'd wait until I had more myself, like this afternoon, after I'd had the much anticipated talk with Frank.

I loved my office. It had been professionally decorated, but I'd added just enough softness to keep it from being too heavy and masculine; a vase of flowers on the corner of the desk, a bright colored scarf stirred on the credenza, with a plant on top. However, today I just wanted to finish my work and get out. I whipped through my morning projects, postponing some, delegating others and tackling those left over as quickly as I could.

"Excuse me, Mandy? You have a call on one," Pat told me from the doorway.

"Thanks, Pat." I picked up the receiver hoping it wasn't a cancel from Frank.

"Hey." The familiar voice of Jill came through the receiver. "Just checking to see how you are. Is everything alright? I haven't heard from you."

"Everything's okay, in fact, you'll be happy to hear that I'm having lunch with that police lieutenant today," I informed her visualizing her face breaking into a huge smile.

"Alright! I knew he was interested. Let me know how that turns out. I'd better let you go, or you'll be late."

As I hung up I looked at my watch and discovered that it was twelve noon. Where was Frank? Poking my head out of the office, I asked if I'd had any other calls. It seemed unlikely that he'd forgotten, but he wasn't here and he hadn't called. How strange was that? Pulling his card out of my pocket I dialed his office number. Perhaps some big crime had been committed and he was involved in dealing with it.

"No Lieutenant Adams is not available, who's calling?" the business like voice responded to my inquiry.

"This is Mandy Minton; we had an appointment at 11:30. Is he tied up on another case?" I asked, twisting the phone cord around my finger, anticipating the day was not going to go the way I'd hoped.

"Mandy Minton, just a minute," the voice instructed.

I waited feeling disappointment creeping into my mind. We weren't going to meet for lunch that was obvious, and maybe not at all today. The disappointment increased as the minutes clicked by. Was it just because I wanted this mysterious business cleared up or was I also disappointed at not seeing Frank Adams? Or maybe both.

"Ms. Minton?" the voice came back on the line.

"Yes, I'm here."

"Ms. Minton, the lieutenant had an accident and won't be able to keep your appointment. Lieutenant John Jarvis will be taking his cases. I'll put you through to him." Before I could speak, the voice was gone and the phone was ringing through to another extension.

An accident? The voice didn't say he wouldn't be able to meet with you today. It said 'he won't be able to meet with you,' period. A male voice interrupted my thoughts. "Ms. Minton, this is..."

"Wait!" I instructed. "I want to know where Frank is."

Silence filled the phone. I waited, and then heard a deep breath as he prepared to answer my demand. "Mandy? Mandy is it? I see in Frank's case file that he has been working on your home break in..."

"Where is he?" I made my demand again not letting him finish his sentence.

"Perhaps we should meet..."

"Where is he?!"

A big sigh surged through the phone line. "Frank is in the hospital. He was involved in a hit and run this morning on the way into the station."

"No!" I told the receiver in my hand. "No! It can't be! Which hospital?"

"Ms. Minton, he isn't receiving visitors."

"You don't understand. He was hit on purpose. This was no accident. Do you have a guard on him?" I asked, my words rushing to keep up with my thoughts.

"What?! How do you know?"

"Lieutenant Jarvis, meet me at the hospital we can talk there."

"Ahh, okay. Good Sam in 20 minutes."

I hurried to my car, only to find that it had a flat tire. Why do these things happen when you're in a hurry? And those are new tires. Retracing my steps back into the building I asked Pat to call a cab. I went back into my office and called the Firestone people and made arrangements for them to change and fix the tire, leaving my car keys with Pat, I headed outside again.

"Hey! Did I hear Pat calling you a cab? Where's your car?" The mailroom kid, Matt, was taking the steps two at a time to reach me. He was probably all of 18 or 19-years-old and had an obvious crush on me always going out of his way to deliver my mail first, offering to run errands, and always wearing a huge grin.

"Yes, I have a flat tire."

"Hey, I can fix that easy," he offered.

"Thanks Matt, but I have someone coming to fix it." Then it occurred to me. What if the military guys had flattened that tire, knowing that I'd call a cab? What if they had someone driving the cab? "Matt, are you off now?"

"No, not really, I'm just on a break," he said looking a little sheepish.

"Do you have a car? Could you drive me to Good Sam, you know, it's just over on NW 20th?"

"Sure I have a car, but it's not much to look at."

"I promise I won't look at it, I just have to get to the hospital right away."

"Are you sick?" A sudden look of concern replaced the smile lines from the lower part of his face and stuck them onto his forehead.

"No, no, it's not me, but someone I know has had an accident," I explained, as we headed into the parking garage to his car.

He was right, it wasn't much to look at. It was an old Chevy, wearing only a coat of primer. Before I could even get in he had to shovel off the front seat. It was littered with junk food wrappers and paper cups. A thought briefly touched down in my mind. What if the cabby was safe and Matt was the one set up to keep me from the hospital?

No, I had to draw the 'fear' line somewhere; besides this kid was someone I knew and he definitely wasn't prepared to have a passenger in his car. I climbed into his questionable chariot, but it rose above its appearance and ran like a top. He probably spends most of his spare time tinkering with it while eating junk food.

At the hospital, the front desk insisted that Frank Adams was not to have visitors. I was about to argue with them when a voice said, "Ms. Minton?" I turned to find a very tall thin man, in a less than fresh gray suit, facing me. His chiseled features looked drawn and serious.

"Yes, are you Lieutenant Jarvis?"

"Yes, madam." He nodded at the girl behind the desk, took my arm and directed me down the hall and into the elevator. We were alone in the small cubical, so I asked, "Did you beef up security already?" I was thinking about the girl at the front desk that wouldn't tell me anything.

He was studying me as I spoke, then without answering my question, he said, "Tell me why you think Frank was hit on purpose." He waited, still studying me.

Then it occurred to me that he was wondering how I could have this information, 'he' already knew that it was no accident. I looked him right in the eye and asked, "You know that it wasn't an accident don't you?"

"Yes," he responded, "but how do *you* know that?"

"It's such a long and confusing story, but in a nut shell, he was checking on more than the attempted burglary. There have been several attempts to kidnap my daughter and I think these same people have now run him down to keep him from helping me." This was as close to the truth as I could come. There was no way I was going to tell him about the dreams, the dog, or about the Boogie Man, who pops in and out of my dreams and my real life.

The elevator stopped, the doors opened and I found myself looking right into the face of the bogus insurance man! I recoiled with a gasp and breathing out came in the form of words, "No! Oh no!" I grabbed Lieutenant Jarvis' arm and said, "That's him…"

Jarvis was big, but he wasn't slow. Without asking questions he immediately stepped in front of the man, blocking his entrance into the elevator. "Sir, may I speak to you for a moment?"

The look the man gave me was full of anger. No it was more than anger, it was pure venom, but his eyes cleared and his face changed before he turned to Lieutenant Jarvis with, "But of course. What can I do for you?"

They stepped off to the side, out of the traffic pattern to the elevator. I looked around for more police, but saw none. A few steps to the left I saw the nurses' station, so I walked to the desk and asked to be directed to Frank Adams' room. The nurse behind the desk was obviously an old hand at her job. Her hair was a no nonsense style, her make-up minimum, her nails short and her professional attitude said that she was capable of handling everything and anything that might happen. I hoped that she could, because she may have to. Unaware of the scrutiny, the nurse looked briefly at her ledger, and without changing expression said, "I'm sorry…"

I interrupted her with, "Yes, I know, I'm with Lieutenant Jarvis," and nodded with a glanced towards the elevator, where Jarvis and the bogus insurance man were talking. The nurse glanced in that direction too. I said in a low tense voice, "There may be trouble, show me the room that's under security, and do it now!"

I watched as her hand reached for the hospital security button on the phone. Nodding my head, I said. "Good, we may need them." That seemed to break the ice. The nurse pushed the button and came out from behind the desk and walked briskly past me, saying as she did, "That military type," and she nodded towards the elevator, "was asking for him, just before you two arrived. He didn't find out anything."

I was certain of that; this woman wouldn't be someone that could be sweet-talked. I glance back towards Jarvis and the bogus insurance man and was surprise to see the area where they had been talking was empty. *How strange, where did they go?* I wondered, as I followed the nurse down the hall. Maybe Jarvis arrested him.

Frank's room was around the corner near the end of a quiet hall. The hallway was clear of people. No policeman sitting in front of the door, as I'd expected. The nurse pushed open the door and we entered the room. Frank lay in the bed covered with bandages, and casts. The only parts of his face that showed were covered with welts, bruises and abrasions. *My God! They must have hit him with a truck.* He lay very still, his breathing was ragged.

"What's the extent of his injuries?" I asked not taking my eyes off of the traumatized man in front of me.

Reaching for the chart the nurse asked, "In layman?" I nodded a yes. Knowing I would be unable to speak just then.

"He has a broken leg, arm and rib, plus extensive superficial wounds. No skull fracture, no lung puncture and no detected internal injuries. He has, however, been unconscious since he came in."

She put the chart back and turned to leave. Then she asked, "Was this deliberate?"

"Why do you ask?"

"Why else the security?" she shrugged.

"Yes it was, so it's important that no strangers get in here."

She nodded and as she opened the door, she was met by two of the hospitals security people. They were alert and looked like they knew there way around. The older of the two looked past the nurse as she quietly talked to them. His eyes met mine and then moved over to the bed.

"Wait a minute. Is that Frank Adams?" he asked, to no one in particular, as he stepped around the nurse and walked into the room. "My God, what happened to him? We worked together back a few years ago, when I was with the department." He moved to the head of the bed and spoke out loud, "Hey Frank, its Al. Al Simons. You hang in there, Frank. I'll watch your back, just like always."

It was very slight, but Frank moved. His mouth twitched. I glanced up at Al. A smile was slowly spreading itself across his face. "He hears me alright. Okay Lou, we've got to talk about shift changes," he said as he turned to the other security man in the doorway.

"You," he said, looking at me, "you with the department? Related?"

He was abrupt, not giving me a chance to answer his first question before moving on to the second, but I liked him. He was experienced, tough, knew his stuff and liked Frank. "Friend," I said quietly.

He raised his eyebrows just slightly and he smiled. "We'll take good care of him." Both men were wearing blue security uniforms, not unlike the local police attire. The big difference was that these uniforms did not include a gun. They had a Billy club, a Walkie-talkie and hand restraints, but no guns. Apparently security in a hospital wouldn't normally require a gun, but I would have felt better if he'd had a gun on him.

The nurse had gone back to her station and Lou was waiting. "We need to talk," I said softly to Al. He seemed like a life raft in a storm.

He nodded and said, "I'll be back." His squared jaw twitching, his five o'clock shadow was well in progress on his well-worn face. Then he left with Lou.

"Oh Frank, I'm so sorry," I said, as I laid my hand over his. "This is my fault. I got you involved."

His hand twitched slightly under mine. Was it a nerve or was he reacting to my statement? Suddenly I realized what time it was. I had to pick up Naja soon. "Listen Frank, I have to go and get Naja, but I'll be back. I think that your old friend Al is going to hang out here, so you just rest and get better in a hurry." As I turned to leave, I discovered Al standing in the doorway.

"You're right Miss, I'm here and I'll take care of him."

"Listen Al. Trust no one, this was deliberate. I have to run, but I'll talk to you later."

He nodded and walked into the room.

As I reached the elevators I remembered Lieutenant Jarvis. What had happened to him, and what about the bogus insurance guy? Where were they? Checking him into jail, I hope. All the way out of the hospital I kept looking for Jarvis. Why did he leave me, a complete stranger to him, to go into a secured room unsupervised? Something was wrong.

I stepped out to the cabstand and the first cab drove up. I'd already been through this. I walked past him and past number two, opened the front door of cab number three and looked the driver over. His face matched the picture on the visor and I didn't get any bad feelings about him, so I got in.

When I arrived back at the office, to pick up my car, I saw Matt's smiling face peering out of the lobby window. He darted outside and said. "I fixed your tire and sent those other jokers away. Both companies." He was grinning from ear to ear.

"Thank you, Matt, you didn't have to do that," I said grinning back at him. "Wait. Both companies?"

"Yea, Firestone and the other company. I don't remember the name."

Two companies? I'd only sent for Firestone.

Then his smile left and he hung his head. "What?" I questioned.

"I did do something else." He glanced at me and then down at his feet.

There's more? "What else?" I asked almost afraid to hear the answer.

"I told the cop and that other guy that your car was over on the other side of the parking."

"Cop?"

"Yea, he wanted to see your car. I thought maybe he was going to give you a ticket or somethin'."

My mind had gone slack. A cop wanted to see my car?

"I'm sorry. I just don't like cops. Actually, all he did was look at the front end of the car that I told him was yours. No ticket."

He just looked at the front end? Frank! He was checking to see if I was the one who ran Frank down. Well, I'm glad that they were checking out everyone involved with Frank, but why me and what other guy?

"Matt. What 'other' guy?"

"That was kinda strange. He came and wanted to know which car was yours, so I pointed out the car that the cop was looking at, but he took one look at the cop and split."

"What did these men look like?"

"Which ones? The tow truck guys, the Firestone guys, the cop, or the other guy?"

"All of them, I guess." Matt was back to his old self. He was the center of attention and loving it. The earring in his ear was dancing up and down as he bounced about.

"Well... let's see. The cop, came first he was here when I got back he was tall, blond and smoked a lot. The Tow truck guys, just your normal excon types," he said grinning. "The Firestone guy was young, about my age with blond hair. The other guy was another excon type."

"Wait, what do you mean 'excon' type?"

"You know short hair, serious face, generally tough looking."

"Perhaps like they'd been in the military?"

"Yea, that's it. They looked like retired green berets."

Oh no, these guys were everywhere. Nothing's safe. "Thanks Matt, you did great. I've got to run," I told him as I hurried towards my car. "It's time to pick up my daughter."

He stood there grinning, as I drove past him. I quickly dialed the schools number. I suddenly had a funny feeling about Naja's safety.

"Hi, this is Mandy…" I didn't get to finish, as Miss Susan interrupted.

"Mandy, I'm so glad you called. Are you alright?"

Oh no, something was wrong. "Yes, I'm fine. Is Naja okay?" My heart was doing flip-flops in my chest. *Oh God, let Naja be alright.*

"Oh yes, she's fine, but I had a call saying that you'd had a problem and someone else would be picking her up. I told them that she'd be staying with me indefinitely unless I heard from you directly. I hope that's all right with you. I just can't let any of my children leave here with just anybody."

Thank God for this blessed woman. I breathed a huge sigh of relief. "Thank you. I definitely agree with you. My problem wasn't that big, a little car trouble, but I'm almost there now. Thanks again, I'll see you in a few minutes." Who called her? Well, obviously the same people who flattened my tire, ran down Frank, and visited my car in the lot.

When I reached the pre-school, there were a couple of parents talking to Miss Susan, so I signaled to her that I'd call her later and she nodded.

"I hear that you had car problems." A mature question from a mature little 5-year-old, I thought as I helped her into the car.

"Yes, just a flat tire. A guy at the office fixed it for me, but I was afraid that I'd be late picking you up."

"Was it Matt?" she asked.

"Yes, do you remember him?"

"Sure, he wears an earring. Miss Susan said that I could stay with her *indef-in-ly*. What does that mean?" she asked, just like she always did when she discovered a new word.

"Well, indefinitely means for as long as necessary."

"Forever even?"

"Yes, forever if necessary."

Naja sat there with a serious expression, on her face, as she digested this information. After she was satisfied that she had that little tidbit filed away she said, "Guess what happened today?"

Oh no, more problems? "What?" I asked thinking of the Boogie Man.

"Jerry fell down and had blood coming out of his mouth!" She looked at me with great expectations. Apparently this was a big deal to her. To me, it was a big relief. "Oh no! Poor Jerry," I responded with a great display of emotion.

"Yes. Miss Susan said his tooth cut his lip." Again she waited for a reaction. I gave her what she was waiting for, but couldn't help thinking of the traumatized face I'd seen today on Lieutenant Frank Adams.

We'd just gotten into the house, when the doorbell rang. Looking out of the little peek hole I discovered my neighbor Mary peering back at me.

"Mary. What brings you calling?" I asked as I opened the door. Mary stood there, silent for a moment, while she and her brown and beige clothing blended into the very space around her. She must have been one of those undercover cops, because I was sure that no one would notice her.

"We need to talk," she said. No hello, no smile, just 'we need to talk.'

"Sure, come in. I'll put the coffee and the cartoons on," I said nodding towards Naja.

"Great!" Naja said, as she ran into the living room, her little blond pony tail swinging along from side to side.

I put the coffee on, set Naja up with cartoons and a snack, and then turned to Mary, who sat at the table saying nothing. She seemed to be a person without humor, her mouth never experiencing that turning up at the ends movement that ends in a smile.

"Okay, what?" I asked, handing her a mug of coffee. This talking with police at my kitchen table was getting to be a habit. Naja liked it, she'd watched more cartoons in the last couple of days than she usually did in a week.

"You tell me," Mary said looking me squarely in the eyes.

I took a sip of coffee before asking, "What is it you want to know, Mary?" How much did she already know? Why was she here questioning me? I cautiously wondered.

"What the hell is going on? That's what! Frank is a good friend of mine and I think that you somehow, know something about what happened to him today." She used strong words, but kept her voice down and did not really show strong emotion. She was very controlled and wanted answers.

I leaned back in my chair. Where do I begin? "Mary…I don't' know where to start." She sat there, sipped her coffee, never taking her eyes from my face, and waited. That must be something they learn in police school. I thought, remembering that Frank Adams had done that very same thing when I met him in his office. "There have been several attempted kidnappings of Naja," I said lowering my voice, and looking briefly towards the living room.

Mary looked surprised, and then her entire attitude softened. Not much, but a little. Perhaps she did have a bit of sensitivity after all.

"I think that Lieutenant Adams was run down by the men who tried to break into my house and who have been after…" I nodded towards the living room. "Probably because he was going to help us."

The coffee mug was forgotten in Mary's hand and she was deep in thought. I watched, as the wheels turned inside of that experienced mind, and waited to see what was going to come out of that thinking. After a couple of seconds Mary returned from speculations and met my gaze. This time it was my turn to wait.

"What about Lieutenant Jarvis?" Mary finally broke the silence and asked, setting her mug down.

"Yes, what about Lieutenant Jarvis? He left me at the hospital when we went to see Frank. He just left."

"Lieutenant Jarvis has disappeared. He was last seen with you." Her attitude had resumed its rigid business like state.

"What! Disappeared! Oh God! As we were getting off of the elevator I pointed out one of the men that's been after…" Again I glanced at the living room, but Naja was deeply engrossed in *Blue's Clues*. "He stopped the guy and I went on in to see Frank. I never saw him again." I was starting to feel sick. This was becoming more than I could handle; Frank in the hospital and Jarvis missing. If the cops couldn't deal with these guys, how could I? I must have expressed my feelings of fear on my face because Mary set her cup down and leaned towards me, her attitude completely different now, in fact, it was almost maternal.

"Relax. You'll be okay. Take a couple of deep breaths, don't let fear get a grip on you."

'Don't let fear get a grip on you.' That sounded familiar. How much did this woman know? Did she share Frank's information? Had she also been in Franks dream meeting? I sat there staring at her, completely unaware of my kitchen, and completely unaware of Mary's presences. I'd retreated to a safe place within. Mary patted my hand and it brought me back. I couldn't afford to retreat, I had to take care of Naja, I had to keep her safe.

"Mary… what'll I do? What if they get my baby?" I was near tears. I was losing it.

Mary dug a nail into my finger just hard enough to cause pain, but not to break the skin. It brought me back into control over my emotions and my fear. Mary was staring hard at me, willing me to shape up.

"I'm okay," I said and attempted a weak smile.

"I'm on my way to see Frank now…"

I interrupted her with, "Oh, I'm going to go back up later."

"No, you stay with the little one and get some rest. I'll let you know if there's any change."

I opened my mouth to object, but closed it at the firm expression I encountered. Instead I asked, "Do you know Al Simon?"

"Yea, I heard that he's security at that hospital now. You see him?"

"Yes, he told Frank that he'd watch his back and Frank's mouth twitched. I know that he heard him."

Mary's eyes came to life and she straightened her back preparing to stand up. "Good! He and Al use to be partners years ago when Frank was a rookie. Al will watch out for him alright." She pushed her chair back, picked up her mug and took it to the sink. Then turning back to me she said, "Why the attempted grab? Can't be money, this is a nice place, but not an indication of big bucks."

Oh dear, now what? I hesitated. I couldn't tell her about the Indigo kid theory. "I don't know," I said simply. I was so tired of saying that.

Mary studied my face for a second and started towards the door.

"Mary, would you tell Frank that I won't be coming up to the hospital? I told him I'd be back. I don't want him to think that I just forgot or something. I'm sure he can hear you even though he's unconscious."

She nodded her head, waved her hand, opened the door and left. Even though I could hear the TV in the other room, I could also feel the silence that was enveloping the house. For the first time I felt afraid to be alone, I'd never felt fear of being alone in this house before. Fear is like a growing cancer, I decided, as I stood up went to the front door locked it and then set the alarm.

Back in the kitchen I put the mugs into the dishwasher, just to be doing something. When I turned back towards the table, the White Dog was standing behind me. He wagged his tail and then walked the few steps to me. His nose was cool and wet as he pressed it against my hand. I knelt down and buried my face in his soft warm coat. I didn't cry, but I did draw strength from this wonderful Guardian Angel of Naja's. Was he here to protect Naja or to give me the security that I needed at this time? I really didn't care, as long as he was here I felt one hundred percent better already.

"Look who's here?" I called to Naja. "Thank you," I whispered to the dog. He licked my cheek in response.

Dinner was simple, Naja didn't care and the dog enjoyed the pasta just as much as she did. Unfortunately, I didn't even taste it and only went through the motions of eating. After getting Naja and the dog settled in, I too headed for bed. It had been a trying day. I was suddenly so tired that pulling off my shoes seemed to be a big project.

I sat on the edge of the bed and wondered about Frank Adams. What had he been going to tell me that was so important that someone had tried to kill him? No! I was too tired to deal with this now. I pulled my clothes off and slid into bed without even hanging them in the closet. Tomorrow. I'd put everything away tomorrow.

~

Whispering voices were drifting past my ears, circling my head and drifting by again. Did I care if someone was whispering? No, I didn't. Then I heard my name, faintly, but it was definitely my name. With a big sigh, I forced my eyes open.

"Well, I guess she's gonna join us after all," said the smiling face directly in front of me.

Lindy! What was Lindy doing here? "Lindy? What's up?" I managed to ask softly, as my eyelids drooped and slowly closed again.

"What's up?! That's what we'd like to know. Are you here or aren't you?"

What was she talking about? Lifting my lids once again, I noticed more faces studying me. "Oh! Good grief! Are we at the Dream Meeting?" I was awake now, glancing about quickly, discovering that we were, indeed, at the Dream Meeting and I, apparently, was the center of attention.

"Well that's a first."

"Yeah, can you sleep in a dream?"

"Honey, are you okay?" Sally's face moved into view, looking very concerned.

"Oh boy, I'm sorry. I was so tired…" I started to explain, still feeling groggy.

"Well, we could see that, but you sure scared us."

"It's so strange, I feel like I've been drugged. Usually, I feel fine at these meetings. Alert and all." The faces and the room were finally settling down, and the faces became normal and no longer looked like bloated balloons drifting aimlessly around my head.

"So Sleeping Beauty, if you'll pull yourself together, we'd like to know how your meeting went with the cop. Is that why you're so tired?" asked a grinning Lindy.

"Let's sit and hear what Mandy has to share with us," came the logical advise from Rachael. She chose a chair facing me; obviously she didn't want to miss a word and wanted to get a firsthand reaction as well.

I just sat there, still not feeling quite with it. "Why would I feel this tired when I'm asleep and dreaming?" I asked no one in particular and expected no answer and got none.

However, there was one possible answer and it made sense, as explained through Rachael's well-organized mind. "You apparently went through a highly emotional situation today. This hasn't been brought on by physical stress or exertion, it seems to be from extreme emotional stress," Rachael was explaining to the group, as well as to me.

I wasn't surprised that she had the answer. She was a very wise woman. I hope that I have that much wisdom when I get older, but then immediately felt sad, as I realized that I may not live that long. Not after today's happenings. The heavy silence in the room brought me back. I hadn't realized that my head was hanging down and tears were slowly making their way down my cheeks.

"I'm sorry," I said wiping my face with the back of my hand, "you just have no idea what kind of a day it turned into. I just don't know what to do next."

"Tell us, Mandy."

"Maybe we can help."

"Is Naja alright?"

As they gently asked their questions I realized that I wasn't alone, at least not in my dreams. They deserved to know and they deserved to have a leader who didn't give up. I pulled myself up straighter in the chair, adjusted my position and smiled weakly. "You know, I think I love you guys!" Cheers went up and there were smiling faces everywhere. "I almost allowed him to win! Fear was overpowering me." I told them, then turned slightly in my chair, looked at the open doorway leading to the hall and said loud and clear, **"Didn't work, Boogie Man! Close, but no cigar!"** More cheers and catcalls from the group. We were working together and the support felt wonderful, like a shot of adrenalin.

"Okay, here's what happened." I began at the very beginning and didn't finish until I'd shared it all. They were quiet throughout the entire story, absorbing the details, holding their questions until later. From their faces I could tell that they were also trying to come up with some answers. I prayed that they would, because I had run out of ideas.

"Oh dear!" I mumbled out loud.

"What!?"

"What Mandy?"

Even though I'd spoken quietly, they had picked up on my words after I remembered that I hadn't called Miss Susan as promised. "The pre-school teacher, I was supposed to do some explaining to her. She deserves to know why police are checking on Naja, why she got a phone call about my car problem," I explained, feeling like I'd really dropped the ball.

"She'll understand."

"Yeah, you've had a busy day."

I looked at Teri and said, "What would your reaction be if all of these strange things had been happening to you and your school?"

Without any hesitation, she answered, "I'd want some answers. If someone, for whatever reason, was possibly putting the rest of the children in any kind of a negative situation that I couldn't control, I'd probably ask them to not come back." She shrugged her shoulders and said, "Sorry Mandy."

"You're right and I feel the same way. Tomorrow I'm taking a long overdue vacation. I'll keep Naja home with me."

"Will you go somewhere?"

"Yeah, you could still join us at night from no matter where you were," Shala encouraged.

"No! Mandy, don't leave. I think you're better off staying in your own home court. You can't ditch these guys, especially the Boogie Man. You need to be where you know your way around and can tell who the players are."

I held up my hand, because I could see some of the others were going to have a lot of conversation about this. "Wait. My leaving is not an option." I held up my hand again, as I saw some of the objections begin with the expressions on their faces. "Really, I'm not leaving. Naja and I could go off to some strange place and disappear and no one would even know it. No, we have to stay here where we are known and would be missed."

"What about some of us moving in with you? Temporarily, of course," asked Lindy. "You know safety in numbers and all that. We could form a commune."

"It's not a bad idea," ventured Sally cautiously.

"Yeah it is," Ron stated without hesitation. "Mandy and Naja have been having all sorts of trouble, while all we've had is that scary jerk creeping around now and then. If we start hanging out with Mandy, we'll be right in there in the front line."

I expected all hell to break loose and have another big debate, but there was nothing but silence sitting solidly in the room. I looked around the room and was unable to meet anyone's eyes. Who could blame them? No one wants to put their own children in the line of fire.

"Besides, I don't think my wife would understand my staying with a lovely gringo woman while she works," Ramon explained logically.

"Thanks guys, but Ron and Ramon are right. The best thing you can do for me is to help me think. I'm really at my wit's end."

"Then let's begin!"

"Yeah, let's begin with the status of the Boogie Man."

"No, let's talk about Frank's comments. He said that he too had been in a dream group. He also said that the Boogie Man usually works alone. Does this mean anything?" I asked, knowing that I was really grasping at straws. "Who are those other guys, and why do they want to stop Naja?"

"They're government."

"Yeah, they certainly sound like it. The professionalism, the big black cars, the military look and actions."

"But why would the government be after a little girl?"

"Or…maybe they're…what do ya call them…?"

"Mercenaries!" Ron filled in the term.

"Yes, ex-military trained and working for hire," added Pete.

"Don't forget the mission."

"The kids' mission, but when was that mission going to be, when they're 20, 30, 40? Do we have to go through this for the next 15 or 20 years?!" I suddenly asked, feeling the pressure and the responsibility. The others were still, considering the situation, but no one had an answer. Children were a lifetime commitment, for better or worse.

Day Nine

"Mommy! Mommy aren't you going to answer the phone?" The dog barked as they both jumped onto the bed following Naja's question. Bedlam reigned, as Naja and the White Dog clamored over me squealing, barking and completely trashing the bed. My day had definitely begun. Scrambling to free my arm from the tangled sheet I reached the phone just as it stopped ringing.

"OUT!" I shouted and pointed towards the bedroom door. Both kid and dog jumped off of the bed and ran crashing through the doorway, still laughing and barking. "Whew." I breathed in relief. What a pair. I wasn't sure what was going to be the toughest job, protecting them or taking care of them.

Pulling myself out of the tangled bed I was just shoving an arm into the sleeve of my robe when the doorbell rang several times. Naja and the dog both became silent at the sound. I glanced into Naja's bedroom before going down the stairs to the door and both were sitting on the floor looking at me. "You two stay here," I told them adding emphasis with a pointed finger. Before I reached the bottom of the stairs, someone started pounding on the door. On the other side of the peek hole was Mary's stern face. I quickly opened the door.

"Mary! What is it? Is it Frank?"

"Whata ya mean, 'What is it?' You tell me! I called twice; I knew you were here, why didn't you answer the phone?" She was upset and angry.

A loud warning beep sounded from the alarm. Mary froze, taking a defensive stance.

"It's the new alarm system," I explained as I stepped over to the wall and punched in the code, shutting down the alarm before it activated.

"Come in, I'll fix some coffee." She stepped past me and headed for the kitchen, as I closed the door.

"Okay you two come on down for breakfast," I called up the staircase. As I entered the kitchen, Mary had just finishing putting the coffee on. Wow, how'd she know where things were kept?

"Thanks Mary. Can I hire you to come in every morning?" I smiled at her, but Mary didn't answer, she apparently wasn't going to be sweet-talked. She just pulled out a chair and sat down. Then she opened her mouth to say something, but never got the chance as Naja and the dog came bounding into the kitchen.

"Who's that? I didn't know you had a dog!" The White Dog came equipped with outstanding manners. He stopped romping with Naja, walked up to Mary, sat down and put his front paw on her knee. She was definitely a dog person, and melted instantly. The dog on the other hand, was definitely a diplomat and knew how to win someone over.

I set Naja up with cereal and milk in front of the TV again, this was definitely becoming a habit, but obviously Mary and I had to talk. Naja started to object, but the dog led the way into the living room just as if he understood.

"Well, you've got a security system and a big dog now, it looks like you're in good shape. Good thing too, 'cause that big black car cruised by a couple of times early this morning."

I started to stand up and automatically glanced at the window. "Relax, I called it in and that's one of the reasons I'm here." I eased back into my chair, but still felt tense. Perhaps I should get dressed and be ready for anything.

"Mary, I think that I should put some clothes on. I need to be ready…"

"Wait a few moments, you're okay. I want to tell you something."

I eased back into my chair and picked up my cup, giving Mary the lead. Actually, I welcomed the fact that an experienced person was here willing to help.

"The car is registered to an untraceable department in the U.S. Government." Mary watched my face for a reaction.

I was aware that I wasn't showing the surprise that would be normal, but the dream group had already guessed this information. All I could say was, "Why would the U.S. Government try to kidnap Naja?"

Mary studied my face closely, trying to decide if I was one of those people who just didn't react instantly, or if I knew more than I'd told her. Finally she said, "Sometimes a splinter group within our government decides to make decisions and act upon them on their own, for whatever reason. I think that this has happened here. The question is…what is it about," she nodded her head towards the living room, "the little one, that makes her a focus?" Again, she watched my face trying to analyze my reaction, and again, she saw that I didn't react as a normal mother would at that statement, an actress I'm not.

"She's only 5, what reason could they have to eliminate her?"

Her eyes narrowed slightly, as she continued to study me. "I didn't say that they wanted to eliminate her."

Oops. I guess that I contributed too much. I tried to recoup. "Well, why else would they try to get her? You said yourself that I don't have enough money to support a ransom." I knew that my answer didn't make sense, but it was the best I could do. "Are you, with your connections, able to find out why they want her?" I asked trying to redirect the attention.

Then suddenly I'm sure that my face did show expression, I could feel my face give way to a very concerned expression, as I leaned towards Mary and said, "Mary, you must be very careful! Everyone who has tried to help me has had something happen to them."

Mary relaxed her stern face and nodded. "Don't worry about me, I've been around a very long time and I plan to be around a lot longer."

"Mary, I'm serious. Look what happened to Frank, and what about Jarvis?"

"To begin with, Frank and John were caught off guard. I have an advantage. I've been alerted. I know I'm up against something bigger than usual and that gives me an edge." She looked like she believed this. She looked like she felt very confident, like she could handle herself. God, I hoped so. Then I remembered the Boogie Man.

"Mary, there's something else you have to know." The expression on her face said she knew that I'd been holding out on her. "I don't know how to explain this, and I hope you don't think that I'm one of those 'fruit loops,' but... there is another man...he isn't one of the military types, he has light hair, blue eyes, and isn't bad looking. He...well, he...just sorta appears. He doesn't talk, but he tries to intimate with fear. Naja's seen him too, she saw him talking to the military guys in front of her day care, and the White Dog doesn't like him." I finished with the last as if that proved my point.

"Are you talking about that blue-eyed man?" A small voice asked from the doorway. "She's right, the dog growls and shows his teeth."

"Really? Well, you know what they say. You can trust your dog's instincts, so you pay attention when he lets you know something isn't right. Okay?"

Mary's full attention was now directed toward Naja. "What does this blue-eyed man say to you?"

"Oh, he never says anything, he just looks at me."

"Does this scare you?"

Naja climbed up into the chair beside Mary as she said. "No, but I think that he wants me to be scared, but I'm not. Why does he want me to be afraid of him?" The innocent question stopped Mary momentarily. She took a couple of seconds to formulate an answer.

"I don't know, some people like to upset other people. How come he doesn't upset you?" She slipped in the question tactfully, and leaned back casually to take a sip of her coffee, like the question wasn't really important; like they were just chatting, while I waited on the edge of my chair for the answer. I considered the answer to that question to be very important and was very interested in hearing why she wasn't afraid of this man.

Naja looked thoughtful and then said, "I think that he's not a very happy man. No one likes him, even the dog. I think that's very sad." She looked up, and cut Mary off, just as she opened her mouth to say something. "I'm careful. He's dangerous you know." She was nodding her head up and down and had a very knowledgeable look on her face. Once again Mary started to speak and Naja spoke, "Mom told me and so did the White Dog." It was as if she was anticipating the questions or... reading Mary's mind.

Mary didn't exactly look confused, but she did look like she'd been stopped in her tracks and had lost control of the situation. This wasn't exactly how she had expected the conversation to go. Police, even ex-police like to be in control of their interrogations. "Well, I'm glad you're careful and that your dog is also doing his job."

"Oh, he's not my dog. Mommy says he's a free soul," Naja quickly told her. "He does what he wants and comes to see me when he wants to. Maybe when he misses me," she added with a grin.

Mary turned and looked down the hallway. "Where is he now?"

"He left. I told you, he comes and goes whenever he wants to."

Mary glanced at me with a huge question on her face. I just nodded and smiled.

"Who let him out? I didn't hear the door open," Mary continued her probing.

"Well you know...that is kinda strange. He lets himself out I guess. He comes and he goes. No one lets him in or out." Naja admitted this as being out of the ordinary, but it didn't seem to bother her.

It did bother Mary, however. She had stiffened noticeably and had a strange expression on her face. Naja must have noticed the change in Mary too, because she leaned towards her and said in a quiet voice, "It's okay, he does it all of the time and it doesn't set off the alarm or anything." Mary sat there, very still. She was either in deep thought or in shock. I just waited.

Finally, Mary turned towards me. I nodded my head and shrugged. There was no way I could help her to understand...I didn't understand myself.

"Ahhh, well...yes, that's good." She struggled to regain her composure.

"How often does he visit you?" she asked Naja. I had the feeling that she was actually just asking the question automatically, until she could get it all back together, rather than gathering pertinent information.

"Oh, whenever he wants to. He always comes when the man with the blue eyes comes around. Yes, he always comes then." Naja was bobbing her little head up and down, in an affirmative action, her blond hair dancing around her shoulders.

Mary suddenly came alive. "Does this mean that the blue-eyed guy was here this morning?" She'd been looking at Naja, but glanced at me as she asked the question.

She obviously didn't understand what was going on with the dog thing, but it only slowed her down momentarily. She'd recouped and was alert to the situation, putting what she didn't understand aside to study later. I marveled at her flexibility.

"He came last night," Naja volunteered, "I didn't see the man, but I bet he was here somewhere."

I decided that it was definitely time to contribute to this conversation. "I have to agree with Naja. If the dog was here, so was the Boogie Man." Oops! I hadn't meant to say that.

"Boogie Man!?" Naja asked her eyes wide.

"Yes honey, that's what I call him, because he tries to scare us." I hoped she'd accept this and not freak at the name most kids get upset about.

"YES! That's the perfect name. He is trying to be a Boogie Man. Ha, Ha." She clapped her hands together and laughed.

Thank heaven, I breathed. I'd completely forgotten about Mary while talking to Naja. Turning my head towards her I found that she was studying me with curiosity. I just raised my eyebrows and smiled, what else was there to do?

"Mommy, are we going to meet Jill and Sam at the park?"

"Oh, I forgot …no, no park today."

"It's because of the guys that came to school isn't it?" She turned and explained to Mary.

"They're friends of the Boogie Man and the police came and everything. They waited for us at the park one day and a dirty woman told us to watch out. We bought her lunch. We have to be careful now." Good grief, I was shocked; I had no idea that Naja was so aware of what was going on.

Again, Mary glanced at me for confirmation. I opened my mouth to speak, but was interrupted by the phone ringing. Both Mary and I jumped a foot, at the sudden harsh sound.

"Mary, it's for you," I said carrying the phone to her.

"Naja, why don't you go and get dressed. Put on play clothes, it's going to be a fun day today." She raced down the hall and up the stairs, giggling and laughing all the way. I turned back to Mary as she was hanging up the phone.

"Sorry, I told the department where I was going when you didn't answer the phone, in case something was wrong. They were just following up."

"Mary, how was Frank? Did you talk to Al? Do they know any more?"

"Whoa girl. First, Frank is the same. Yes I talked to Al and he spent the night in Frank's room, and they do not know any more, including where John is. Now…"

I held up my hand to stop the questions I knew were coming and that she deserved to have answers to. "Mary…I know…but she'll," and I pointed to the ceiling, "be back way too soon for me to fill you in right now. It's a long…long and strange story. I sure wish Frank were awake. He knows about this Boogie Man, the White Dog and…" I broke it off, before saying the dream meeting.

Mary nodded as she stood up. "Okay, but we **are** going to talk. You really have a lot of explaining to do. A lot!"

"I know," I muttered, wondering how I was ever going to explain all of this to her.

"Now, what are your plans for today?"

"Well, I want to go up and see Frank, then maybe lunch and some shopping."

Mary fished around in her pocket and pulled out a card. Here is my number I want you to call me every two hours." She held up both hands as I started to protest. "Either that or I'm going with you." She looked like she wasn't about to back down, so I nodded my head and took the card. Then she added, "Are you sure that you want to take her to see Frank in his present condition?"

I considered for a moment, I hadn't thought about that, he did look pretty bad. "I guess you're right, we'd better skip the hospital visit. Perhaps, we'll shop, do lunch and pack it in with a couple of videos to watch here at home, but I can't just hole up here forever." I wasn't happy with the idea of being forced into hiding out in my own house, even if it was the safest place.

Mary was heading for the door; she turned and pointed to the card in my hand. "Every two hours."

"Gotcha." I closed and bolted the door after Mary. I noticed that her foot steps didn't leave the porch until after I locked the door. She certainly was thorough, and she didn't even understand what was going on. It must be automatic with her, and if it involved her fellow officers she'd do her thing and sort it all out later.

I quickly went to the phone and called Jill. When she answered I told her that we would not be going to the park and that I would call her back later this afternoon and explain a lot of things to her. Then I looked up the number to the pre-school and called Miss Susan.

"Hey, Susan this is Mandy and I have to make this quick because I don't want to talk in front of Naja." I spoke quickly, not giving her a chance to speak, as I walked down the hall to check on Naja to make sure that she couldn't hear me.

"There is a possibility that someone is trying to kidnap Naja." I heard the gasp on the other end of the line, but continued rapidly, "I don't want to endanger you or the other children, so I'm keeping her out of school until this is settled." I heard Naja humming as she came out of her bedroom, "I'll let you know more when I can."

Susan spoke quickly before I hung up. "My God, Mandy take care. If there is anything I can do, let me know."

"Thanks, I'll keep you posted. Bye for now." I felt like a spy quietly talking in quick sentences and glancing around for listening ears.

"Mommy, you're not ready!" The reprimanding voice came from Naja as she came into the kitchen.

"No, but I will be by the time you finish this cereal and toast," I said as I dashed down the hall, making an elaborate display of frantic hurrying up the stairs. I could hear Naja laughing as I reached the top. *At least her spirits are up, now we just have to get through this day*, I couldn't help thinking, as I quickly changed into my clothes.

The day was passing very slowly for me. I'm not used to having idle time on my hands, but I did get a lot of household chores out of the way. I cleaned and rearranged cupboards, drawers, and closets all with the help of an extra pair of little hands. I guess it was time well spent, but I'm not used to being the domestic mom, staying home all day doing chores and taking care of the kids. When bedtime came I was ready, not because I was tired, but because I was bored and remembering to call Mary every two hours was a real pain.

~

I was the first to enter the dream meeting since I'd gone to bed so early. It seemed like forever since I've had such an uneventful day. Others soon began to filter into the room. As everyone settled into their chairs, I began the meeting. "Glad to see you this evening," I said to them, meaning it. It felt like a relief to be with others who knew what was happening, others that I didn't have to hide things from.

I glanced up and was startled by the look on Cindy's face. Her deep auburn hair framed her round pale face as usual, but it was her eyes that drew my attention. They were wide and focused on something behind me. *Oh no! The Boogie Man is here*, I thought as I slowly turned to face my tormentor.

"Oh my God!" I whispered. "Frank! It's Frank!" I quickly skirted the chair and rushed across the room to Frank Adams, who stood solidly in the doorway. He was not wearing the bandages or the cast, and his face was without the bruises. His attitude was not that of a sick man, apparently the body was injured, but not the man inside and not in his dreams.

"Well, this is slightly déjà vu." He smiled at the group. "Not to be alarmed, I've been here and done this before, so relax." He escorted me back to my chair and then walked over to an empty chair that had gone unnoticed, picked it up and carried it to put beside mine. The rest of the group still sat in surprised silence. He placed his chair next to mine and said, "Okay, tell me what's happened so far."

Sally reacted first by saying, "Hooray! The marines have landed," which broke the ice and reactivated everyone.

"Welcome, we've come to a dead end."

"Boy are we glad to see you. Mandy, you didn't tell us that the cops you deal with are so handsome," smiled Lindy as she pulled her chair in a little closer to the group.

"Okay, okay, this is Lieutenant Frank Adams. Frank this is Sally, Bill, Lindy, Teri, Ron, Cindy, Hally, Ramon, Pete, Shala and our group wise woman, Rachael." I introduced the group, and noticed that some were still acting a little reserved towards this new member.

"I don't want to rush you, but in the dream state, your time is limited, so let's move right along. We need to cover some ground here, I don't know when I'll be able to join you again, or even if I will be able to join you again," Frank explained to the twelve people in front of him, ignoring those who seemed distant.

"Rachael," I made eye contact with her and asked, "you are good at keeping things in perspective, would you like to fill him in?" She let go of the crystal and leaned slightly forward as if she were about to tell a group of children a story. As she finished filling him in, she leaned back and picked the crystal off of her chest and began to trace its curved lines with her fingers again.

"That brings you up to date. Now, how about you? What's your story?" asked Pete. Curiosity was written across each face. They had all visibly leaned in towards the circle.

"My story can wait, because it doesn't seem to have any direct bearing on this situation, except to allow me to understand what you're going through and know about your Boogie Man and the White Dog. So let's shelve it for now and put our heads together to protect these kids."

He got no argument from them. The key words were 'protect these kids.' Everyone physically relaxed at his statement, leaned back in their chairs and waited for the next step.

"Frank? One thing. Was your hit and run connected to this situation?" I couldn't help asking, even though I felt that I already knew the answer, but wanting to have it confirmed, and setting up a starting place for him to jump in and help us.

"I'm sure that it was, although, I didn't see it coming and I don't have any information about it. However, the fact that I'm here…here in this dream of yours kinda validates it for me, and if it wasn't, it is now. I don't like being run down by cars!" he stated with emphasis.

"**Ya hear that Boogie Man? Now you've made 'The Man' mad**," Lindy sang out looking over at the doorway. Others hooted and laughed. Frank looked confused and turned to look at the door.

"He lurks around here sometimes too," I explained. "We never know."

"Sounds familiar."

"Okay, tell us what to do."

"Yeah, how do we handle this?"

"Well, as I remember we, the group that I was in, struggled along sharing information until we became a team working together, instead of a group of individuals, working separately. We eventually joined in a common idea and understanding, but your situation seems a little different.

"You do have the White Dog and the Old blue eyes, or as you call him, the Boogie Man, and you apparently have reached the point of working together, but you also have a group of people trying to stop these children. My guess is that the Boogie Man has incorporated help from a 'fear' based establishment. He promotes fear and controls people through it."

He stopped and thought for a moment, then spoke to Rachael, "If these

Indigo children, as you described, are actually here to help change the world and the mess we've allowed it to become, and I hope that you're right because we sure need some help, then the Boogie Man along with any others who would have a lot to lose would try to stop them.

"He has the insight, and keeps the fear boiling, while they have the ability, through money, and power, to try to stop this mission."

There was a general shuffling around as the group acknowledged, but didn't like what he was saying. He held up his hand, and continued, "You notice that I said...'try to stop this mission'? We're going to stop them."

"But how?"

"Yeah, we're up against some mega stuff here."

"Get a grip you guys, nobody said it was going to be easy," stated Ramon in his deep accented voice. He looked ready to do battle.

"Yeah! These are our kids. WE WILL WIN!" Hally's eyes flashed and her shiny black hair bobbed as she nodded her head for emphases.

Out of the corner of my eye, I sensed a movement. Turning my head I saw the Boogie Man, in all his scariness, standing in the doorway. I stood up, in an unhurried manner, to face him, and said as I was turning.

"Look who's come to join us?" Everyone except Frank stood up facing the door. No one showed fear; in fact, you could feel strong solid energy surging from the group. The Boogie Man said nothing he just stood there.

Finally Frank slowly stood and turned to face the man of fear. Their eyes met and everyone could feel the electrical current that jumped from one pair of eyes to the other. The energy between them was far stronger than the energy coming from the group.

"So, we meet again," Frank spoke with a soft, but strong voice his eyes never wavering.

The Boogie Man never uttered a word or changed expression. The room was as still as if it were empty even the sound of breathing was missing; everyone was holding their breath.

I couldn't stand the silence so I said, "So Boogie Man, have you come to apologize for picking on little kids?" I was amazed as he broke his focus on Frank and turned his eyes towards me.

His eyes met mine and I felt the strongest emotional contact I'd ever felt. I struggled to hold my own and not show him his power. I worked at blocking my feelings by thinking of Naja. I thought of my daughter's innocent face, her beautiful blond hair, her wisdom, her boldness, all of her attributes surfaced in my mind, keeping me from succumbing to this man's overwhelming mental power.

He suddenly broke contact, turned and left. It was a full minute before anyone moved, and then quietly someone let out their breath in a soft exclamation. Movement followed and Lindy walked over to the doorway and looked down the hallway. Then she made an obscene gesture in the direction that he'd taken.

"Mandy? Are you alright?"

"Wow, I could feel that contact clear over here."

Frank took my arm and directed me back into my chair, as he indicated to the rest of the group to be reseated. I was feeling shaken, but okay, I'd actually held my own with the Boogie Man!

"Frank, did you see that? She stood toe to toe with him!"

"Listen, any of you could have done that. He's threatening our kids," I stated with feeling.

"Okay, let me tell you something. This Boogie Man is not the person you have to worry about. You all proved that you're not going to let him scare you...so...that means he has to scare someone else into hurting you."

"...and this is where the military guys come in, isn't it?" asked Pete.

"Yes, you all have to be very careful now. Mandy, you and Naja are probably still the main target, so we're going to have to do something about that."

A sudden thought occurred to me that had nothing to do with what Frank was saying. "Frank, is your body still unconscious?" He looked kinda blank, as though he didn't know the answer.

"I'm not sure. I didn't know that it was unconscious." He scratched his head, still looking a little confused.

"Hey..." said Lindy. "Frank, tell Mandy what's wrong with you, so she can tell the medical people what to fix."

"What an idea. Can that work?"

"Why not?"

"Yeah, he's got an inside track." Laughed Lindy, totally thrilled with her idea.

Frank looked at me and said, "I don't know what's wrong, but I'll think about it later. Do you think it will work?"

I shrugged. "What do I know? It's certainly worth a try, but why would they believe me?" Then I thought about Mary. "Listen Frank, how much does Mary know about this dream thing?"

"As far as I know, nothing. She wasn't in *my* dream group."

"Are there 'other' dream groups?" The whispered question floated towards us.

"We're not alone in this?"

Silence fell over the room. Not a disturbed silence, but a thoughtful absence of sound.

Frank watched as the others assimilated the possibility that there were 'others' having dream meeting. Then he said, "I originally assumed that other dream meetings would be as mine was…I mean similar in subject, but now I can see that the meetings happen when a group of souls need to bring their human selves together when something important needs to be figured out, organized, and dealt with."

"So you think that this is a way, maybe a faster way, to bring people who have some type of important mission or goal, together?" Rachael asked him.

"Yes, I think it's possible. My group would never have gotten together if it hadn't been for the dream meetings. We didn't even have the common bond of kids."

"Not that we would have found each other in this century even with the kids," commented Lindy.

"Right."

"Yeah, we even resisted when we did find each other."

"So, do you think that this has always been happening or is this something new?" asked Ron cautiously.

"I don't know, but if it's always been around it's sure been underground."

"Perhaps…it's happening now, because…well, because, things are happening faster now, and there isn't time to take years to figure something out."

"That's true, I read that the energy around the earth has escalated. So we do, as a whole, need to move faster to keep up," Rachael contributed her slant.

Suddenly Sally said, "Does that mean that we'll be meeting like this forever?"

"Yeah, do you still meet in your group?"

"No, we don't meet anymore, and you probably won't once you get the idea and have worked out what your role is," Frank told them. "But that doesn't mean that the meetings won't start again if the need arises."

"You mean these dream meetings are kinda like a crash course in what we need to prepare for?" asked Cindy, her eyes wide and questioning.

"Well, I don't know for sure, but it seems like it to me."

"Wow."

"Yeah, double wow."

"So now what?"

"Yeah, now what?"

The group went silent, thinking, wondering, *Now what?*

Day Ten

I woke with a start, looked around and realized that I was in my own room. *Oh No! The meeting couldn't be over. I hadn't finished talking to Frank. I had more questions and I wanted more answers.* "Damn!" We never know when those meetings are going to end. It's like ready or not we're through. *Damn.*

Then I remembered that I didn't get to find out what was wrong with Frank's body, why he was unconscious, so I could tell the doctors. *Double Damn!* I quickly made up my mind, and I didn't care what Mary said, I intended to see Frank today.

Hunger wasn't my main concern, but Naja was acting like she hadn't eaten in days. She was polishing off her second bowl of cereal when the phone rang. I suspected it was Mary as I picked up the phone. "Hello. Oh, hi Mary, I thought it might be you. Listen, I've got to see Frank today…"

Mary interrupted with, "Yeah, that's why I called. Frank's awake and he insists on seeing you right away." Her voice sounded more animated than usual.

"Awake! Great! What about Jarvis? Is there any word on him?" I asked, fearing an answer.

"No nothing yet," came the answer that wasn't as bad as the one I'd feared. Mary continued with, "Why don't you run up and see Frank and I'll take care of the little one for you?"

I hesitated and was taken back, I didn't leave Naja with sitters and even though this woman was a cop, I still didn't know her, and felt uneasy.

Mary sensed the problem and said, "I can come over there or she can come over here and meet Toby, my dog, he's not nearly as big as hers, but he has a big bark."

Still I hesitated, "Mary, I'm just not comfortable with her away from me lately. Why don't you come to the hospital with us and she can spend time with you while I go in to see Frank?"

"Deal! I'll be over in 20 minutes," she said and the line went dead. No good-byes for this intense lady. I smiled as I hung up the phone, apparently she also doesn't want to be very far from the action so going with us worked for her too.

"Well little one, are you finished yet? Mary's coming over and we're all going to visit a friend in the hospital today."

Naja looked at me in surprise. "We have a friend in the hospital?"

"Well, yes. Do you remember the policeman from the school?"

"The one that was at the park the day they made the little girl, in the red shirt like mine, cry?"

Wow, what a memory. "Yep that's the one. Well he was hit by a car the other day and I want to go up and see him."

"Oh no! Did the Boogie Man do it?" How can one so innocent be so wise?

"No one knows who did it. Why do you think it was the Boogie Man?"

"I don't think that they're friends and I don't think that he likes policemen. He looked mad when he saw them drive up at the school."

"Okay, chop, chop, let's get ready before Mary gets here." We raced for the stairs, Naja squealing and laughing.

At the hospital, I decided to give in to Naja's repeated request to visit Frank, which was greeted with big time scowling from Mary. I explained, "I've prepared her for the worst, explaining how he looks and that he is very sick and she could only stay for a minute and then would go to the cafeteria with you for a treat."

The three of us entered the hospital room together, each with a different agenda; Naja out of curiosity, Mary to see how "this kid" would react to seeing a man in Frank's condition, and I to see how Frank was doing, and maybe pursue some of the unanswered questions I didn't get to ask last night at the dream meeting.

All of us were surprised to see Frank sitting up with most of his bandages gone, the bruises were still there, and he had a cast on one leg and arm, but he looked alert and almost as well as in the dream meeting last night. I glanced at Naja to see her reaction and was not at all surprised to see her smiling at him, with no fear on her face. She marched her tiny body over to the side of the bed and said to a grinning face that looked down on her, "You look awful, I guess getting hit by a car isn't much fun, huh? I brought you a present." Then she reached into her pocket and carefully pulled out a rock. This wasn't just any old rock this was her favorite polished Rose quartz. She had spent a great deal of time, one weekend, picking this rock from a collection of hundreds at a stand at the Saturday Market.

"Naja, what a wonderful gift! Thank you," Frank said, sounding like he meant it. He had not acknowledged either Mary or I, but had kept his focus on Naja, which made her feel important.

"I hope you get well soon. We all miss you. Are you going to come back and visit again?"

"You bet kiddo, in fact, maybe sooner than you think." And then he winked at her.

"Have to go now, I only got one minute. Mary's taking me for a treat," she told him looking pleased. Then she walked over to Mary. Mary, on the other hand, stood there with surprise written all over her face. Naja slipped her small hand into Mary's. Mary took her hand, glanced at Frank and said, "I guess we're going now." Then they turned and walked out of the room.

When I looked back at Frank I was startled to see him bending forward, holding his mid-section, and groaning. "Oh my God! Frank shall I get a nurse?" I asked, feeling panic rushing through me.

He held up a hand, lifted his head and said through clenched teeth, "No, no. It just hurts like hell to laugh."

I let out my breath and relaxed. "I guess Mary was a little surprised at Naja's complete control of herself and the situation."

"Oh yea! I think she's definitely met her match." He bent forward again groaning. "Damn!" he muttered and groaned again.

I waited until he had almost regained his composure and then couldn't wait any longer.

"Frank, do you remember last night?" I waited for his reply, praying that he'd be aware of the dream meeting.

He started grinning, which didn't look comfortable either, as his lips pulled at the stitches along side of his mouth. His eyes met mine and he said, "Yes Mandy, I certainly do."

I felt relieved. Actually, I felt more than relief; I felt a surge of happiness. *What's that all about?* I wondered. No sooner was the thought completed, than I answered my own question. Of course I was happy. This man could help us.

"Frank, there were a lot of questions that I didn't get to ask last night." I was feeling the need to hurry, afraid that someone would come in and interrupt us.

"Wait Mandy," he said and took a couple of shallow panting breaths, holding his mid-section again. I moved towards him to help. He said, "It's alright, I just took too deep a breath. That hurts too. Mandy, I understand from Mary that you've pulled Naja out of school and are taking some time off to stay home with her." He waited for my confirmation and when I nodded, he continued, "Now if you don't like this plan, say so, but it kinda consolidates a lot of problems." He hesitated like he was searching for the right words to use.

"They won't release me from the hospital because I live alone and need someone to help me." My heart jumped. "Mary has insisted that I come to her place and she'll wait on me. It's close to you so we could also keep a watch on you at the same time." He was studying my face as he spoke.

I felt a passing disappointment flow through my body. I stood there wondering about this reaction. Why in God's name did I feel disappointment? Was this the old, but common, feeling of competition between women? Was I in competition with Mary? Why: Because he was bringing her into my problem? Because I thought that I could take better care of him? Or... NO! No way! I am not interested in this man except for his skills, connections, abilities and knowledge of the dream thing, After all, it's certainly not everyone that I can talk to about the dream meetings, or the White Dog.

"Mandy?"

His voice brought my focus back to him and the question hanging between us. He was so physically damaged by the hit and run, but you could still see that he was a handsome man, not the knock you dead kind of handsome, but nice looking. Actually, it was more than physical looks; he had a kind of charisma about him.

"You don't like the idea?"

"Oh. No, it's a great idea. I was actually thinking of you and what has happened to you because of me... and Naja." Again I tried to put my feelings into perspective. This wasn't completely untrue. Yeah, it was. It was a complete lie. I then said. "Would this put you in more danger? You have Al and security here."

He laughed. "You've never seen Mary in action."

"Did I hear my name?" The question came from the doorway.

"Mommy, I had ice cream, and it's not even lunchtime yet." Naja was thrilled with the idea that she'd gotten away with something. I was thinking that was certainly fast. Mary must have had her eat it on the way back. Obviously she didn't want to miss anything.

"Let's go girls, I've got some furniture rearranging to do," Mary said as she turned to go.

"I guess we're out of here," I said, looking at Frank.

"Bye ladies, see ya later." He was grinning and rubbing the stone that

Naja gave him.

"Is this a lucky stone?" he said looking at Naja.

"Yes. Yes, it is," she replied seriously, as she waved goodbye to him.

In the car, I said to Mary, "I'll come over and help you with the furniture."

"Not a good idea. We need to keep this as low key as possible. No connection between your place and mine. In fact, we're bringing Frank in under wraps later tonight, for security, and Frank's room is going to continue to be listed in his name for a while, with Al keeping an eye on it or any interested parties."

"Oh good, I was worried about that. So… how will we be communicating, certainly not by phone?"

"No, we've got some cleared wireless equipment to hook up, so we'll be able to hear every sound coming from your place." She looked at me, grinned and added, "So don't be saying or doing anything you don't want us to hear."

"Oh boy!" I muttered. "Just like the movies."

"Yep. It's a stake out, however, my place is too far away and at the wrong angle for a complete visual, but we can sure do audio."

"Well, thank God for small favors," I answered.

Mary laughed. "Yeah, you can still run around in the buff if you like."

We dropped Mary off and went back to our house, where we planned lunch.

"It's the TV repairman," the voice came from the front porch. "Mary sent me." He continued in a softer voice. I peeked out the hole and the man was facing the door, but his eyes were looking upward. Following his eyes up I saw a police badge, pinned above the bill of his hat, in place of the TV company emblem. Clever.

"Okay, we've checked the place and there are no bugs here now, and the phone is clean on this side, but I wouldn't use it for anything confidential." He looked at me and I nodded. However, my mind was playing a commercial song that Naja always thought was so neat.

'There ain't no bugs on me, oh there ain't no bugs on me.

There might be bugs on some of you mugs,

but there ain't no bugs on me.'

His voice continued and I came back to the present. "Also, these mikes, one in the upstairs hallway and one here at the lower level, can pick up any conversation, but they are one-way units. In other words, you can be heard, but you cannot hear."

I opened my mouth to ask how we were going to communicate, but he held up his hand, and said, "This is your communication devise. It looks like a Walkman, but it really works like a headpiece phone. You can just say out loud that you want to talk and put on your piece and they'll pick up. However, if they want to talk to you… it's not as easy. This does have a small signal, but it's subtle, so as not to draw any unwanted attention to it."

"Okay Mary, give us a signal," he said out loud.

The small box in his hand vibrated, but made no noise, I looked from it to him, with a question written plainly on my face.

"Yes. You'll probably have to wear it most of the time, preferably out of sight."

I let go with a big sigh. "Okay, is Frank in place yet?"

"No, he comes later. We didn't want too much activity on this block at the same time. Questions? No? Okay, I'm gone." He walked to the door, opened it, stood in the open doorway and wrote on a paper handed it to me, said goodbye, and left. As I closed the door, I looked at the paper he'd handed me, and saw written there, *Don't forget to turn the alarm back on*, and then he'd added a smiley face.

"Okay Mary, all's clear here," I called out as I headed down the hallway to see how Naja was doing with her watercolors at the kitchen table.

"Wow Naja, what's that?" I questioned as I looked at the picture that was unfolding. It was mostly black with many little strips and stripes and blobs of color here and there.

"It's a dark cloud and these are kids," she answered very seriously. I was shocked. It was very similar to Rachael's muddy dream with the Indigo kids fighting the bad energy. "Are you in there?" I asked, holding my breath.

"Yes, I'm here," she answered pointing to a bluish green blob right in the center of the picture.

Letting out my breath I asked softly, "What does all of this mean?"

"I'm not sure, but I think it's serious trouble!" she said nodding her little head up and down. "Yes, serious trouble."

"How do you feel about this…'serious trouble?'" I waited for her answer. How much did this wee child know about her mission?

"It's okay, I picked it." Then she scooted off of the chair and carried the water cup to the sink, where she waited for me to take it and pour it out.

Obviously the conversation was over. "I'm hungry, Mommy."

"Me too. It's been a busy day, and tonight we get to watch *Rugrats* on the video." I was glad to be doing something with my hands as I prepared to fix our food. However, I knew it wasn't going to stop my thinking and worrying.

Naja loved *Rugrats*, she laughed and giggled all the way through it. I have to admit, it is well done. Those kids are something, and a kid named 'Dil, Dil Pickle'? Somebody out there had a good imagination.

"Okay little one, let's do it. Bedtime."

"Awww…"

"No, no, don't start. It's upstairs with you." I turned off the TV set, turned off the lights, checked the alarm, said goodnight out loud to Mary and headed upstairs. Wonder how Mary liked listening to the *Rugrats* movie? Better yet, I wonder how she's going to like listening to the bedtime story that's a ritual.

~

Just as I became aware that I was sitting alone in the dream meeting room, I found myself back in my bed reaching for the Walkman communicator. I'd taken it off of my waist band and left it on the nightstand beside the bed and it was rattling around on the top of the table, furiously. Fumbling with the headphones I finally got them in place and punched the button. **"Hello Mandy! Mandy don't go to sleep."**

"Frank? What's wrong?" I was fully awake now and straining to hear any sounds that didn't belong there.

"Mandy, it's okay so far, but I have a gut feeling. Stay awake for a while, okay?" He paused and then said, "I know this is strange, but … talk to me, Mandy?" He sounded upset and anxious.

"Okay Frank. Are you alright? How did the move go?" I threw my legs over the side of the bed, found my robe and slippers and quietly walked to the window that looked out to the street. Standing to the far right side I could just make out Mary's house, where I tried to visualize Frank sitting in the dark watching my house.

"Yea, I'm bone weary after they wrestled me in and out of beds and trucks, but I'm okay and glad to get out of that hospital. Maybe that's the problem. Maybe I'm just exhausted." He paused for a moment sounding completely done in.

"Frank, what's the news on Jarvis?" I asked to change the subject a little, as I walked up and down the room.

"You know, that is so strange. Jarvis is a good man, no one can figure out why he'd just up and leave."

"What do you mean leave?"

"He sent a message saying that he had to make an urgent trip to Eastern

Washington, because of a personal family problem." A chill ran through me. He was last seen with that military type and suddenly he takes off for Washington State. This didn't add up…

"I know what you're thinking, Mandy," he interrupted my logic. "I had the same thought; it's just too much of a coincidence. I've already got someone on it."

"Jeeze Frank, first you, and now Jarvis. Is everyone associated with me a potential victim?" I was near tears, feeling the weight of responsibility.

"Listen Mandy, I know the dangers and so does Jarvis. It goes with the job. You are not responsible; those who are behind all of this are the responsible parties. You need to focus on keeping Naja safe, that's your responsibility, and I'm going to help you."

His words helped me pull myself together and I asked, "How much does Mary know about these dream meeting things?"

I heard a chuckle trickle through the earpiece. "Well…" he began, "actually nothing… yet. I'm planning on telling her tonight. She has a right to know what she's up against. However, she's a very solid, by the book person and this is going to be a lot for her to swallow." He chuckled again. "I know she'll come through, it won't interfere with her job, even if she does think we're fruit loops. It's going to be interesting to see how she reacts."

"Poor Mary," I said, "she thought she was retired and now she's into something beyond her wildest imagination."

"Beyond any of our wildest imaginations I think," he added, with another chuckle. He was getting his sense of humor back. Perhaps he was starting to feel better.

"I'm sorry, Mandy. Go ahead and go to sleep. I think I'm just a little over anxious because this is your tenth day. It is the tenth day or rather night, isn't it?"

"What are you talking about Frank? Tenth night for what?"

"You've had nine nights of dream meetings. You're getting real close to number twelve. You have twelve people and I think there will only be twelve meetings, which means that things could escalate at this point."

"Really! Why? How do you know?" My questions ran together. Were we really almost at the end of this nightmare? I felt excitement and fear all at the same time.

"Well, I don't really 'know,' but my experience in a dream meeting had twelve people and only went for twelve nights. This one could be different. I don't know the rules for this game."

"Game? Do you think someone is playing a game with us?" I asked quickly.

"No, it's for real, but... Uh!" I heard a lot of confusing sounds, then from a distance, **"Mary! Mary! It's going down!"** Then Frank's voice came on the line clear and closer. "Mandy! Get to Naja. **Now!** Stay on the line, so I can direct you."

I was running down the hall before he finished the sentence. Naja's room was quiet and I could hear her breathing as she slept peacefully, unaware of any problems. Where was the White Dog? Wasn't he supposed to be protecting her if there was a problem?

"Mandy! Get out of the house! Get Naja and go out the back door. Mary will meet you." Frank's voice was controlled but anxious.

"No. No Mary! The gates are locked she can't get in and she'll only draw attention to us," I countered his instruction, as I gathered Naja and her blanket up in one bundle. Naja opened her eyes, looking surprised. "It's okay, honey. We have to go outside and we have to be very quiet."

"Are we hiding from the men in the black car?" How could she understand so much so quickly?

"Yes, we are." I grabbed her tennis shoes and jammed them into my robe pocket as I headed for the door.

"Wait! We can't leave JoJo!" She squirmed around looking for her favorite stuffed toy. I couldn't see it and didn't have time to stop and hunt for it.

"We can't take the time, honey, we have to go now." I felt the little body relax, but sensed her unhappiness, but we just couldn't take the chance.

"Mandy, don't take the time, get out now, I think they're going to torch the house." Frank's voice came through my earphone I'd forgotten that he could hear us. I was half way down the stairs when I heard a loud popping sound coming from the street. I rounded the corner still heading for the back door. Grabbing the doorknob I suddenly remembered the alarm. If it sounds, they'll know I opened a door. Quickly I ran back into the hall and punched in the code turning off the alarm.

As I turned to retrace my steps back to the door, I bumped against the wall and the phone set flew off of my head and skidded away down the hall, I wasn't about to stop and look for it in the dark. Sirens were screaming from somewhere in the distance.

Jerking the door open, I stepped into the cool night air. It only took a moment to scan the area and decide that the best place to go was the tool shed in the left corner of the yard. I hesitated for just a second to listen. Hearing nothing near by, I quickly ran to the far side of the shed.

"Okay, we're going to put your shoes on now. Are you all right?" I fished the tiny shoes out of my pocket, not waiting for an answer. Squatting on my heels with my back braced against the shed wall, I improvised a lap for Naja who held out one little foot to accept the shoe.

"I'm okay, Mommy. Are we hiding here? This isn't a very good place. You always find me here when we play hide and seek." She was right, it was pretty obvious, but how could we get out of the yard without going through the front gates and right into all of the action? Security works both ways, keeping some out and keeping some in. Suddenly I remembered the ladder I'd shoved behind the shed earlier in the season.

Dragging the ladder out of its small space was harder than putting it in there, but I finally had it out and secured against the fence. I was spurred on by shouts from the front. "Okay, how are you at climbing ladders?" I whispered to Naja. "I'll go first and you follow me. Okay here we go." I took a couple of steps up the ladder and paused to make sure Naja was with me. "Great. Now, I'm going to lift you over the fence and drop you to the ground."

Naja looked a little startled, but nodded her head. She had a small frame and didn't weigh much or I would never have been able to lift her up from one side of the fence and lower her down on the other. Even so, I felt muscles pulling and stretching. My leg muscles were strong, but I hadn't exercised my arms much since my college days. *I'll be feeling this tomorrow. If there is a tomorrow*, I thought grimly.

"Naja, you must be pretty close to the ground, so I'm going to let go now, step back out of the way, so I can jump over."

Letting go of the small hands, I quickly hefted myself over the fence and dropped to the ground looking for Naja as I touched the ground, knees bent. Before I could straighten up, a figure stepped out of the shadow. My heart stopped. The Boogie Man had Naja!

"Mrs. Minton, it's okay. Stay quiet," whispered a male voice from the shadow. I hadn't moved, but was straining to see who it was and if he had Naja. He stepped closer and there was my precious child clutching his neck, while he held her against his chest. I flexed my knees again ready to physically rip his heart out if I had to in order to get my little girl back. He moved closer and I saw his face. My mouth fell open.

"Lieutenant Jarvis! John Jarvis is that really you? Wh…"

"Shhhh. We must be quiet. Follow me quickly," he instructed, and stepped around me and started across the neighbor's yard towards the next street.

We were moving quietly alongside of the neighbor's house that sat behind mine and had almost reached the front when a movement from the walkway ahead stopped Jarvis. He shoved Naja at me and reached inside of his jacket. I was struggling to get Naja into a secure position when I noticed a large White object move in front of us.

"Wait!" I whispered loudly as I grabbed for Jarvis' arm. "It's our White Dog!" Jarvis relaxed and swore, shoving his gun back into his shoulder holster. The dog stood and studied Jarvis, as if he were sizing him up. He wasn't growling, but he wasn't wagging his tail either. I watched wondering what was wrong. I stepped further away from Jarvis suddenly not feeling so trusting.

Jarvis looked at the dog and then at me, slowly understanding that I was acting upon the dog's judgment. I took another step away. Suddenly there was the sound of running feet from the street in front of us. I took the opportunity and bolted back around the rear of the neighbor's house, across their patio, ducking behind an outdoor fireplace in the corner, I hesitated just a second to see where Jarvis was and if he was following me. The only thing I could make out in the dark was a large white shape in the yard, between Lieutenant John Jarvis and us.

Quickly I ran behind a hedge, and then along the backside of a fence next to mine and then turned into the yard belonging to the neighbor two doors down and on the left side of my house, putting me closer to Mary's house.

The street in front of my house was alive with movement and voices. Was it the good guys or the bad? I hesitated, should I go out? Who could I trust? Who was out there? Mary's house was across the street. I'd be seen if I tried to get to it. A sound so soft that I didn't really hear it, but only sensed it, drifting towards me from the direction I'd just come. Turning I saw the White Dog moving towards me.

Thank God, I thought, as I leaned against the house and slid to the ground, sitting on the cement walk. The dog approached Naja dropped JoJo in her lap, and licked her face. She squeaked, grabbed both the stuffed toy and the large White Dog in a huge hug.

"What about me?" I mumbled, and to my surprise the dog leaned forward and licked my face. Naja giggled and then clamped her hand over her mouth, remembering that we were supposed to be quiet.

Setting her down, I removed the light blanket which was in complete disarray, folded it lengthwise and placed it over her shoulders. "Can you wear this like a coat, if I tie it around your waist with the belt from my robe?" I asked.

"Sure, then I can walk, too," came the logical reply, which I appreciated because my arms were definitely experiencing stress.

The White Dog moved a few steps away from us, then turned and looked over his shoulder. "He wants us to follow him, Mommy," She was right. I struggled to my feet, finished arranging the blanket and reached for the little hand that was already extended upwards towards me; the other hand had a tight grip on JoJo.

We followed the Guardian Angel past the house, around a shed through another back yard and behind shrubs in the front of a house with a big fence enclosing its back yard. I followed the dog blindly and with complete trust, until we ended up several blocks away at the side of a house with a large fenced in yard. The dog turned to walk to the back of the house where the gate was standing open. He went through without hesitation, and we followed him. He stopped at a doggy door at the rear of the garage. *Oh, oh*, I thought, hoping the occupant wasn't home. The White Dog pushed through the swinging door then stuck his head back out to look at us.

Naja scrambled through the doggy door, giggling all the way. I took a deep breath, got down on my hands and knees and crawled through the door. There was no question that I'd fit, the White Dog had more bulk than I did and he fit. Of course, that means that the dog that lives here was also very big. Then suddenly I looked at the dog in front of me. Maybe it was the White Dog who lived here! He certainly acted like he was at home. He walked over to a large overstuffed doggy bed and lay down. Naja joined him, throwing her free arm over his back. He sighed, and she smiled.

Well, I decided, *it looks like this is the place for us to stay for a while.* So I walked over, sat down on the bed and leaned my back against the wall.

~

The conversation in the room stopped as Ron saw me standing in the doorway, and nodded his head towards me. "Here she is."

"Oh my God, Mandy!"

"We've been so worried about you."

"Are you okay?"

The questions were coming fast, without waiting for answers. I'd forgotten all about the dream meeting. "I'm late. I'm sorry, I've been... well, I've..."

"Here honey, sit down and take a deep breath." Lindy was on her feet and ushering me to a chair, before she dragged up another one for herself.

"She's in her night clothes," someone whispered.

"Shhhh."

"Jeeze am I glad to see you guys!" I managed before the tears started rolling down my cheeks and dropped on to the folded hands in my lap. "Sorry," I wiped the tears away with the back of my hand. "I don't have time for this. I have things to tell you."

"Yes!" Lindy stated as she made a fist, raised her arm up and brought it down with force.

"Considering your appearance and the fact that you are very late, I'd say something big has happened," added Sally as she leaned forward in her chair.

Quickly I gave them the headlines. Frank being moved across the street, the audio security system, then about Frank yelling to Mary, 'it's going down,' and then running into Jarvis, and my dash through the night with Naja and the White Dog and hiding in someone's garage.

"My God."

"Wait a minute. What's with this Jarvis guy? Where does he stand and where has he been?"

"Indeed and why was he there when you fled into the night?" Rachael murmured as she reached for her crystal pendant and placed it on her forehead, closing her eyes.

"I didn't get a chance to ask him, and considered him a knight in shining armor there to save us until the dog appeared to have reservations."

"Wow!"

"Say, what do you think has happened at your house?"

"Yeah, do you think that they burned it?"

"Listen you can stay with us."

"No problem, you can stay with us too."

"In fact, if you moved around a lot, that would keep them confused and they wouldn't be able to trace you."

"This is true, it would work."

"Wait. Thanks, you guys, but wouldn't it put you and your children in danger?"

There was only a slight hesitation before Ramon said, "I think we are past that now. We are all in this together and Naja might be safer if the military guys realize that there's not just one kid to deal with...but many."

"He's right."

"We need to be sure that everyone is in agreement," I said. "I won't even consider it if all are not okay with the idea."

"Not a problem. You only go to those who are okay with it," Shala, the quiet one stated matter of factly.

Movement and a cold draft alerted me to a new scenario and brought me back from the dream meeting. Naja was curled up beside me, but the dog was gone, the swinging doggy door evidence of his leaving. Naja apparently missed the warmth of the dog, because she scooted closer to me, seeking heat while she slept. I waited to see if the dog was going to return. Perhaps the danger was gone now, or maybe he was just out on a recon mission.

Then I heard it. Barking! Somewhere off a few house down the street and to the right of where we were, but it definitely sounded like the big White Dog. Then other dogs joined in. Well, this would certainly wake up the entire area. If anyone were creeping around this would not help them to stay unnoticed. Most people got up and checked to see why their dog barks in the middle of the night. I could picture lights going on all over the neighborhood, just like in a Disney movie that I'd watched with Naja. It was a ploy to keep anyone from checking the neighborhood and the yards too closely. What a dog!

I cuddled Naja closer and wished that I could contact Frank and Mary, but losing the head set and not grabbing up my cell phone made that difficult. Originally, I thought about circling around to Mary's house, but the dog changed all of that. Now I planned to just stay put for a while.

Shortly the White Dog quietly pushed his way through the doggy door and with a sideways glance at me, dropped on to the mat with a grunt. Would he still be there in the morning? I wondered, and how would I explain to the owners of this garage why we were sleeping in their dog's quarters, or even more important, how would I explain to the dog that lived here, if he showed up? What about walking down the street in my bathrobe when the time came to leave here, and how would I know when it was safe to go back to my house?

My eyes closed, I was just too tired to worry about these problems now.

"She's back! Look, she's back."

"God, what is going on?"

"Mandy? Mandy, honey, talk to us."

"I'm sorry I seem to keep popping in and out of this dream." I told them about the dog and his barking ploy before asking, "What am I going to do in the morning? And who do I trust?"

The voices around me were still. No one had an answer.

"The good news is…you guys are here…" I opened my eyes, which had slowly drifted shut again, to find the only person listening to my words was the White Dog. "You especially," I muttered and closed my eyes again.

Day Eleven

"Amanda Minton's residence," the very professional woman's voice came across the telephone line. I was startled. Who was answering my phone?

As morning light crept slowly in through the garage window, I'd found that we were alone, just as I had suspected we would be. The dog was gone, which probably meant that the coast was clear and we were no longer in immediate danger.

Not wanting to walk the streets in my nightclothes, I'd opted to just knock on the back door of the house whose garage we'd been hiding in. The smell of coffee made the idea seem even more acceptable. However, judging by the look on the face of the 70-something-year-old woman who opened the door, I realized that I hadn't really thought the idea completely through.

The sight of Naja sleepily clutching her JoJo toy helped clear us of the harmful intent category in this grandmotherly woman's mind. My request to use her phone apparently seem reasonable to her considering our appearance. The woman pointed to the phone in the hallway just off of the kitchen, but her attention was on Naja. The woman fussed over Naja, getting her settled into a chair and discussing JoJo. I had decided, almost on a whim, to call my own phone number, and now a woman had answered.

"Hello," the voice said again, sounding more curious than professional now.

"Who is this?" I demanded, the feeling of being violated seeping through me. Who dared…

"Mandy? Mandy is that you?" The professional voice now sounded excited and familiar.

"Mary?"

"Oh my God, Mandy! Where are you? We've been frantic." I could hear other sounds in the background, other voices.

"Who's there, Mary?" Automatically my voice had taken on a sharp edge.

Who could I trust? Who were the good guys? "Apparently my house is still standing. What's going on, Mary?"

There was a shuffling sound and then I heard, **"Mandy! Where the hell are you?"**

"Good Morning, Frank. Tell me what's going on. Why are Naja and I not safe? ...Even from the cops?"

There was silence on the line, and then Frank said in a low voice. "What are you talking about?"

Suddenly I felt like Frank and I weren't the only ones on the line and immediately hung up the receiver. Standing there with my hand still on the phone, I heard someone clearing her throat behind me. Turning, I discovered the woman holding a hot cup of coffee towards me.

"Well," I said taking the coffee. "I guess it's time to share a couple of things with you." I glanced towards the kitchen where Naja was eating a bowl of cereal and watching the small TV that was cleverly hung under the cupboard. TV watching again, just two weeks ago Naja watched selective TV on a limited basis, now she was watching it regularly while I talked privately to people I didn't even know. Our lives had really changed dramatically and I had a feeling that this was only the beginning.

I sat down on the Mission style bench, next to the telephone stand, where I could keep an eye on Naja and hugged my robe closer to my body. What should I tell this woman? How much had she overheard of the phone conversation? "My name is Amanda Minton, and my five year old daughter's name is Naja," I began. "My husband was killed before Naja was born. We live over on Clarendon Street. Last night someone tried to break into my house. I called the police, but it didn't look like they were going to get there in time, so I gathered up Naja and ducked out the back. I thought someone was following me. We ended up in your garage." Part lies, part truth. What else could I do?

The woman was sympathetic, patting my hand and muttering, "You poor thing."

"I don't know how to get back home, during daylight hours, in..." I hesitated, looking down at my nightgown and robe. "Plus, I'm not sure what's happened at my house or who's there. I don't want to walk Naja into a situation."

"Of course not," the woman agreed. "Here's what we'll do. You'll both take a nice hot bath. You'll feel much better. I can find clothes for you...probably not for the little one though." She pursed her lips as she studied Naja's small form. "No matter, I'll wash and dry her pajamas so she can put them back on. We'll take this one step at a time. Oh, by the way, I'm Ethel, and my husband is dead too. My daughter is about your age." She smiled as she started up the hall towards the kitchen. "She lives in California now. Let me show you to her room, I keep it ready in case she comes home to visit. It even has its own bath."

"Thank you, that would feel good. By the way, where's your dog?"

"Oh, Toby is really my daughter's dog and he's with her in California. You need some food; I'll fix you a good breakfast while you're getting cleaned up."

I bathed Naja first and then sent her off with Ethel, wrapped in an oversized towel, and ran a hot steamy shower for myself. A shower never felt so good. I love that dog, but he does smell like a 'dog.' Clean body, clean hair, I even used my finger and the toothpaste by the sink for clean breath. I felt like a new woman. I definitely needed to be in good shape because I didn't have a clue as to what I'd be walking into at my house.

Ethel had provided me with one of her daughter's jogging suits. It was purple and very comfortable. When I walked into the kitchen, Naja was wrapped in a huge terry cloth robe, while her pajamas were in the dryer. She was smiling from ear to ear.

Ethel motioned me to sit while she piled a stack onto my plate. I dug into the best pancakes I'd ever eaten. Coffee, good food, warm comfortable clothes, and an ally. I felt like I just might get through this after all.

Ethel handed me a pair of tennis shoes, and said, "These might be a little big, but if you wear these heavy socks, they'll probably work just fine. In any case, they'll be better than those flimsy slippers that are in the dryer." She was obviously happy fussing over us like a mother hen, and we were enjoying it too. We'd been alone and depending solely upon my abilities for a long time, so this was an enjoyable change. However, I did need to check out my house and I didn't want to take Naja with me. Could I impose upon this woman further? Could I trust Naja to her care? Certainly the White Dog wouldn't have brought us to this house if it hadn't been safe.

"Ethel…" I started and then tried to think how I could suggest leaving Naja here for another hour when Ethel broke into my thoughts with, "Amanda, why don't you scoot on over to your house and check things out? Naja and I will stay here and make cookies."

Well, it looks like she was reading my mind, I thought as I glanced at Naja to see how she was reacting to the suggestion. Naja smiled and said, "It's okay, Mommy, the White Dog will help Ethel take care of me."

What was she talking about? "Is he here?" I quickly asked, feeling tension build.

"No, but he will be if I need him," she stated matter of factly.

"Right!" I'd given up being surprised at Naja's awareness of things. "Okay, but you have to promise to save me a cookie."

I left the house clutching a paper with Ethel's full name and phone number on it. As I walked, I also noted the exact color, house number and street name. I was nervous about letting Naja out of my sight, but had to take a chance. And I had to admit that I did feel comfortable with Ethel.

Stuffing the paper into the pants pocket I started jogging toward my area, keeping track of the streets and the houses, something I hadn't done in the dark last night. I jogged along a street that ran parallel to mine, but was two blocks west. I was planning to come in from the opposite direction so there would be no clue as to where I'd left Naja.

As I turned the corner, I could see three cars parked in the street near my house. Everything else appeared to be just a regular morning. A paperboy rode his bike down the other side of the street, a cat ran across the street to avoid the boy and in the distance, I could hear someone's wind chime gently ringing in the breeze. Everything seemed normal, but why? Things happened here last night that were not normal.

Slowly I walked towards my house, staying on the same side of the street and staring hard at the parked cars, but they were empty. Who did they belong to? The only cars that sat out in this neighborhood were visitors. Who had three visitors this early? I did, of course.

I turned onto my walk, and as I approached the porch, the door was flung open and Mary rushed out, grabbed my arm, and pulled me inside. Frank was struggling to rise from the couch while another man helped him.

Mary let go of me as she turned to Frank. "Don't Frank!" she called out to him. He stopped, hesitated a moment and gently lowered himself back on to the couch, beads of perspiration lining his upper lip.

"Frank, you look like hell," I stated as I circled the end table and walked towards him.

"Well, you look great, all fresh and nice," he said casually. Then he added in a stronger, angrier voice. "Where the hell have you been?" He was staring hard at me. Suddenly he looked past me, and said in softer voice verging on fear. "Where's Naja?"

"She's fine. Where are the others?" I answered.

"Others?"

"Yeah, the drivers of the cars out front."

He smiled as he looked down. Raising his head back up, he nodded to Mary. "Call em in."

Mary raised her hand to her mouth and said, "Recon in one." She was speaking into a small wrist communicator.

I heard the back door open and footsteps coming down the hall. From the top of the stairs a man appeared and headed down towards us. "These men have been searching for clues to your whereabouts."

"Are they police?"

"Yes, of course. What's going on, Mandy?"

"Thank you, gentlemen," I said smiling at them. "Did you find anything that I should know about?" The man from outside glanced quickly at Frank.

"Okay, that's enough. Pete, Harry, take a break, Joe you too." The three men headed for the front door.

"Mary?" He tipped his hand up like he was drinking coffee. Mary grinned, turned to me and raised her eyebrows into a question. I shook my head no. When I looked back at Frank, he was studying me. I ignored his scrutiny and sat on the chair across from him, leaving the space beside him for Mary. I wanted to be able to see both of their faces when I told my story.

Mary handed Frank his coffee and took her seat. "You make good coffee," he said to her after he'd taken a sip. "She buys good coffee," she said as she lifted hers to her mouth. *Aren't we all acting like this was a social get together?* I thought as I watched them.

Looking around, I softly mouthed. "Is this place 'bug' proof?" Frank looked startled. Mary did not change expression, but she did stop her coffee cup midway to her mouth. I reached over and retrieved Naja's note pad and Crayola from the drawer in the end table, and wrote. "What about the house across the street? Blinds never closed, day or night." They both glanced at the house with its blinds tightly closed.

Mary was out of her seat and on her way to the door in an instant. Saying, "I'll get it Frank." Frank held up his hand to indicate that I should stay seated. As he said, "So Mandy, would you get me some more of this coffee, while Mary gets my file?" He was studying me hard and slightly shaking his head no, sending me a message that said, 'sit tight.'

One of the cars slowly and casually turned around in the driveway and headed up the street. Mary waved and turned back towards the house. When she stepped inside of the door, she looked at Frank and nodded her head up and down slightly, then returned to her seat.

"Let's see now…" Frank stalled.

Mary stood up and walked to the kitchen through the dining room which was in view of the bay window, and instantly returned down the hall, which was hidden from the window. She stood on her tiptoes and peered out of the peek hole. I was sitting on an angle, which allowed me to casually view the window without completely turning my head towards it, or really be seen.

Suddenly, a green car came crashing out of the garage, which was partially behind the house, and skidded sideways as it turned to race off up the street. The remaining policeman was apparently ready for this because he jammed his car into gear and attempted to block the car's get away. The other two cops ran from the back of the house. The cars, with front fender to front fender, looked as if they were in a wrestling match. The two cops on foot had their guns drawn and were approaching the cars, one on either side.

It all happened fast and was over fast. The get away car stopped struggling with the cop's car and seemed to relax into a settled position. The tall cop that had been upstairs jerked open the door of the green car and a man stepped out with his hands raised.

I glanced at Frank and saw that he was grinning. "Nice call," he said as he settled himself back onto the couch. Mary had moved to the window, her gun in hand, but made no move to go outside. Instead, she was talking to her wrist, giving instructions to one of the cops outside.

Suddenly, from the corner of my eye, I saw something move in the hallway. Half turning, I discovered the Boogie Man. Mary sensed something and turned at about the same time that I did. She raised her gun and said, **"Don't move!"** He moved. She crouched, both hands on the gun now and said again, **"Don't move!"**

Frank was standing with his gun also pointed at the Boogie Man. "Well, here we are again," he said, addressing the intruder. The man just stared at all of us with a slight smile on his face. Then he turned and made a jumping move towards Mary. She fired three shots rapidly. I automatically closed my eyes, my hands covered my ears as the deafening sound filled the room. Opening my eyes, I saw Mary standing with gun still in hand, looking at the spot where the Boogie Man had been, but no Boogie Man. To say that she had a confused expression on her face would be putting it mildly. She was in complete shock.

"Mary!" Frank's voice tried to break through her stupor. **"Mary! Disengage! Pete's coming in!"** The door flew open and Pete burst though the opening. He stopped inside of the door and looked at Mary.

"Out the back," Frank said, and Pete took off. Mary was still standing there. I walked over to her, lowered her arms and led her back to the couch. She was completely dazed.

Harry came running in, puffing and holding his gun. "Pete's got it. Are we secured in front?" Came Frank's professional, no nonsense voice. "Yeh, but..." he indicated the back door, feeling he should be backing Pete up. "Go," Frank said. Then he grabbed Mary's gun and her wrist and spoke into her communicator. "Joe, secure back door of other house no one in or out."

"Mandy, could you stand over by the window and tell me if anyone comes out of that house." Then he picked up his cell phone and called into the station, requesting additional back up.

Suddenly it occurred to me that if the Boogie Man were in the neighborhood he'd be able to find Naja. **"Naja!"** I said out loud, as I turned and headed for the door.

"Wait! Mandy wait!" Frank yelled, but I was out the front door and running down the street. I focused on a direct line to Ethel's, cutting across yards, over decks and through shrubs, using strength that I didn't know I had. As I cut across the grass of a corner house, I could see Ethel's house next to it and there was the Boogie Man standing in the driveway. He turned when he heard me coming, and if he hadn't stepped sideways, I'd have run him down, because I didn't even slow down.

"Naja!" I yelled, as I banged on the back door. Naja opened the door, and there at her side, stood the White Dog. "Oh thank God!" I fell on my knees and hugged her to me. The dog moved past me, placing himself between us and the Boogie Man.

Naja and I stepped out onto the step and stood beside the White Dog. The three of us facing the blue-eyed Boogie Man. He looked at us for a moment and then turned and disappeared around the hedge next door.

"Amanda?" Ethel's voice spoke from the doorway. She looked concerned. "Are you alright Amanda?" Amanda. No one had called me that since my mother died. I walked over to Ethel and gave her a big hug. "Yes, I'm alright."

"Mommy, we saved you a cookie." I laughed out loud as we went back into the house, relief causing a slightly giddy feeling, the dog following us in wagging his tail. "I suppose you want part of my cookie?" I asked him. He wagged his tail and let his tongue fall out in a huge doggy grin.

I called my home phone number once again. "Hi Frank. She's okay, but he was here, however, so was the White Dog," I explained smiling and munching on an oversized and misshapen oatmeal raisin cookie.

Very calmly he asked, "Where's 'here,' Mandy?"

"Frank, how's Mary?" I countered, suddenly remembering poor Mary and her shock at shooting a man and having him just disappear before her eyes.

"Where's here, Mandy?" he repeated not raising his voice.

"Frank, get things squared away there and I'll be back soon. Are you going to be there or at Mary's?"

He sighed and said, "Here."

"Good, we'll send out for Chinese and have a long talk."

"Mary will be here too. I'm going to try to fill her in."

"Well, I'm glad it's you and not me trying to explain this."

"Thanks," he said sarcastically and hung up the phone.

After thanking Ethel again and promising that we'd keep in touch and come back to visit, the four of us; Naja, the White Dog, JoJo, and I headed for home. On the way, Naja explained that the White Dog scratched on the door and they let him in. Ethel, she told me, thought that he was our dog, and that he had tracked us to her house. Naja thought this was funny, but liked the idea that she had this secret about the dog. She changed the subject and talked about her cookie experience, but I was thinking how interesting it was that the dog just shows up inside of our house, but had the wisdom to allow them to open the door and let him in at Ethel's.

"Oh dear," Naja's sorrowful voice exclaimed, as we entered the house and she spotted Frank looking very ragged as he sat there on the couch. "You don't feel very good, do you?"

"To be truthful, I don't, but don't tell the ladies, or they'll start fussing over me," Frank answered, grinning at her.

The dog joined us, giving Frank a gentle lick, and then waited patiently for Naja at the bottom of the stairs. He apparently felt that a nap was in order.

Mary was functional again, but looked drained and didn't meet my eyes. Clearly she was having a difficult time with the information that Frank had given her. I wondered if he'd told her about the dream meetings too.

"Mommy, dog and I are going upstairs to sleep. We're both tired," Naja informed me as she leaned across the dog's neck.

"Good idea. I'll come and get you settled." I knew the place must be secured, but still had to check it out myself. Naja's room was just as we'd left it, covers in disarray, blinds down. I tucked Naja in, hugged the dog, who nuzzled my face, and checked out my own room. Everything felt okay, so I headed back downstairs. I had to talk to Frank while I had the chance.

Mary had delivered three cups of coffee and donuts to the living room and the two of them were waiting for me to join them. I couldn't resist saying, "Donuts? Is it true what they say about cops living on donuts?"

Frank almost chuckled as he said, "Only out of necessity." Mary didn't respond.

"Okay, let's compare notes, while we can," Frank said seriously, looking at me. "To begin, where have you been, and what happened after we lost phone communication last night?"

I told them about getting out of the house and over the fence, then I hesitated and glanced at Mary. "As I dropped over the fence, I discovered that a man was holding Naja."

Frank sat straight up and even Mary came alive. "What!?" Frank uttered.

"Yes and that man was John Jarvis." This time Mary reacted, while Frank sat with his mouth open. "John? John Jarvis? Where is he?" She was on the edge of her chair.

"Well, I don't know where he went. He was leading us past the neighbor's house in the back when we met the White Dog and the dog didn't seem to like him. When we heard something in the street in front of us, I bolted a different direction with Naja and then the White Dog led us to another area and we hid out in an unused dog's quarters." They were both silent. Both had that deep in thought look on their faces. I sat sipping my coffee and waited for them to come to some conclusions.

"Okay, I guess this qualifies as a need to know basis," Frank said. "John has been working on an undercover job." Mary looked surprised. "He was borrowed by another agency, and when he disappeared at the hospital, I was told that he'd had to go underground."

Mary and I both started to speak, but Frank held up his hand, anticipating our questions. "I don't know the job and I haven't a clue as to what he was doing here. I do intend to find out though."

"What happened here, after I left, last night?" I asked, still confused about things I'd heard outside.

"Well, while I was talking to you on the headpiece, I notice a car without lights slowly coming down the street. It stopped across the street and two houses up. That's when I called for Mary. Then I noticed a man, I don't know where he came from, but he was already in your front shrubbery. I saw a flicker of light and figured he was trying to torch the place."

"And was he?" I asked, trying to remember if the outside looked scorched.

"Yes, he was, but several things happened at once. Mary ran out the door, the White Dog jumped out of the bushes, and your outside lights went on. It was all too much for him and he took off with Mary after him. She fired a couple of shots in the air when he wouldn't stop, but he got away, when the car tried to run her down."

"Wow, Mary. Are you okay?" I asked concerned about this retired woman still having to perform such active feats. On second thought, I think she's better equipped to handle the physical than the strange information that Frank gave her.

"The Dog was here from the beginning? Why wasn't he inside protecting Naja?"

"He couldn't very well stop a fire starter from inside."

"Oh, right. Why did my automatic outside lights go on? They don't include the front, only the sides and back."

"Obviously, someone triggered them, someone who was in the back," Mary said, looking thoughtful.

"Oh! Why didn't they go on when Naja and I ran across the yard? I'd completely forgot about them."

"Why, indeed?" Frank's voice repeated my question quietly. Mary was out of her chair and headed for the back door. I jumped up to join her.

"No, stay," Frank said quietly. He waited until we heard the door open.

"Listen, Mary is not handling this well, I told her everything, but I don't think she completely believes me. She's a very by the book person and this is not exactly by anybody's book. Spooky stuff, she calls it."

"And she's right. It is spooky stuff and I wouldn't believe it either if I wasn't living it," I told him.

The back door closed and Mary walked back into the room holding a broken piece of glass. "The lights on both sides and the back have been disabled. One side was unscrewed the other broken," she stated returning to her chair and placing the broken glass on the table.

"What's your thought?" Frank asked her.

Matter of factly, she said, "After triggering the first side light, which is what we saw, he disabled the others."

"Yeah, sounds right."

"This must have happened before I went outside," I said softly, thinking to myself. "Was it Jarvis?" I added looking at them.

"I guess it could have been, since he was here," Frank answered.

"Or it could have been someone else and John was watching him," commented Mary in Jarvis' defense.

"That's true too," he said, looking up at Mary.

I tried to stifle a yawn, but was beginning to feel tired from lack of sleep and the rush of adrenalin that I'd been working from was definitely gone.

"You know, I'm beat, I think I'll join Naja and squeeze in a nap and from the looks of you two, maybe an afternoon nap is in order for everyone," I suggested.

"She's right," Frank said. "Mary, go home tend to your dog and catch a few winks, I'm going to get someone on this and then doze a bit right here."

She hesitated as if she were going to argue and then relaxed and said, "Yeah, you're right, I'm beat, but call me if… say, is that head phone audio monitor still hooked up? I'll be able to hear if you call out."

"Mandy, where is the monitor located?"

"It's here in the hall, so it picks up from all directions, but I don't know what happened to the headpiece."

"It's on the kitchen counter, it was on the floor in the hall."

After Mary left I peeked into Naja's room and the dog raised his head, but Naja slept soundly. I didn't know why the dog was still here, but was too tired to worry about it. Cops, audio monitor and the dog all on duty, I was going to sleep.

Hunger pains woke me up and it took a few minutes for me to figure out what time it was, or for that matter, what day it was. Looking at the clock, I was surprised to see that it was 5:30 in the afternoon. No wonder I was hungry, I'd missed lunch and now it was dinnertime. I tiptoed down the hall and wasn't surprised to find that Naja was still sleeping but I was surprised to see that the dog was still here. Maybe he'd decided to move in.

I peeked over the top of the staircase and saw that Frank was still sleeping, but Mary had returned and sat dozing in a chair near Frank. I crept down the stairs and into the kitchen going over in my mind what I was going to cook for dinner. I was very quiet, not banging around like usual. I finally decided on spaghetti, most people liked it. I had almost finished pouring the sauce when Mary walked into the kitchen.

"Hi Mary, hungry?"

"I could eat a horse and chase down the rider."

"Well no horse here, but we do have spaghetti, salad and garlic bread."

Good thing Naja and I went to the store and stocked up.

"Do I smell food?" the call came from the living room.

"Can Frank get to the table or should be serve him in the living room?" I asked her.

"Hey Frank, wanna join us or special service?" she called into him.

"Table." He was already up and hobbling to the main floor bathroom.

"Hi," said the small voice.

"Hey Naja, you're awake. Ready for dinner?" I asked her.

"Yes, but I'm too tired to set the table," she answered. As she leaned against the White Dog for support.

"No problem kid, I'll do it," Mary offered eyeing the dog suspiciously now that Frank had filled her in.

The four of us had a pleasant, but quiet dinner. We were all so tired and hungry that we just ate and didn't bother with small talk.

Naja, the White Dog and Frank retired to the living room for a lesson in creating pictures out of puzzles, while Mary and I cleaned up the kitchen. I asked if there was anyone outside that needed food and she replied that the department thought that the two of them could handle any further disturbances. I'm sure the department did think that, but I wasn't sure.

Naja and I retired early, leaving Mary and Frank to their own devises.

~

I stood in the doorway without being noticed. The same room, the same people, but somehow it seemed different. I seemed different. I walked into the room, my eyes searching for an empty chair.

The group turned almost in unison as I approached them. Ramon jumped up and offered me his chair. The group was silent as Ramon darted out into the hallway and returned with another chair. They waited. Waited for Ramon and then waited for me.

"Sorry, guess I'm late again," I said.

"Cut to the bottom line, Mandy. We're dying of curiosity," demanded Ron abruptly.

Heads nodded on all sides.

I smiled and didn't blame them. "It's a long and wild story..." I began filling them in on the entire activity. No one interrupted, no one moved. They were completely mesmerized. Even after I'd completed the wild night and morning story they sat there absorbing what I'd said.

"So I guess that I'm late because my afternoon nap took the edge off of the evening sleeping," I added. Still no one spoke. This was certainly different; usually they had questions, challenges, and opinions. I decided to wait for them to assimilate the information that I'd given them.

"The pieces are finally falling into place," Rachael spoke softly to no one in particular. "From very early in my life, I've heard stories of the 'new breed of people', who would save us from ourselves. That there would be conflict and difficulty, but these people would come in waves and they would be our salvation." She looked around, realizing that we were watching and listening to her, but not understanding what she was talking about.

"As I told Mandy, I'm Sephardi, Spanish Jew, and my grandmother and her mother before her were seers and I remember as a child hearing them tell of these people. It always sounded to me as if those who would save us were going to come riding in on horses from some other country. I didn't put it together until just now, but these 'people' are these children. Our Indigo children! Who will, of course, grow into 'people,' with our help.

"As I remember…they are only the beginning, they said 'waves of people.' I can only assume that after our Indigos do their job, they will have children who will carry on and possibly be even more advanced."

The group sat silently absorbing this new bit of information. No one objecting to its logic, this group had never been so quiet.

Finally, Lindy turned her head towards me and asked, "Mandy, what about this cop Jarvis? Whose side is he on?" This brought the group back to its normal diverse character.

"Yeah and what about the guy they arrested?"

"Yes Mandy, go on with the story."

"Well, Jarvis is still undercover, I guess. Frank couldn't get any information on him that wasn't classified. The fellow they arrested is a criminal from way back and was only hired to listen and record. He apparently knows very little."

"What about the people that live in the house across the street? What became of them?"

"They were called away to a sick family member in Iowa. However, when they got there no one was sick."

"Mandy, what about the White Dog? Is he still in your house?" Sally's curious voice asked.

"He is. Isn't that interesting? He's never stayed this long before." There was no response.

"I know it may be because Naja is in more danger now than before. I've thought about that. I'm just glad to have him."

"Say, has anyone seen the Boogie Man lately? Anyone besides Mandy, that is," Pete suddenly asked.

"Nope."

"Not even a glimpse."

"What do you suppose he's up to?"

"I would suspect that he's rallying together his troops," came a voice from the doorway. "Boy you guys go to bed early."

"Frank!" I called out happily. Then I noticed Lindy watching with the beginnings of a smile forming on her lips.

"Better bring in a chair from the hall, we've been short tonight," added Ron.

Frank stopped dead in his tracks, half way across the room and turned towards the hall. "Short on chairs?"

"Yeah, there wasn't one for Rachael, Mandy and now you," he answered.

"Get out of here, Rachael! Mandy wake up and get home. There are always enough chairs for whoever is supposed to be here. The rest of you call me tomorrow when you're awake, Lieutenant Frank Adams, they'll find me. This now needs to be dealt with in the real world. **Mandy wake up!"**

I was sitting up when my eyes opened. Quickly I threw off the covers and headed for Naja's room. Pushing on her door, which I always left ajar, I stood face to face with Naja. She was standing up in bed facing me. Her eyes were open, but she was still asleep. I reached for her, but she said, "I want Dog." I looked around the room, but the White Dog was nowhere to be seen.

"It's okay sweetheart, he'll come back," I reassured her. "Come on, why don't you sleep with me until he does." I gathered her up without further resistance, and headed back towards my own bedroom. On the way, I looked over the upstairs railing at the living room below. Frank was sprawled out on the couch sound asleep and possibly still at the dream meeting. I began to wonder, *Why did he think Rachael and I shouldn't be there because we didn't have chairs? Just when I was thinking that I was beginning to understand and even accept this strange situation it becomes confusing again.* However, I wasn't about to challenge Frank's experience. If he thought I shouldn't be there tonight…I'd be out of there. Rachael didn't hesitate either; in fact, I think she was gone before I even left.

It must not be dangerous here, because the dog is gone, so I took Naja and curled up in my still warm bed wondering where this would all end. I didn't immediately fall asleep and was thinking about this strange situation, so didn't immediately connect the sound that was bothering me. Then suddenly I realized that I was hearing voices. Male voices coming from downstairs in the living room where I'd seen Frank sleeping a short time before. I disengaged myself from Naja and the covers, slipped my robe on over my pajamas, tiptoed to the bedroom door and quietly pulled it open.

To my surprise the White Dog stood at the top of the stairs, bristled and in an attack position, although, he wasn't making a sound. He didn't look at me, but one ear turned in my direction, he knew that I was there. I stood still listening and trying to figure out what was happening. Where was Frank? Why wasn't Mary monitoring the communication system from her house?

I was sure, now, that I'd heard two male voices quietly arguing before I opened the door, but now I heard nothing. I was just about to take a step forward to peek over the railing when I head Frank say, with a big sigh in his voice, "Okay so what do you plan to do now?"

"It's not up to me, Frank. I'm not calling the shots here."

"Well who in the hell is! This is getting out of hand," replied an angry Frank.

"Get 'em out of town. At least until this is over."

"John, you don't get it. That won't help, because they are 'it.' They are the entire reason for this." Frank spit the words out at the other man.

"No, no. It's bigger than a woman and a kid. This involves big men with big money, but for some reason these two seem to be in the way, these two and anyone who tries to help them. That puts you and Mary right in the middle with them. Get them out, Frank, do it tonight, it's coming down real soon. In fact, it may already be too late."

"It is too late John, but not for the reason you think. It's too late for **them**; it's not a woman and a kid, it's an entire new generation of kids, a new breed of kids that are going to give these power seeking men, the government and everyone else a real run for their money. Stopping this one kid and her mom isn't going to put an end to **their** problem. They'd have to get rid of all the kids, plus all those still to be born." I heard a shuffling noise and the Dog stiffened.

"These kids are being born with a mission that's implanted in there little heads, it's to change the world. That means those who are using power to control, those in government, and those with all the money." When Frank stopped talking silence filled the void.

Then John's voice, sounding stiff and formal, said, "Frank, you've gone over the edge. You need a vacation. No! You need help. I can't believe that you expect me to believe this hogwash. I'm out of here; I've been gone too long already. Don't say I didn't warn you, Frank."

Suddenly the front door burst open and banged against the wall. Men's voices filled the room. The dog shot past me pushing into the bedroom. I turned, closed the door and hooked a chair under it and then groped in my purse for my cell phone and dialed 911. Where in the hell was Mary? While giving the address to the 911 woman, and instructing her that my house had just been broken into and I needed help right now, I got Naja out of bed.

"Naja, Naja honey, wake up. I want you to hide in the storage space with the White Dog, Okay? Okay?" I gathered a blanket, pillow and JoJo from the bed and shoved them inside the 2x2 foot door of the storage space in the corner beside the dresser. Next I led a sleepy little girl inside and she automatically curled up on the blanket. This was one of her favorite hideouts when she played with her dolls so she had no problem with it. I then held the door open and looked at the Dog. He walked past me and into the small space, and lay down next to Naja.

"Yes, they are downstairs now. I'm upstairs in the bedroom. I'm hanging up now, you do your thing." Retrieving the straight chair from the door, I placed it in front of the small door in the corner and threw my extra pillows on it then my robe. Then quickly I climbed back into bed and pulled up the covers just as I heard someone coming up the stairs.

"Okay lady, rise and shine," the raspy voice called out as a strange man flipped on the overhead light.

"No one in the other room," said a second voice.

"What?" I feigned surprise. "Who are you? What are you doing here?" I said in an angry, indignant voice.

"What?" the first man said to the second man. Then he turned back to me and said. "Where's the kid?"

"What?" I echoed his response, trying to sound confused. I jumped out of bed and started toward the door. "Is she gone?" The men let me run past them to Naja's room. I flipped on the light and made a pretense of searching the bed. They had followed me into the hall. I ran to the top of the stairs and looked over the railing. Frank sat on the couch, John Jarvis stood in front of the window, another man stood in the middle of the room pointing a gun at Frank. I ran down the stairs, praying the two men would follow me. I ignored the gunman, and staring hard into Frank's eyes hoping that he'd read my signal. "Frank, where's Naja? She's gone."

Frank never blinked an eye, but said. "Don't worry, I sent her away where she'll be safe. She's well guarded, and out of harm's way."

I visibly relaxed and said, "Well I wish you'd told me."

"And I wish you'd tell me. **NOW!**" demanded the man holding the gun. I looked at him as he spoke, as if this were the first time I'd noticed him. I also noted that the two men had followed me downstairs. Then I realized that this was the bogus insurance man and also the same man that Jarvis and I had seen in the hospital, the man that Jarvis had been talking to before he just up and disappeared. He slowly turned the gun towards me, but continued to look at Frank.

"Drop it!" The voice was firm, familiar, and female. Mary stood in the doorway to the kitchen, her gun held in both hands pointed directly at the gunman. He hesitated and then lowered the gun, holding it by one finger through the trigger guard. Frank was instantly on his feet, his gun retrieved from the coffee table, pointing at the other two men standing at the bottom of the stairs. Jarvis just stood there watching the entire scenario.

Red lights flashed outside as the Cavalry I'd called arrived. Jarvis casually moved towards the door, and let them in, but after opening the door he turned and disappeared down the hall and out the back door in the confusion of the uniformed men coming in and finding the bad guys already standing with their hands in the air.

I glanced at Frank, but he didn't let on that he'd noticed, even though he couldn't have missed seeing Jarvis duck down the hallway behind the two men with their hands in the air.

I took the stairs two at a time during the arresting process and pulled the chair away from the hiding place and opened the door to discover Naja sleeping soundly, but no dog. Grinning, I could only shake my head. I'd stopped wondering a long time ago how he came and went. While I was tucking Naja into my bed, I did wonder about Rachael. Why was she not supposed to be at the meeting? Was her little Dina in danger now too?

After things settled down and Mary had gone with the arrested men to the station, 'just to make sure nothing goes wrong,' she'd said, I poured Frank a cup of coffee and told him I had a few questions.

"Just a few?" he asked with his eyebrows raised and a grin on his face.

Day Twelve

I woke to the smell of coffee. Turning over, I expected to find Naja curled up beside me, but she was gone. I immediately sat up ready to do battle or whatever, but then decided that if I didn't see a White Dog and did smell coffee... things must be okay. I really doubted if the Boogie Man or his friends would stop off in the kitchen and make coffee. Mary was probably back, fussing over Frank.

Pulling on a robe, I headed for the kitchen, I could use a cup of coffee, even though I'd consumed quite a bit last night. Frank and I spent half the night hashing and rehashing the wild and crazy time we'd had. I glanced at the clock as I left the bedroom and was shocked to discover that it was almost eleven o'clock. *Wow, I really slept in.* I hadn't done that in years, in fact, since Naja was born.

"Well good morning, sleepy head," called out Frank as I entered the warm, cozy kitchen. He didn't seem to be suffering from sleep derivation. Naja was sitting up on one of the high stools that she was never allowed to sit on, swinging her legs and stuffing her mouth with a bagel. "Hi, sleepy head," she finally managed to say through the huge bite she'd taken, mimicking Frank's greeting.

"Boy are you two chipper. Where's Mary?" I asked as I gently lowered myself onto the closest chair, leaning my elbows on the table.

Frank set a steaming cup, filled to the brim with coffee, in front of me. "Here, drink this. It'll make a new woman out of you. Mary dropped off some bagels then went home to tend to her dog and catch a few winks."

"Was she at the station all night?" I asked, feeling guilty that I'd had even the little bit of sleep that I did.

"Yeah, pretty much. I think she caught a few nods between paper work though. So, what'll it be? Eggs? Pancakes? Or both?"

"You cook?" I couldn't help showing my surprise.

"I do and I'm pretty good too."

"Wow! How about the pancakes? Will I have time for a quick shower?" I asked, thinking that I'd certainly be in better shape after freshening up.

"Yeah, but not long, fifteen minutes max."

I leaped out of the chair and ran down the hall towards the stairs, Naja's gleeful laughter ringing behind me. "Hurry Mommy, hurry."

As the wonderfully refreshing hot water ran over my head and down the length of my tired body, I thought about Frank and our conversation last night. He didn't have all of the answers, but he did shed a little light on some of my questions.

Lieutenant John Jarvis was and still is assigned as an undercover agent to a group of people who were new in our town but had friends in high places, not only here, but on the East Coast as well. They knew he was a cop, but considered him to be there man on the inside. He had actually been working with them before Naja and I came on the scene so he knew the man at the elevator in the hospital and cemented his position when he escorted him out and let him go.

Frank couldn't convince John that Naja and others like her were the big threat to these men; their positions of power, their bank accounts, and their entire system of control. We had to agree, that it did sound rather farfetched, but we had the advantage of having lived out the situations in dreams, and we knew about the Boogie Man.

After we'd discussed the Boogie Man and his role, I had suddenly had a deep fear for John Jarvis. "Frank, Jarvis could be in trouble." I'd explained that the Boogie Man had seen John here and he always knew everything, and he certainly knew that Jarvis was a plant. He'd surely tell his accomplices. Frank agreed and quickly called and got the head man out of bed to tell him to pull Jarvis immediately, saying that he'd been compromised during the raid here and didn't know it.

We'd also discussed Mary. Apparently she had been monitoring Frank and Jarvis' conversation from the back yard with the headpiece, so she was close enough to step in at just the right time. It seems that she'd never retired completely, but had been on a 'as needed' standby, so she was still qualified to fill out the reports and give instructions to officers of a lesser rank.

As I watched the steam cloud the shower door, enjoying the warm water on my stressed shoulder and back muscles, I suddenly remembered Rachael. Were she and her little one all right? I rushed to get dried off and dressed. "Frank, what about Rachael? How can we contact her?" I asked as I rushed into the kitchen.

"I've been worrying about that too. Do you know her phone number or even her last name?" I shook my head. "I'm afraid we don't have any way to contact her," he said as he turned around and slid two perfect pancakes on to a plate sitting on the table in front of my coffee cup. "She split as soon as I said the words. The others are supposed to contact me today. I want to know who they are and where they live, in case the Bad Boys start going after any of them."

Naja sat quietly listening to the conversation but saying nothing, which was unusual for her. She usually wanted to know everything that she didn't understand. I noticed and wondered about the reaction. My mind flashed a thought that wasn't logical... *perhaps she does understand...*

The pancakes should have been delicious, but now I couldn't really taste them, I was worried about Dina and Rachael. From what I'd gathered they also lived alone, as we did. The ringing of the phone startled me out of my speculations. I looked up and saw that both Frank and Naja were watching me toy with my food. Frank reached over to the counter and picked up the phone.

"Minton residence." He listened silently for a minute and then said, "By all means, can you pick them up? Okay." Now Naja and I were both watching him as he placed the phone back into its cradle. "Are you up for a playmate this afternoon?" he said looking at Naja.

She looked surprised. Playmates were something she only had at school, especially since we'd stopped running with Jill and Sami. "Yea," she replied with a big grin on her face. "Who is it?"

"Who is it?" I repeated.

"Are you up for a visitor this afternoon?" he asked looking at me this time.

"Frank!" I all but shouted at him.

He held up his hands as if to protect his body and laughingly said. "Okay, okay. It's Rachael and Dina. Seems she just called the station and said she wants to see me."

The pancakes were suddenly the best I'd ever eaten and I asked for more. Frank was ready. He produced two more. "I knew you'd like them," he said with a chuckle. *Is this what it was like being a family?* I wondered. Apparently Naja was wondering the same thing, because she said. "Isn't this fun, can he stay with us?"

"Don't ya think that you should keep the doors locked, especially after last night?" Mary's voice preceded her into the room. Her face, however, said that she'd heard Naja's request and had rescued us from answering, rescued Frank more than likely.

"Mary, how do you feel? Did you get any sleep at all?" I asked quickly.

"Some," she told me, and then she turned towards Frank. "Frank what are…"

"Don't start on me, Mary. I'm fine, cooking and moving around is therapeutic." She walked around him and poured herself a cup of coffee.

"Try the pancakes, Mary. They're terrific!" I stood up and took my dishes to the sink. "Come on Naja, we have to get ready for company." We effectively made our escape to the privacy of the upstairs before Mary could spoil the mood we'd been enjoying. I really wanted to hang on to that feeling for a while longer.

Dina was a beautiful little girl with black curly hair and dark brown eyes. She was small in size even for 4 years old, but her little mind was quick and she seemed older than her size and years indicated she should be. It was almost déjà vu for me as I watched her; she was so much like Naja in every way except coloring. The girls took to each other instantly. We set them up with some of Naja's toys in the living room so that Dina's short legs wouldn't have to negotiate the stairs. While Rachael was bending forward to hand Dina a toy, her crystal pendant swung out away from her body. Naja noticed it and said, "Oh, that's a pretty necklace."

"Thank you Naja, this is my crystal," Rachael answered as she fingered the stone.

"Crystal? Did you say Crystal?" Naja asked looking surprised.

Little Dina also looked surprised and muttered, "Crystal."

Both girls stood staring at the necklace in Rachael's hand. "Dina, you've seen this before, I wear it all of the time."

"I didn't know it was Crystal."

"What do you know about Crystal?" Rachael asked the girls.

Naja said, "Only that they are coming later."

"Who are 'they'?" Rachael asked.

"The Crystal kids."

"Yes," Dina added, as the two girls turned to the coloring book and began to pick out the colors they wanted to use.

Rachael looked at Frank and I. "What do you suppose that was all about?" Neither of us answered and Rachael murmured, "You can bet I'm going to check it out."

Then Rachael, Frank and I retired to the kitchen table, which had becoming the favorite meeting place in this house. Mary had gone back home for more much needed sleep.

As soon as I poured the coffee, Rachael leaned across the table and confided, "You were right Lieutenant, I did need to be home. When I woke up, I heard the strangest sound coming from the living room. When I investigated, I discovered 'your' White Dog," she looked at me before going on, "all bristled and growling at the Boogie Man. I think that Boogie Man is afraid of the dog. He left right away, and I don't even think that he saw me. The dog saw me, wagged his tail, and then settled himself outside of Dina's room." She leaned back and waited for our reaction.

I looked at Frank, "What does this mean? Has the Boogie Man given up on Naja and switched to a new child to frighten?" I asked him quietly, glancing towards the living room.

Frank sat there rubbing and pulling on his ear, a habit I'd noticed that he did when he was thinking. "I don't know. I do know that he works through fear, and he has an uncanny sense of knowing who's going to be a threat to his mission."

"Mission?" both Rachael and I said in unison.

He hesitated took a sip of his coffee, and then said, "It's difficult, but here's what I think. He represents 'fear' and his mission is to keep 'do gooders,' like these kids, from completing their mission, which as you've already discussed, is to change the world for the better."

"Why 'fear'? Why doesn't he use more physical means, wouldn't it be faster?" I asked feeling confused.

"I don't think that is within his means. He can, however, draw those who would and could use physical means to a person once he's instilled enough fear either in them or the would be bad guy. Negative draws negative, you know."

"Do you mean that he can still get to us by creating fear into someone else and then they can harm us?" I asked, feeling shocked and slightly ill. "How can we possibly protect ourselves against that type of situation?" I was feeling very vulnerable and felt fear creeping in. The very fear I didn't want to give in to.

"Easy Mandy," Frank's voice filtered through to my logical mind, as I swam back to the kitchen and the problem at hand.

"Mandy?" Rachael's quiet voice pulled me back the last few inches. They were both looking at me with concern written clearly across their faces. "Mandy, you've been through a lot already, don't slip backwards now. You're not alone anymore, and we will win," she continued.

They were right, "…but what about the rest of the group?" I finished my thought out loud. "What if he tries each one until he finds one that will cave in? We can't let that happen!"

"We're going to talk to them, warn them, however, it's possible that every kid won't make it to finish the mission, we can only do so much," Frank stated and then gently explained, "Each individual takes a shared responsibility, and that means the little ones too. It's not impossible that some soul may change their mind about being part of this mission or decide that they can be more useful somewhere else. I'm not saying that it will happen, but it could and we need to understand, if it does."

We sat silently thinking of the job ahead, a very big job, a lifetime job, a shared job. Finally Rachael extended her right hand across the table to Frank and her left hand across the table to me. We each took her hand and then took each other's hands. We had formed an alliance, a triad, a trinity. We looked at each other and smiled then we just naturally raised our connected hands upward towards the ceiling. It felt good. We could do this together.

I sat almost facing the window and as we lowered our arms, I caught a glimpse of a shadowy figure as he turned and moved away. *Ha!* I thought, *How's that grab ya Boogie Man!*

After Rachael and Dina left via their private police car, Frank spent an hour on the phone, gathering information on the case, giving directions, and contacting the rest of the Dream group who had called in to the station. Finally when he stopped for lunch, which was pizza delivered by a squad car, he said, "You girls," and he looked pointedly at Naja and then at me, "better prepare yourselves for a party."

"A party?" we parroted together in question.

He nodded his head and said, "Yep."

"Oh boy, a party!" exclaimed Naja in her high little voice. "When?"

"The party is going to be right here," then he hesitated, dragging the when out as long as possible, while Naja sat expectantly on the edge of her chair waiting, "tonight!"

Naja clapped her hands and chanted, "A party, a party."

I sat there wondering why. Why have a party at a time like this?

Frank laughed and told us, "It's my birthday. So you guys get some rest while I go to the office and attend to some business. Party begins at seven o'clock sharp. Mary will be here too." Then as if on cue, the doorbell rang and it was Frank's ride. Mary came in as Frank left, muttered something about babysitting. This time she brought her little short-legged dog and Naja was delighted. Surprisingly the dog too was happy. I had expected a dog that had been raised and lived with an adult to be skittish around kids, but this little guy was gentle and followed Naja all around the house. The house now seemed so empty, even though it contained three people and a dog. Isn't it funny how a man's personality and energy can make a house feel so full?

"We have to have presents!" Naja said, looking stricken. Well, she had a point, whoever heard of a birthday party without presents? Mary and I stood there staring at each other.

"Well," I said looking at Mary, "I suppose going to the mall is out of the question?"

She nodded her head, "Completely."

"Let's make some," said a wee voice. Amazing how children find the simplest answer for a complex problem. Mary looked at me and shrugged. We put our heads together and ended up making him presents out of anything we could create.

Mary wrote a poem, which was quiet good, Naja colored him a picture and I bent and twisted part of a trailing vine into a halo, of sorts.

Mary and I scrounged the cupboards and fridge for ideas for our feast, first choosing and then rejecting many items. Finally, we came up with a green salad with dried sunflower seeds, thawed frozen peas, onions, and tomatoes thrown into the mix. We even had a couple of different choices for dressings. Baked potatoes with a special bacon and cheese filling provided by Mary, and after much debating over our limited choices, we baked a canned ham, decorating it with cloves and the last of the orange marmalade.

Dinner was a great success, not because of our culinary skills, but because of the work we put into it together and because it was a relief to be doing something normal, acting like a family, sharing jobs and ideas.

Right after dinner, Frank was forced to open his gifts, which were wrapped in the Sunday funnies, because neither Mary nor I had any birthday wrapping paper. He exclaimed, ohhh'd, and awww'd, much to Naja's delight.

Later, we spent the evening playing games, which involves a lot of creativity and flexibility when a five-year-old is involved, and ended the evening by eating our celebration cake. It was a mix cake and for some reason, when finished, listed slightly to the side. We found one candle to top it off with, that and the ice cream, which we shared with the officers on patrol outside. Apparently the chief decided we did need help here after all.

~

I sat alone in the Dream meeting room wondering where everyone else could be. I went to bed late, but was the first one here. *How odd*, I thought, then my mind wandered back to Frank's birthday party, which had turned out to be great fun. I can't remember that type of fun since I was a little girl at home with my mom and dad.

"Hey! Where is everyone? I thought I'd be late," Ron said as he strolled into the room, looking almost pleasant.

"Sorry to be late..." Sally's voice trailed off as she looked around at the nearly empty room. "Where is everyone?" she asked.

"I was wondering that myself, but there are twelve chairs, so apparently everyone is going to be here," I explained as I looked around the room.

Then Ramon, Hally and Cindy came in almost together. They were laughing and acting very social. Before they even got seated, Lindy, Bill, Pete and Shala arrived.

"Better late than never," called Teri as she and Rachael strolled into the room arm and arm.

Wow, what a jolly group. No fear here. "Okay, what's going on? You guys look positively jovial," I challenged them.

They took their seats still smiling and chuckling. "What?!" I challenged again.

"I just feel good. I've decided that this is a good thing and I can handle it," Lindy said as she stretched her long legs out in front of her.

"Yeah. Me too."

"Yeah and having support sure helps."

"Sure this is no tougher than we can handle."

"Okay, what'd I miss? What happened after I left last night?" I asked them still confused by their jovial attitudes.

"Well we did talk some after the three of you split, but I think it was this morning that your friend the lieutenant helped me to feel more secure about this whole thing," Hally added.

"Yeh, it sure helps to know someone understands and will help."

"You bet!"

"Yeah, your lieutenant is okay, Mandy."

Everyone was nodding and confirming. "What are you talking about?" I asked still not understanding what had made such a difference.

"Your lieutenant talked to all of us today, he's going to help us." Lindy filled me in.

"Yeah, he's okay," repeated Ron, nodding his head up and down.

"Yeah, his understanding of what's going on is a big help by itself, but he's going to have police patrol our houses on a regular basis."

"Yes, 'a show of force,' I believe he called it."

"Plus, he's working on this case from the inside. It feels good to have the security of the police force personally behind you. He even set up a direct line that we can call at anytime, day or night."

Lindy looked right at Mandy, grinned and said, "Of course, some of us don't need a direct phone number, since we have the real thing just a whisper away."

I felt my face flush, "It isn't like that."

"I know, I'm just teasing, but I'll bet it will be. He kinda lights up when he mentions your name, and it doesn't hurt to have cops all over your place."

He lights up when he mentions my name? Really. I tried to digest this information, but noticed the attention and smiling faces I was getting.

"Not to change the subject, but what's next?" I asked.

"I suggested we pool the kids, but he ruled that out saying that we needed to keep them spread out," Sally added.

I need to think about getting back to work. What then? I was trying to plan my own options.

Rachael broke into my thoughts, with her soft voice. "We have to learn to be very aware, very cautious, and yet try to lead normal lives for our children. Keeping them safe is on the top of the list, but we can't wrap them up in cotton and stick them in a closet. We have to let them live and experience life. Allow them to develop and learn, so that they can complete their mission. My people have had to struggle with survival issues for centuries.

"This, however, is not an issue of being in danger because of nationality, culture, or religious beliefs. Our children are all from different backgrounds, but have a common mission, which has become a survival issue for us at this stage. It's our job to see that they make it." She stopped talking, looking at each one of us.

"We've taken on a big job."

"Yeah, but we can do it, we have each other and now professional help too."

"It's a challenge."

"I love a challenge."

"Twelve," I spoke out loud.

"Well leave it to Mandy to move on to another subject without the rest of us," Lindy said smiling, but looking at me with a questioning expression.

"What about twelve?"

"Oh, a couple of days ago, I think it was a couple of days ago, Frank mentioned that we didn't have much time, because the dreams go for twelve nights, something about the number twelve being important. Something about twelve people."

"Yeah, so?"

"Well, this is our twelfth night. This could be our last night together."

"No!"

"We need each other."

"I can't go this alone."

"Thirteen!" I said.

Eleven faces looked at me, waiting for an explanation. "Frank is number thirteen! He's joined our cause."

"Right!"

"Yes and a welcome addition too."

"Is that going to change things?"

"I vaguely remember there's also something significant about the number thirteen..." murmured Rachael.

"What does this mean?"

"Well, if you ask me, it means we're not like all the rest. Twelve has always been a magic number throughout history, calendars, disciples, clocks, measurements, and who knows how much more. I think we've gone past all of that. We are in a new era," Shala explained in her quiet style.

"Right! We definitely are experiencing different things than what parents in the past have experienced during child rearing."

"Yeah, I don't think my parents had to deal with 'real' Boogie Men with blue eyes."

"I feel like a pioneer, and I'm so glad that we're doing this together," said Ramon, expressing the feelings of all of us.

"Amen to that."

"Here's what I'm getting," Rachael said quietly. "We are going to be doing this differently. We have thirteen people, not even counting the kids, **and** we are going to be taking our meetings together into the awake world. We will continue to meet and see each other even after the dream meetings are over. In fact, I believe that they are over. They brought us together and as Frank pointed out, as soon as we figure out what we need to know, we no longer need to meet in dreams."

"Yes, because Frank joined us and is making it possible to continue our contact with each other in the real world," stated Sally, picking up Rachael's idea.

"You know, when we're not doing this meeting thing during the privacy of our dreams... we're going to have to include our spouses," Ramon stated.

"Yes, those of us who have spouses are going to have a lot of explaining to do if we just run off to 'secret meetings.'"

"You're going to have a lot of explaining to do in any case."

"Right!"

"Another challenge!"

"This is going to be okay, we can do this."

"Yes, we can."

"And will!"

"We'll all help you guys with the explanations," Lindy told them. "...and don't forget we have Portland's finest to back up our 'unbelievable' tale."

Rachael and I confirmed the idea. "I love you guys," I threw in. "You're like an extended family."

The warm secure feeling that I'd felt for these people in the past was back. Whether they liked it or not we are in this together and everyone was willing to cooperate and work together. I started smiling as I reached for the hands on either side of me. Rachael noticed and did the same thing. The entire group held hands in a circle.

The energy flowed from hand to hand, like electricity lighting up each human station as it charged our emotions, our minds and our physical strength, creating a strong unspoken bond between us. A bond between twelve people who had been complete strangers just twelve days ago, and now were on a tract together that skipped back and forth between two worlds with our children in the middle.

I watched as every face took on the look of determination, but there was something else that slowly superimposed itself across those faces, it showed other faces. Other faces with the same determination, faces we didn't know, but faces that were dealing with the same situation that we were dealing with. Faces of other parents and guardians of Indigo children on a mission, our group wasn't alone.

I broke into the esoteric drifting of the people around me with a chuckle, bringing the group back to reality. "I think the Boogie Man and his accomplices have taken on a bigger job than they bargained for." Laughter and cheers rocked the room.

A silent shadow stepped away from the door, and disappeared slowly down the hallway, as the people who stood up to *fear* celebrated their first victory.

Epilogue

I knew that I should open my eyes, but I didn't want to. The cold dread of fear had gotten its icy fingers wrapped around me. I prayed that it would be all right. It had to be. A small hand squeezed mine, and I heard Naja's excited voice say, "He's coming, Mommy. He's coming."

I allowed one eye to partially open, and peered through the lashes. There he was. My other eye popped open and I watched as Frank walked purposefully towards us a big smile on his face.

"Well girls, I've pulled the car around to the front. Shall we go home now?" He scooped a squealing Naja up into one arm, locked his other arm through mine and propelled us out through the double doors. Naja's newly adopted grandmother, Ethel, was grinning and blowing kisses to us, as we swept past the cheering crowd of people and into the waiting car.

It was a wedding day that hadn't ended in tragedy, and there wasn't a Boogie Man in sight. I turned to look out the back window of the car as we pulled away. My maid of honor and best friend Jill, her husband Fred and little Sami stood with Miss Susan, the pre-school teacher, both women dabbing at their eyes. The rest of our new friends stood at the curb waving; the Dream Meeting people, their spouses, their kids, most of the police department, my office team, including an ear-ringed Matt, and off to the side Mary and Alice, the bag lady, stood together. It was definitely the beginning of an entirely new life. Not just for us, but for many people, perhaps the entire world!

It's been almost a year since the Dream group's last meeting, the night we decided the Boogie Man and his henchmen had bitten off more than they could chew, and what a year!

Jarvis narrowly escaped being killed by the Boogie Man's friend, but managed to close his undercover work by bringing down the organization that was in the beginning stages of taking over our lovely city and destroying the kids' mission. This threw a block into the Boogie Man's plans as well; all he could do now was say boo. I've seen him a couple of times, but, only from a distance, he seemed to be just checking things out. Frank expects we'll see him again sometime, but we're ready, we're all ready.

Frank recovered completely from the hit and run accident and since the

Dream group wasn't being pulled together at night anymore, he kept his promise and arranged for us to meet while awake. We've all become very close both personally and with a determination to see these Indigo kids through to their mission.

Naja had her sixth birthday and Frank surprised her with a puppy. A white Shepherd! Needless to say, she was thrilled and the two have been inseparable.

I smiled as I ended the recap of the past year. I rolled over facing Frank in the bed. "Frank? Are you awake?"

"Yes," came the quiet answer.

Little strips of light filtered into the room through the vertical blinds on the window, giving me just enough light to make out Frank lying on his back with his hands behind his head. He looked relaxed and happy.

"Frank?" I said again then hesitated… "do you suppose that the white puppy… well, that he could somehow have the same powers that the White Dog had?"

He immediately said, "I'd say yes."

I sat up, staring down at him. "Really? You would? Why?"

He started grinning, "'Cause just before Naja's party, the White Dog showed up at the back door with the pup in tow."

"The White Dog brought the pup? Where was I?"

"You were letting kids in the front door for the party. Don't you remember when Naja disappeared and you were calling her to tell her that her friends had arrived? We were in the kitchen accepting the puppy from the White Dog."

"What?! You told me that you'd gotten the puppy."

"No, you just assumed that."

"And you just let me think it!"

"Well… you were so delighted with me that I decided to let you keep thinking it and tell you later."

I grabbed a pillow and started hitting him all around the head and chest. After he'd received a few whacks, he grabbed me and wrestled the pillow away holding me close against his body until I stopped struggling. As his grip loosened enough for me to move my head back, I looked into his face and saw his eyes filled with laughter. Relaxing I slipped my arms free, reached out and pulled that wonderful face, with those laughing eyes and that too tempting mouth down to my lips. Frank and a White Dog… Naja and I were definitely in good hands.

Printed in the United States
63560LVS00003B/301-375

9 781592 864041